Contents

Golemian Calendar   3

Prologue: Shackled Words   4

Chapter I: Appendix Addendum   6

Chapter II: Flower   21

Chapter III: Their Dreams   24

Chapter IV: Aerbith   26

Chapter V: A Scourge All Its Own   29

Chapter VI: Blade of Humanity   31

Chapter VII: A Memorable Tower   35

Chapter VIII: The Aborted Shade   40

Chapter IX: The Coveted Saviours   42

Chapter X: A Veiled Sacrifice   46

Chapter XI: The Other One   51

Chapter XII: An Eternal Venture   70

Chapter XIII: To Live Forever   77

Chapter XIV: To the Ruins of Old Halia   82

Chapter XV: A Master and His Subjects   87

Chapter XVI: The Betrayer's Stand   91

Chapter XVII: The Cleansing Canvas   98

Chapter XVIII: My Gift to You   112

Chapter XIX: New Golem 122

Chapter XX: The Reverent Fortress 134

Chapter XXI: A Cherished Novelty 148

Chapter XXII: Outcast 158

Chapter XXIII: The Unfolding 170

Chapter XXIV: Empyrean Wings 187

Chapter XXV: A Vow Transcending Lifetimes 206

Chapter XXVI: To Another Life 217

Chapter XXVII: The Gift of Empathy 228

Chapter XXVIII: The Dove in the Rain 234

Final Chapter: The Crow in the Sun 257

Epilogue: A Good Night in Water 267

Acknowledgements 272

Glossary 273

This is a work of fiction.
Names, characters, places, and
incidents either are the product
of the author's imagination
or are used fictitiously. Any
resemblance to actual persons,
living or dead, events, or locales
is entirely coincidental.

Cover design by Flos Nullius
Editing by Destyn Hehr

Golemian Calendar

1. TALANS - 48 DAYS

2. MOHRENS - 27 DAYS

3. SAHN - 53 DAYS

4. RIUNDA - 15 DAYS

5. HALTH - 63 DAYS

6. DURADIS - 39 DAYS

7. EOS - 45 DAYS

8. VITHARD - 21 DAYS

9. YULGENS - 39 DAYS

10. INGRIVE - 54 DAYS

Prologue: Shackled Words

In the desolate city she stood, clenching her limp arm and the ribbon of blood woven within the crevice of her punctured shoulder.

She and that woman stood alone on the pulverised road, the scrap of what used to be a one-manned aircraft smouldering amid the coming tumult, biting at a brisk air with a draft of warmth.

The light of daybreak cascaded from the darkness of the surrounding buildings, eclipsed yonder by a giant saucer hovering above, weapons mounted along its rim. Try as its pilot did to draw attention from below—speaking in military jargon she did not care to heed—the wounded woman's attention lingered elsewhere, towards the prideful smile and longing emerald gaze mocking her as she suffered.

But that gaze deviated towards the wreckage as she narrowed her own eyes in fury and resolve—towards a battered young man collapsed beside it, alive but barely alert. She could read well the sentiments of she who wielded those eyes, her greater half who had awaited this moment since time immemorial: *Don't be so arrogant to think you could take him from me.*

Lyaphend scowled at Watcher. So be it—if she lacked the power to challenge her directly, she would beat her at her own game. She would run away and survive anything Watcher threw at her; she would spite her for as long as her legs could move before dying a horrible death; she would leave her frustrated and bitter for having given so much effort to kill a worthless coward. And so, as she had done thrice before, she turned her back to

Watcher, throwing one foot in front of the other again and again —journeying off into the depths of the desolate streets with no particular destination in mind. Any ground upon which she stopped would invariably amount to the same thing—her final resting place.

"I can— please."

Watcher's voice echoed within, her words faltering alongside Lyaphend's senses. Was it a threat or a veiled plea for help? Who was she? What was her name in life? Her suffering was not of one who sought to live against all odds, but of one who yearned to reclaim the identity stolen from her.

Halth 38ᵗʰ Reign, year 999 In Golem's Reign—that day had etched itself onto Lyaphend's heart, burning into its depths whenever she recalled it, profound yet incomplete. She would never wash away the tarnish of giving up her old identity in the name of survival upon reaching that bridge over the lake.

She would never forget the moment she learned through her own body which of them was truly the monster.

Chapter I: Appendix Addendum

Ingrive 48ᵗʰ Reign, Year 999 I.G.R.

A well-dressed man stood in front of the screen of a weather forecast.

"Curtains and moonlight, my curious night owls! It's your favourite nighttime weather forecaster, Sam Dean, so sneak in some late-night snacks, have a seat on the couch, and get ready for our latest predictions to keep you on your toes before you head off to bed to tackle tomorrow!"

Tap.

A woman with a microphone stood before two rugged men in a roadside field.

"Witnesses say that the Cold Creek Killer is still at large, having deftly escaped out of sight of his pursuers shortly after the brutal stabbing of two local fishermen, who were pronounced dead at the scene. Here's Tristam at the scene with two disgruntled townsmen."

"Cold Creek? 'Most secure town in the suburbs,' my ass. If you dumb fucking idiots would just bend the knee and let the government set up some real fucking security around these parts instead of praying to your fatass vigilante overlords, maybe we wouldn't have to take so much murderous dick up our asses every weekend. Ever think of that?"

"Wrellord can't come soon enough. Gede's been getting lazy these days. Know what I mean?"

Tap.

Grainy footage of a dark trail shooting through the morning sky played alongside the logo of the local news station, *Prime Centrum*.

"The 'Black Comet,' as it has been dubbed by observers, reportedly ascended from a quiet street in the South District before soaring and descending towards the North. Our diligent operatives of FOG Central promptly trailed the object to its approximate destination, and we eagerly anticipate their full report by the end of this week. As always, we think of nothing less than the absolute safety of Golem's people and her rulers. Coming up next on the FOG Channel are more exclusive footage and stories of the White Monument, where Wrellord, son of Gede Haizer, is scheduled to present his inaugural address."

Swipe.

Lyaphend rested her phone on her lap and quietly exhaled a sigh. From the view of the window beside her, the black, illuminated buildings and skyscrapers of Prime District pierced the cloudy night sky, foretelling a heavy rainfall. She leaned sideways, laying her entire two-metre frame along the lengthy, velvet back seat of the driverless luxury transport cruising above the bustling metropolis of Golem's capital city. The neon lights bordering the roof clung to her eyeglasses as she fixed her eyes towards a holographic screen positioned between the two front seats, relaying footage of the aerial gridlock courtesy of several detached cameras hovering above the taillights.

This city was her birthplace; she was but an infant when she was whisked away to another city. When she returned eleven years later, the bustling metropolis was a desolate ghost ravaged by an unspeakable calamity. She could at last witness the capital in its desired glory, yet a foreboding air flooded her nostrils with her every breath, growing brisker with every venture towards her destination. The harbinger of her upbringing was near—of that, she was certain. What remained to be questioned was what would become of her identity once she claimed it. Even now, the craven within her begged to set loose and flung back into the comfort of home.

I pitied that she had forgotten just how far from home she was.

Before she could relax to the jazzy tune playing over the

radio, her phone trembled in her grasp, notifying her of an incoming text:

CALL ME.

She playfully rolled her eyes, withholding the urge to text a witty gripe at the sender, Yona Igens. Far from friends, she and Yona were what the latter referred to as *transient business partners*. Although Lyaphend had Yona to thank for granting her some semblance of freedom when she last journeyed to Prime District—as comical as it was to be grateful that she was kidnapped by a clandestine cult to be delivered to a cyberterrorist organisation—her gratitude extended only as far as to abide by their contract until it was fulfilled. She dialled Yona's number and repressed the uncooperative layabout within her before speaking sweetly, "Yes, Igens?"

"Enjoying the ride, Ms. Farwalth?" Yona asked in her usual sly tone. "On a scale of one to ten, how nervous does the sight of Prime District leave you? Considering what happened last time you were there, I take it your heart isn't exactly fluttering with joy."

Lyaphend lifted an eyebrow. "That doesn't sound like a question in the interest of business."

"Maybe it's business, or maybe I've decided to test you somehow—which makes this my business alone."

Lyaphend twiddled the black tresses of her otherwise faded green fringe with her index finger, staving off the added stress. "I thought you already trusted me."

Yona left Lyaphend lingering in a moment of silence before responding, "So, anyway, you're a grown woman, aren't you? How much have you been keeping up with politics?"

"Should I be interested?" Lyaphend asked, deciding against the first response that came to mind: *Not much at all.*

"Gede's sixteen-year-old son is scheduled to give his inaugural address in a few days. Wrellord is a bit of an enigma for the populace at large. His upbringing was more or less what you would expect of a coddled son of the ruling family. He was locked away in his posh estate and privately tutored in his room. Much of his free time was spent playing with his toys in the courtyard. Occasionally, he could even be spotted standing by his window during the rain, contemplating whatever secrets stirred in that reserved little brain of his. It goes without saying that he exists solely to inherit the burden of his two-centuries-old father."

"Not for two hundred years, I hope," Lyaphend japed, drawing attention to Gede's unusual age.

"The Haizers are far from your usual family, but that shouldn't come as too much of a surprise for a magic girl like you. Golem's poor civilians are unaware that this entire world is far from what it seems on the surface."

Lyaphend rolled over and opened the transport's sliding door with a button on an adjacent panel, exposing the exterior to the unpleasant low temperatures. She clasped the outer rim of the door's foundation and used her hand as leverage to swing herself up to the roof. Vivid colours swirled around her—the medley of lights of the vehicles, the tiny surveillance automations circling above, and the holographic advertisements affixed to the surrounding buildings. But the sight most demanding of her attention was that of a giant building approaching from the left, comprised of a cascade of balconies from every angle. The King's Tower was the tallest building in all of Golem, reserved for government use except on the most special of occasions.

And tonight was a very special occasion. Wave Haizer, the sister of Wrellord, would be hosting a party in celebration of her brother's ascension to the crown of authority, and the tower was scheduled to become dense with the presence of every man and woman belonging to Golem's aristocracy, including Lyaphend herself through adoption. If her intuition served her, the King's Tower also concealed her object of interest—the object with which she was delivered to Golem.

With any luck, it was not under the possession of the

ruler-to-be's sister herself.

"Still there?" Yona asked.

Lyaphend lifted her phone. "Still here. I'm close."

"No one knows what to expect from Wrellord, but for all we know, he's lived a good life. His father is hailed as one of the greatest rulers in Golem's history; he'll get to decide whether he wants to build upon that foundation or tear it apart with extreme prejudice."

The transport came to a stop at the final aerial intersection to Lyaphend's destination, where traffic was directed by a box-shaped automaton hovering above in the middle. "What would you prefer?" Lyaphend asked, daring to pry into Yona's sentiments.

Yona replied after a long pause, "Well... Gede's not exactly famous in the criminal underground—though I know you have yet to get your hands dirty yourself—but I hate wildcards far more. And speaking of wildcards..."

A green light emitted from an orb embedded in the automaton's chest, and the transport made one final turn before approaching the balcony of the King's Tower serving as the reception area. Straight ahead, men and women in fancy ballroom clothing disembarked on a raised walkway leading to a detached segment of the balcony's glass window, their abandoned vehicles assorting themselves within a nearby cascade of pink holographic grids serving as an aerial parking lot.

"Yes, Yona?" Lyaphend asked with some hesitance in her tone.

"Speaking of wildcards, you should know I'm contemplating killing you."

The omen of Yona's genuine killing intent presented itself even as the woman's tone remained stagnant, and the back of Lyaphend's head already grew warm with the touch of imaginary blood drawn from a fatal bullet. She gritted her teeth with resolve. The curtain of impending death had already stolen her innocence not long ago; it would take more than a passive threat to intimidate her into submission. Yona was a dangerous woman, but so was she, even if she was more the type to make it clear through actions rather than words alone.

And as far as actions were concerned, she was confident she was the more intimidating one of the two. "I thought I'd already earned your trust."

"Not while I'm left with so many questions about you. What kind of woman are you? What do you want in life, and how are you planning on getting it? What do you have now that is most valuable to you? I need to know these things before I trust you with my life and trust myself not to take yours. Until then, I'll keep my gun on you, and if you have any iota of wisdom, you won't shove it away from the back of your head."

Lyaphend snickered. "I have two little brothers and a father to look after now; they are my most valuable possessions. You can keep as many eyes on me as will help you sleep peacefully at night, but I hope you have something better than a gun to point at me in the case you fire and somehow... *miss* your mark."

Lyaphend lingered in silence and amusement, awaiting Yona's response until the call abruptly ended. She dismissed the tension with a sigh and refocused her thoughts on the task at hand, tucking her phone away in the back pocket of her jeans. Evidently, Yona was equally terrified of her. "Shouldn't you be thinking about retirement by now anyway, old girl?" she mumbled with a smile.

With the transport coming to a stop, she jumped onto the walkway with a fancy forward flip, earning her the gawks of several bystanders. The marble interior of the twentieth floor of the King's Tower stared at her beyond two glass doors at the end of the vast balcony; the space was overlooked by the presence of several tall men in black suits, the two nearest to the entrance carrying handheld devices that appeared to be chip scanners. Lyaphend waded through the line in the walkway and the overcrowded balcony until the time had come to introduce herself. "Hello. My name is Lyaphend Farwalth, but you seem to be getting ready to confirm my invitation for yourself."

The guard to her left nodded before pointing a laser from the rectangular nozzle of his device into her chest, scanning the identification chip embedded in her heart. He flashed the resultant readings to the other guard, who turned away and contacted someone over his phone with a hushed tone before tilting his head at Lyaphend. "One of the Farwalths, eh? Looks like you've kept out of the public eye for a long time."

Lyaphend smiled. "I prefer a more modest lifestyle."

"Got any special business here? That's an interesting party style you've got." The guard drew particular attention to her flowing, silver-piece-embellished black vest.

"I have a busy schedule and don't intend to stay long, but I hoped to run into a few familiar faces and catch up a little bit."

The guard to her left flashed a smirk. "Hope you'll stick around for the banquet, at least. Be on your way."

As Lyaphend stepped through the soundproof barrier of the front door, she was deluged with sensory information. From the seats of the assorted dining tables shrouded under gingham cloths and decorated with vases of lacquered black roses, the innumerable voices of the prattling guests loomed over the song of an opera playing on a holographic television hanging behind the room's golden chandelier. The entire space graced her nostrils with a polished scent like that of a pair of new shoes, but even the presence of fine paintings hung upon the calacatta marble walls did not distract her eyes from the presence of state-of-the-art cameras and miniature turrets along the ceiling to remind her that the building existed for government officials first and foremost. Her own mind began to prattle over possibilities. What was the main purpose of the King's Tower? How many floors were accessible to the guests? How many of them would she need to peruse before she stumbled upon her objective?

With the discovery of a row of electronic guideboards hidden near the corner of her eye, she had found the means to glean some answers. The touchscreen inputs provided her with several menus of information— the number of floors accessible to the guests, the first names and surname initials of the guests present on the current floor, a surprisingly intimate detailing of the building's layout, and exotic beverages served by the counter. Were it her business to waste the night in pleasure, she would have enjoyed throwing on a sensual dress, dancing and fraternising with her fellow guests as though she were free of burden and leading a life no different than that of an ordinary woman who chanced upon wealth and sought to indulge in it. Alas, the fancy bun restraining her hair would have to settle for the relatively casual drab of a potential thief in the making, and her fantasies would have to come to fruition another night.

She stepped away from the board and withdrew her phone as it began to vibrate in her pocket. Yona had sent her another text:

> IF YOU HAPPEN TO RUN INTO WAVE HAIZER
> AT SOME POINT, CHOOSE YOUR WORDS CAREFULLY.
> SHE'S EVEN YOUNGER THAN HER BROTHER, AND
> I KNOW NOTHING ABOUT HER AT ALL.

She kept her response simple:

> ACKNOWLEDGED.

But before she could put her phone away, it vibrated in her grasp as another text came, the sender anonymous with the following message:

> HELLO, LYAPHEND FARWALTH. I HAVE WHAT
> YOU'RE LOOKING FOR. TAKE THE ELEVATOR TO
> THE TOP FLOOR. YOUR ID HAS ALREADY BEEN
> GRANTED THE NECESSARY PRIVILEGES.

"What?" she whispered under her breath, coming up with three possibilities as to where the message originated: An unnamed hacker setting up a trap, an agent sent by Yona to assist her, or some sort of government official—perhaps even

Wave Haizer herself. She texted Yona again while fiddling with the guideboard to appear natural.

SOMEONE ANONYMOUS JUST TEXTED ME.
THEY'RE TELLING ME THEY HAVE WHAT I'M LOOKING
FOR AT THE TOP FLOOR. FRIEND OF YOURS?

Yona's curt response followed quickly:

NO. DEAL WITH THIS YOURSELF.

Lyaphend shoved her phone back into her pocket and groaned. "There's one way to know for sure, I guess."

She made her way towards the opposite end of the floor, weaving through the dense crowd until she found an elevator within a long corridor. Upon attempting to call it to her floor, a light above the door cast a red laser scanner shifting to and fro across the ground as if searching for a target. She took several paces backwards and waited in the middle until the laser stopped at her chest, and the elevator began to move, allowing her to step inside and ascend to the top floor—the rooftop.

She paused the elevator just before the elevator could open, having received another text from Yona:

HERE'S A TIP: THAT COULD BE A
TRAP. THINK CAREFULLY.

She lifted her empty palm, curling her fingers slowly. She had never taken the life of a human; as far as she was concerned, she had no enemies. Fighting was survival; defeat was death.

But whenever her heart thrashed as it did now, she could never tell if she was more afraid of killing or being killed. She was a dangerous woman, but so too was Wave Haizer. The apparent lack of security made that much clear to her.

The harsh air rolled into the inside of the elevator as the doors slid open, unravelling the night sky and the spacious rooftop beneath it, illuminated by an unseen object casting a bright light from above. Near the precipice of the building, three figures stood with their backs turned towards her. Two of them were unremarkable—tall men in suits not unlike the ones from before, as far as Lyaphend could tell, given the considerable distance she stood from them. What drew her attention was the drape of long silvery hair between them, contrasted by the flowing skirt of a frilly black dress—a figure too frail and feminine to be called that of a man or a security guard or even that of an average grown woman.

"I knew it was you," Lyaphend whispered before making her move. But as soon as she took her first step off the elevator, her heart skipped a beat. Two rifles flanked both sides of her face. She shifted her eyes to the sight of two armed guards who had slipped by her senses.

"Hands up, girl," the man to her left calmly ordered.

Lyaphend regained her composure with a brisk breath, hoping her words would be enough to protect both herself and them. "Stop. I wasn't intending to—"

"Hands fucking *up!*" the man repeated, jolting his weapon forward.

The man to her right was more attentive towards the edge of the building, and he lowered his rifle as he noticed the girl in the dress swaying her raised hand without turning to face them. "Looks like we're letting you off easy," he chuckled.

Lyaphend nodded at him before glaring at the pointed rifle of the one to her left. "Hands down... pretty please."

The man's face twitched with mild irritation before he managed to lower his own rifle.

With the two men following closely behind her, Lyaphend carefully walked forward, squinting her eyes briefly after glancing at the source of the light, a hovering mechanical sphere with a radiant core sizeable enough to illuminate the entire rooftop.

Refusing to turn around even as Lyaphend stood a few metres away, the girl extended her other arm sideways, revealing the screen of a phone in her grasp. "I would guess I needn't ask if you got my text!" she shouted in a refined tone.

"Lyaphend Farwalth, I am pleased to grace your presence."

Lyaphend folded her arms in front of her, patient but sceptical. "I appreciate the hospitality, but I'm afraid you have me at a disadvantage."

"At a disadvantage? Whatever do you—" The girl caught herself with a gasp. "Oh, yes! My sincerest apologies!" She stepped away from the glass railing and turned around to formally introduce herself, her innocuous expression belying a considerable intellect. Her eyes, coloured like a deep blue sea, delved under the curtain of her long eyelashes as she bowed politely. "I am whom I believe you were expecting—I am Wave Haizer, daughter of Gede and sister of Wrellord. If I have inflicted undue stress upon you, I apologise once more. Rest assured, your life is in no danger by my doing; all I ask is that you and I discuss a proposition I believe you will find equally beneficial for us."

Lyaphend tilted her head slightly away, curious but unanswered. "Interesting. You seem to know quite a bit about me."

Wave rested her forearm on the railing, staring at the vacant spot beside her. "Please, come closer. You deserve this wonderful view, even if the wind is biting." She dismissed the two guards next to Lyaphend with a quick gesture.

But upon standing beside Wave, Lyaphend first noticed their impressive height difference. That she was once intimidated by the thought of standing close to Gede's daughter became a laughable memory. In fact, the city in its entirety suddenly felt as though it could fit within the palm of her hand. From atop Golem's tallest building, the city of Prime District was reduced to an incomprehensible jumble of lights, blinding her to all but its tallest and most recognizable landscapes. She could see the Great Divider, a vast bridge connecting all four of the city's major subdistricts over the Heart of Golem, a lake comprising around half a quarter of the entire city.

She would never be able to look fondly upon that bridge after her first near-death experience.

"As you say, I know quite a bit about you," Wave continued, gazing towards the city alongside Lyaphend. "In fact, I had gone through the trouble of arranging these festivities simply so that you and I could meet in private—not under the prying eyes of my family nor our government lapdogs at FOG. I am well aware of the Farwalths' allegiance to the Dalka Clan, the cyberterrorist organisation FOG is so wary of, and I knew you would come to me with the bit of freedom you now possess—one way or another." She chuckled. "Honestly, I did not believe you would appear as one of our guests, but this is more convenient."

"So, FOG doesn't know exactly where I'm hiding yet." Lyaphend glanced at the guard standing a short distance from her to her other side. "And these men are…?"

"Worry not. They are my personal security detail; they answer only to me."

"More to the point, what do you want with me? My association with the Dalka Clan makes us technically enemies, does it not?"

"The Dalka Clan is of more concern to FOG than it is to my family. Furthermore, my understanding is that you, as a FOG 'deserter,' are merely using them for your own protection. Needless to say, I know about the incident in which you were kidnapped and 'forced' to switch allegiances."

"If you know I'm that same woman, you must have scanned me with something other than a chip reader."

"No matter how much you change on the outside, there is nothing you can do to change what you are inside, sadly." Wave looked directly into Lyaphend's eyes. "Hiding in the criminal underworld does have its difficulties, I'm sure. Lyaphend, I offer you freedom the likes of which will allow you to even depart from Golem at your leisure. Your slate would be wiped clean; you would be considered nothing more than an aristocrat, or even just common folk if you would prefer."

Lyaphend narrowed her eyes slightly, her scepticism growing. "A tempting offer, but how does it benefit you?"

A tiny smile crept upon Wave's lips. "It benefits me because

I alone would have by my side the greatest weapon Golem has ever possessed—you."

"I am not a weapon."

"But you are not human either, are you?" Wave leaned slightly to her side, reaching for an object beside her leg—something about the same length wrapped in kraft paper. "I am no mere daughter of nobility. I like dolls, pretty dresses, and fairy tales, but nuance is my greatest obsession. When I closed the book of one fairy tale in particular, I was told it may not be a fairy tale at all. I, being obsessed, did my own research. Evidently, my father decided I was too minute to deserve the truth. You, on the other hand, saw the truth with your own eyes. That was when you realised you were not what you thought you were."

Lyaphend looked at the back of her right hand—rather, the black marking that was upon it, a double circle that wove into an elaborate pattern around her forearm. In a usual outing, she kept it partially concealed under a long-sleeved dark blouse, and tonight was no exception. Her arm would quiver and freeze whenever she focused upon it, as though it possessed a life of its own and begged for an offering to do as it pleased. Few people could say they had lost an arm and gained it back moments thereafter, but it seemed no injury could keep her and it forever apart.

"If I may speak somewhat untowardly," Wave continued, "you are a human with the power of an eldritch heart—you are among those monsters that prevail in the world outside our colony. It is of mere courtesy that I refer to you by your adoptive name and not as Enlenea, the name you possessed in your past life a thousand years ago as one of the Elegies—as one of the few eldritch hearts to have reclaimed the sanity you once possessed as a living mortal."

Enlenea... It was a name which carried with it profound emotions and untraceable memories. Although Lyaphend could vaguely remember a moment in which she spoke with the voice of the long-departed entity, the experience was fleeting;

Enlenea's powers and recollections were slipping from her grasp day by day. She remembered a pact between Enlenea and an unnamed woman—one that would result in the rebirth of one or the other as a human over a millennium later. Guilt took her by surprise every time she thought about it. She had transgressed, but she could not remember how.

And whenever she delved deeper into her heart, she drowned in a black sea of infinite, irrational, and uncontrollable madness. That was a part of her inner self she did not wish to recollect.

Wave lifted the object in her grasp between her and Lyaphend, crudely tearing away the kraft paper with her nails to reveal an engraved broadsword with a golden hilt, rusted from years of neglect. "This is what was delivered to Golem, and it is what you were spawned from eleven years ago; now, it is what leads you to me. I would task you to eliminate a certain threat to my family, but you are of far less use to me if you cannot recall the identity of this threat. This sword, wherever it originated, resonates with you, and I suspect, should you touch it, you will reclaim all of your memories. That is Enlenea's power, is it not? Even if you do not agree to my terms at this moment, I will leave this with you as an honorary gift."

Lyaphend reached for the sword, enchanted by its vaguely familiar hilt, but hesitated. "I would be of no service to either of us if I lose my mind in the process," she murmured.

Wave extended the sword further towards Lyaphend. "I have faith in your resolve. Remember that hiding will not disappear your problems, nor will procrastination."

"Fair point," Lyaphend sighed. She placed her hand on the sword's hilt as surely as though she were opening the door to her room, but she could never have prepared herself for the deep plunge. Reality itself spun into an indiscernible swill before abandoning her to uncountable visions of the past—not only Enlenea's past, but that of several other individuals. With concentration, she reclaimed the beginning; from there, she pieced together the end.

All that remained was to walk the completed tale of the forgotten pact and reclaim all she was in a single instant.

Chapter II: Flower

Year 153 Before Golem
Darkness.
Silence.
A sanctuary lost and so far away.
A warm breeze upon fertile soil.
A new land which she could not comprehend.
A tenuous crawl to a new destination.
A novel feeling, a pause.
A pleasant vibe within the clasp of her palm.
Sunlight, nature—all that now lay bare before her sight.
War, chaos, forgotten peace—everything
acquired from her new recollections.
With new life, she stood upon her delicate legs.
With remorse, she watched as the final petals
fell from the flower wilting in her hand.
With allure, she strolled.
With resolve, she dreamt.

Many lands would be known to her; many seasons would come and go with nothing to be found in their wake. With few answers, the woman found many more questions to come. Many remaining civilizations fled from the mere sight of her; others would take arms and stand against her. But even as she wandered the barren lands, her shadow was ever trailed by an assembly of cloaked individuals bestowed with a power she did not understand. Proclaimed by themselves as adherents to the reclamation of their dying world, they were known only as Halians by the powerless. She had soon given up and forfeit her life to these Halians only to discover that she could never truly die. Such could be said for all creatures born of the Scourge, as it was revered by humanity, but she was as ignorant as they to its origins.

War persisted between humanity and the tainted, but the woman could not say she belonged to either side. All things she knew in life were taken from the memories of the meadow, along with her curiosity of the world and desire for peace. Before that moment, she was but a meaningless wayfarer, her emptiness embodied well in her faceless visage. And in some way not yet apparent to her, she was unique amongst even the tainted. Surely the others did not share her beliefs, but neither were they alike in how they came to be. The tainted began as humans; they had little recollection of their former identities but nevertheless once possessed mortal sentience. The faceless woman began as nothing—only from the flower was she given an identity, for such was the gift her power could bestow upon her. From that power alone could she forge an identity to call her own.

She cherished nature; she valued all life beyond her own. And so she would discover a means to die, a means by which she could banish the tainted along with herself. She would journey in solitude to her prospective grave, thinking fondly of a world without her—a world whose rightful inhabitants would thrive forevermore.

"Could you be...?"

"Do you sense me?"

"Can you see me?"

"Do you hear me?"

"Do you know what I am?"

Upon a barren tundra amid a storm, a man would one day approach her bearing those five questions. From but a glance, the woman could feel his tainted presence, yet strangely he harboured no ill intent. The smile he wore on his delicate face left the woman at ease and oddly content, as though her journey had already reached its conclusion. At last, with some effort, she could speak her first word.

"Yes," she replied to no question in particular, her voice echoing as if it had spawned from the land itself.

At this, the man smiled with glee. "Finally, my efforts bear fruit!" He solemnly offered his hand to the woman. "Have you a name, O faceless woman?"

She shook her head after a moment of contemplation.

"Then, henceforth, you will be known as 'Enlenea, the Painted Woman'—such on behalf of your visage. Stand alongside me, and never again shall you be alone or lost."

A ring pierced the blanket of weeping clouds overhead. She and the man stood in a lone ray of sunlight as the morning sky began to overtake the storm, ironic for two beings bathed in obscurity.

Nevertheless, another tumultuous storm had begun to fade along with it—the one in which she had wallowed since the day of her birth.

"Enlenea? That is a beautiful name." She clung to his hand and the ray of light in her own heart, eager to unravel this mysterious identity before her.

Chapter III: Their Dreams

Year 148 B.G.

A group comprised of tainted who stood above the rest; a group comprised of tainted with one common goal; a group accepting of all the faceless woman was. They were known together as the Elegies. Enlenea, at last, found herself accompanied by four tainted beings who shared her beliefs, all named as follows: Astot, Herald of a New Era; Inguis, the Trophykeeper; Constius, the Insidious Creator; and Regnal, the One Ideal.

Astot was their leader and the long-haired man Enlenea first encountered. It was his faint memories and an excerpt from a fable of a peaceful world that led him on a journey to discover his Begetter—the author of the fable and the original transgressor that created the Scourge which had birthed the tainted. To that end, he sought others who would listen to his story—tainted that could comprehend every word he spoke. But although he alone had gathered each of the Elegies, he could not surely say it was his benevolence or a desire they all shared that kept them together. As for his own objective, he would meet with the Begetter before embracing his own death, and that would be that. It was his belief that his powerful devotion would earn him the audience of the Begetter.

Inguis appeared as a disembodied head in the skies with the shape of a six-eyed black hound and the height of a mountain, an entity as looming as his appearance suggested. A suspicion amongst the other Elegies was that he was more knowledgeable of the origins of the Scourge than he seemed. The mightiest of all tainted, as claimed by Astot, Inguis favoured wanton destruction, and he alone made claim to the genocide of many populations. His every breath was accompanied by the immortalised screams of those deemed worthy to suffer eternally in his coffer. It was his belief that destruction without purpose would guide the Elegies to the Begetter.

Constius was one who could be easily recognised in common folklore. Indeed, amongst all of the Elegies, Constius made himself known throughout most human civilizations. With a sleeved black sheet to drape over his human torso as well as his stallion lower body, he was identified most by the gleaming red insignia upon his cloaked face. He was often considered a god who would bestow great power to those of his favour. Such blessings would often come at great cost, and in the end, the Elegy would always claim his satisfaction of it, lending those many civilizations to disarray and ruin. It was his belief that through deceiving mankind could the Elegies convince the Begetter to appear.

Finally, Regnal, the One Ideal. Whilst the others were named by Astot, Regnal had given himself a name of his own accord before he even learned of the Elegies' existence. Before that day, he had simply observed mankind from afar. He had no form to call his own, so he would seek something worthy of his imitation. Regnal did not seem to hold any interest in the Begetter; more so, it seemed he did not wish to die but to stand as an absolute being, encompassing every conceivable existence. Although the 'One Ideal' was scarcely looked fondly upon by his equals, Astot had never denied his usefulness. It was Regnal's belief that the Begetter would make himself known through a reckoning, a decisive battle between him and a rival. Regnal himself would become that rival, an ultimate being beyond the Scourge in its entirety.

Enlenea had yet to decide upon her own methods, and so she would merely do what Astot had done before—to find another tainted being of power and insight,willing to lend it all for the meaning of the Elegies.

Chapter IV: Aerbith

Year 141 B.G.

A black tower stood as an ominous fixture upon a forest of crumbling snags. Since the day it first appeared from the depths of nothing, the tainted swarmed in countless numbers. Nearby settlers cowered in fear, knowing well their powerlessness before the plague. Where the humans saw a calamitous augur, Enlenea saw a promising opportunity. Such an elaborate structure must surely have belonged to a creature of purpose.

The interior was a deliberate and hushed dungeon with grand windows and bells hanging from its intricate walls. She made her way through its dark corridors until she felt a presence beyond a pair of sturdy metal doors. She curiously caressed their cold, dusted surfaces before gently pushing them aside, the resultant creaking echoing throughout the corridor.

The moonlight peered from a lone window behind steel bars. What lay in that small, solitary space was a slumbering beast, a silvery hound with three tails. A pen and parchment lay on a wooden table in the corner of the cell, the pen writing upon the parchment seemingly of its own accord.

The beast calmly opened its gleaming gold eyes before Enlenea's presence. It observed her silently like a tame animal, but she would not be so easily deceived by appearances.

"Do you sense me?" Enlenea asked.

No response.

"Can you see me? Do you hear me? Do you know what I am?"

No response; a moment of silence.

"Shall I then ask… what you are doing here?"

Letting out a prolonged breath, the beast stood on its legs, tall enough to reach Enlenea's shoulder, before turning away and laying back down with a low-toned growl. But Enlenea did not falter; she could sense the creature's mounting frustration, and she would need only to remain in her spot until her words were acknowledged.

"What is it you seek to gain from me?" the beast finally asked, its maw motionless as it spoke without a discernible means.

"I seek only to know you understand my words," Enlenea replied.

"You had known this already; I need not speak. Now begone with you, for we do not seek your lecture—we do not need it."

"How strange. What lecture have you in mind? And, what 'we' do you speak of?"

"Have you not paid heed to the anguished clamours of our tenants? Are you yet deaf to our master's calling? Then you are oblivious—here, an unwelcome sight. And now I understand why you dawdle in my presence."

"You speak half-truth. Indeed, I knew naught of your so-called tenants. Your master, however, beckons well my curiosity, and so I am here." Enlenea lowered herself to align with the creature's turned back. "Pray, odd creature, tell me all you have seen."

Finally, the beast turned until it met Enlenea face-to-face. "All you need do is await my master's calling and hearken. I have naught to gain in prattling for one such as you."

"You know it as your master, but dare I wonder if you linger here not of your own will?"

A grating noise came from the pen and parchment behind the creature as the pen began to tear through the parchment and carve the table underneath. "Impertinent fool, I COMMAND my own fate!" the beast roared.

"Ah, you appear to loathe being likened to a feral beast bound in a cage. But, truly, you try so little to be any different than that. 'Tis such a pity." She stood up. "Very well, lost creature, I will leave you be. Should you least possess a name—"

"My name is Aerbith," the creature interrupted.

"Ah, Aerbith. If anything at all—pray tell me this, at least—what could I have done to earn your favour?"

"Know only that I stay in wait of amnesty."

"Amnesty?"

Aerbith closed his eyes and let out a weary breath. "A pardon of my own foolishness. But only I may provide that pardon."

"And so you retire yourself to this degrading den," Enlenea softly mused. "Now I know all I wish to know from you. You have my gratitude." With that, she took her leave of the isolated room, closing the doors behind her and allowing the creature to once more wallow in its self-imprisonment.

Chapter V: A Scourge All Its Own

Enlenea would not depart from the tower until becoming witness to its hidden master. She spent countless days in the tower's great archives, reading the numerous books recording the origins of both it and its masters. Eventually, she could speak of it as though she belonged there.

In life, the master was a powerful leader known far across the land in an era of three great monarchies. Powerful as he was, he would keep himself from the eyes of his people, secluded always within his grand castle, to be observed only by those amongst his closest subjects. Rumours would spread of his appearance and rulership. Some would say he was a malicious entity who manipulated the hearts of his people; others would say that he was, in truth, a child or a woman or perhaps did not even exist at all. In the end, he would die alone, known not for the man he truly was, but the undecided husk created in the minds of all those he ruled over.

Regardless, the master was no longer present, for he had departed without a word on an unknown journey. In his place, Enlenea could faintly sense the permeation of some corrosive influence throughout a wing of the tower formerly unventured by her—the presence of an intruder unwelcome to all but her, harmless but foreboding in nature.

Having exhausted her interest in much else the tower offered, the time had come to explore the crumbling depths, whether a wise master would await her or not. The ceiling shuddered as the doors creaked open, revealing a corridor infinite to mortal eyes, alight with trails of subtle blue flames seeping from gashes in the walls. Enlenea ventured through the blazing corridors until one became a spiralling stairway, and she ascended the stairs until the sound of flowing water balanced the tumult of cackling flames; she found herself standing before a paved, shallow basin of bleak water flowing in from narrow gaps on either side of the wall. In the basin, upon which wisps of the black flame lingered, a small mass of dark flesh protruded from the surface, round enough for Enlenea to grasp it in her arms. She could barely conjure the words to describe this small creature she cradled like an infant. Was it a pupa to possess its stubby, underdeveloped eight legs? Was it a caterpillar with how it wriggled against her arms?

But who was she to even compare it to an ephemeral creature, this malicious entity who threatened to engulf the tower entirely in flames undying? She shook her head at her own folly before returning the tainted to its watery nest, content to leave it to its vices until, with any luck, it would dine upon the boundless knowledge of the tower alongside her, and she would have not only the ally she sought but a friend who shared her special gift: The power and will to evolve into something greater.

Chapter VI: Blade of Humanity

Year 139 B.G.

Be it from the presence of the pygmy tainted or the challenge of his journey, the master would not soon return to the tower. Enlenea could see nothing of interest from his replacement in its pitiable state. She considered two options— wait for the tainted to grow cognizant at its own steady pace or risk its fellowship by forcing its evolution through a trial of her choosing. In doing the former, she could at least present herself more time to her studies until the tower either disappeared or collapsed from within.

The tower's long history was marred with stories of humans wandering its corridors out of daft curiosity. They would be tasked with ringing eight bells hung upon the walls of eight rooms each, whereupon an emissary would appear and bestow a great reward. Those unfortunate men and women blindly paved the way to their gruesome deaths at the hands of the tower's bestial guardians, their bodies maintained as trophies for the ever-slumbering master. From what Enlenea could tell, only two guardians yet remained in the master's absence, sealed within respective prisons. She was already familiar with Aerbith the Hound; she would concern herself with the other later.

"Stumbled upon a cave... got swallowed by a black flame outta nowhere... and then I ended up here, somehow. Guess we're on the same boat."

"Shouldn't we just stay here and wait for rescue? The others should be on their way by now."

Enlenea had become nigh omniscient within the tower's

boundaries, a power she surmised was a gift to the master's subjects. She could perceive every sound, no matter her own location. She could not believe her own senses the day two foreign voices suddenly appeared.

The toll of a bell would soon follow those voices, followed by another, and another still. Before long, the trespassers succeeded in ringing all eight bells.

"Those fools," Enlenea muttered to herself. Who were these trespassers? What did they seek? None of it mattered when weighed against what was to come, or so Enlenea thought. The tower remained silent, its guardians unaroused by the toll of every bell. With that, she was presented with a comforting opportunity.

The trespassers would await their reward in the Chamber of Trophies, a grand hall before the master's statue. Antiquated coffins lay in rows against the walls as adornments, the remains of all those who had come before the unknowing pair.

One of the trespassers, a woman with yellow-tinted skin, messy blonde hair and curiously red eyes, looked upon her surroundings anxiously. "I did everything right, didn't I?" she asked.

Her fellow trespasser, a rather staunch orange-haired woman sitting plainly upon one of the coffins, looked at her with an amused grin. "Don't look at me; that was all your idea."

"Right..." Trailing off in thought, the red-eyed woman sluggishly approached the entrance, but she would not step far before the Painted Woman stood in her path, taking form instantly. The woman's instincts overtook her, and Enlenea sighed as she turned to flee before Enlenea herself could utter a single word.

"You are a tenant, I presume?" Enlenea inquired, inspecting the woman's knowledge.

The woman paused with the first word Enlenea spoke, looking at her partner, who paused with a curious look, before turning around to respond, or rather, answer a question with a question. "A tenant?"

Enlenea's fears lay bare before her—trespassers who knew nothing of the consequences of stepping foot upon this accursed dungeon. Moreover, they did not appear to be among the humans she had seen before, those who lived not far from the tower's territory. They did not dress nor act as though ignorant of any danger. Tools that Enlenea presumed to be weapons were clenched tightly under their grips. Were they warriors who wished to bask in the glory of heroism? Where had they come from? How much time had passed since she discovered the tower?

"We're just looking for a way out," the red-eyed woman continued. "Who are you? Can you help us?"

Help them? Did they not know of whom—of what—they were speaking to?

"Perhaps," Enlenea hesitantly responded. "What do you know of our master, he whose statue you now stand before?"

"No, I don't know anything about this place. I was just... sent here to investigate a tower that appeared a few kilometres from a settlement. Something happened on the way, and when I woke up, I was here."

From what Enlenea could make of the woman's words, she and her accomplice had been captured by the pygmy tainted on the way to prospect the tower for some unspoken end. Was the tainted itself what they sought, to vanquish the tower's presence from the territory of humans?

"What last had you seen ere you found yourselves here?" Enlenea asked.

"A fire, I think."

"So all becomes clear." Enlenea turned sideways and pointed to the entrance as the woman looked bewildered, eager to claim the opportunity that had just presented itself. "Our master is no longer present, for he has abandoned his servants. In his place now lies this insect of which you speak, a meddler whose presence we do not desire. If you would vanquish it here, this tower may cease to be. If not, I shall aid you as you will aid me."

33

"So I guess it's a fight after all, then," the staunch woman griped while approaching the two. "C'mon, Cyg, let's go."

"How can you be so sure of yourself?" the red-eyed woman asked. "What *is* this place, exactly? Can we trust what she's saying?"

"Hey, I'm not the newbie here, remember? Not like we got many other options, anyway."

Enlenea admired the woman's courage and pitied her ignorance. She was of no help to these two trespassers. The pygmy tainted, however pygmy it was, was a tainted all the same, one whose only instincts were to survive and protect its den. It would overcome this trial and grow stronger, for humanity would never overcome the Scourge.

But that fateful day, something would happen which Enlenea never deemed possible. The trespassers attacked; the tainted resisted with rivers and weaves of ebony flame, but it stood against a human who yet possessed some middling control over the Scourge. In the end, the tainted was vanquished, felled by this newfound might of humanity. Alas, Enlenea, as awed as she was of the inexplicable power of the staunch woman in particular, could not have fathomed the chaotic chain of events she had begun.

Chapter VII: A Memorable Tower

Hours had gone by since the tainted was vanquished, and night overtook the sky, but even left without a master, the tower remained. Whether it remained in its original location or had moved elsewhere, Enlenea did not know; she did not desire that knowledge. She had spent long enough there to expect nothing in return for her numerous efforts. The time had come to return to the Elegies. All that remained was but one final task, one last attempt to make her presence known to the tower's proper master.

Documents scattered about the tower's library told of ways one might reach the master in his absence. By standing before and speaking to the master's very statue, one's words could apparently be heard by the master no matter his distance from the tower. And so there, Enlenea stood in the middle of the night, the moonlight beaming from the windows behind the statue, a depiction of a headless giant with a segmented body draped in a long gown. She pointed a finger forward and spoke the question she had spoken once before.

"Do you *sense* me?"

No response.

"Can you *see* me? Do you *hear* me? Do you *know* who I am?"

No response. After all she had done, there was nothing to be found. She kneeled in utter defeat. Were she human, would she have wept by now? Would she have pitied herself, surrendering all hope?

"Ah... yes, I understand," she murmured after a silence. "To have sought dark solitude, enslaved by vestiges of mortal instinct, knowing not of what you would lose in turn... Poor, senseless creature, how I pity you and your rapt subjects." She stood up and turned away. "There will be no end to your anguish, but I will rejoice that you do not know even that."

"Is it your right to speak with such impudence?" muttered a voice from a black cloud amassing on the opposite end of the hall. An impressive four-legged beast, bulky and dark to match the tower's gloom, stepped forward from the depths of that cloud, its burning crimson eyes wandering every direction as though it had newly been freed from its prison.

From the presence of this beast, Enlenea found a sudden relief. "Are you that guardian I had yet to meet?"

But the guardian would not promptly respond as it approached the Painted Woman until it stood close enough for her hands to grasp its snout and horns. The otherwise frightening beast wore a comforting countenance as though it, too, had eagerly awaited this meeting. And with a solemn nod, this final guardian affirmed Enlenea's hope that it might understand her words.

"What is your name, guardian?" Enlenea asked.

"I am Madcow, the master's favoured trophy," the creature answered.

Enlenea gently caressed the cold, damp surface of the creature's nose. "Madcow... What a curious name, truly."

The creature proceeded to share with Enlenea his own story. Madcow, as he had been so mockingly named, was born as a beast no different than his ilk. He preyed upon the helpless and destroyed all else, for why else would a beast so mighty as himself exist? Before long, he found acknowledgement from the man he now called master, and for all his barbarism, he was taken prisoner as the master's feral pet, given a name he deeply loathed. But with his desolate solitude came a new opportunity, for now he could ponder his own existence—meditate on his own emotions. Thus came the realisation that would set him on a path of enlightenment, for he soon understood the purpose of his own name. Madcow—a fitting scorn for a mindless beast, but would a mindless beast be ever so concerned with names?

Madcow loathed his name, for he saw his existence as something greater. And if he loathed such a name so deeply, then did that not mean he was something more than but a mindless beast? Such was his master's wish all along—to set a mindless beast towards a path of wisdom.

Enlenea followed the enlightened beast as he led her into his dungeon. Several candles on the walls of either side of the bars that once contained him illuminated a small space of the dungeon with blue flames. Human remains littered the rat-infested grounds, and a deathly stench persisted. With Enlenea by his side, the beast faded back into the confines of his cage; the two stood on opposite ends, gazing curiously at one another until Enlenea spoke first.

"Why do you submit to such a hollow existence?" she asked. "You are a caged beast, left savage and athirst... yet you comprehend every word I speak. Why, then, do you choose to submit to that arid husk of a sentient life?"

Madcow cackled at her words. "Is it your belief that he acts of mere instinct? Were his guiding acts merely of my own machinations? Meddling wayfarer... am I merely blind in your own eyes?"

"Why is your master yet deaf to my own words? Why have I trifled before this tower to be given naught in turn? Wayward creature... am I merely not worthy of his words?"

"I am, as you have said, a ravenous beast like every one of its ilk, but my yearning for knowledge is why I may become something more than that. I differ in that I know wisdom; 'tis why our master knows me and why I, in turn, know him as my teacher."

"So he does not know me... because I do not require him, as he himself believes?" Enlenea mused. "Ah, that only he knew how wrong he was..."

Madcow narrowed his eyes at her suspiciously and slumped his head until his nose rubbed against the steel bars of his prison. "What *do* you require of our master?" he asked in a deepened tone.

Enlenea resigned to a moment of silence whilst she contemplated whether or not the beast would find anything of interest in her words or be ever too concerned with his own master. "Why do we exist? Why must we continue to exist? Do you know what happens should we ever die?"

"We cannot die; our wills are everlasting," came Madcow's curt answer. "I, too, have been felled by mortal hands so long ago. I closed my eyes, and my body was taken from me. I saw darkness and heard only sounds of the wind until, somehow, I could open my eyes once more. And there I was again, as though naught had happened. 'Twas a curious sensation, but one I desire not to understand.

"We are undying; we shall ever be undying. To die would be to forfeit the meaning of my existence—to cast myself aside into an everlasting void. 'Twas such a lonely, empty state I found myself in. Why would I condemn myself to it for time eternal?"

Enlenea swayed her head from side to side. "We are not humans. We are but tainted fools who know not of why we exist. We shall herald ruin alone upon this world... and what then? How could you be so unconcerned with our purpose if you value knowledge and wisdom so highly? I come to offer you a place among my people and our master, tainted like us who seek more than just to live."

"What, then, do you and 'your people' seek? Would you waste away your eternal life in a meaningless war for a dying breed of ignorant cravens?"

"If I am to choose between fighting an unending war and knowing an unending state of wishing I could win such a war, then I will walk the journey in lieu of dreaming idly of the destination."

But Madcow would not immediately respond to Enlenea. A prolonged sigh escaped his breath before he turned his back and left into the darkness of his prison. "You are not a human; do not pretend to be as one. I care not of the fate of this world, and neither should you."

"And yet... I do." Enlenea sighed before turning away.

"Farewell, lost beast. Should we become mutual in our beliefs one day, I pray we meet again."

Though Enlenea was soon to return to the Elegies, her link with the tower was everlasting—it would eternally travel to and fro across lands of the master's former interest, but she could return at her own whim in an instant. And she would continue to return for as long as the beast remained, not to admonish him but to converse with a beloved friend.

Chapter VIII: The Aborted Shade

In the wake of the pygmy's quietus, silence and rest had resumed in the tower's decrepit wing. Enlenea ventured into its corridors once more. Though nothing remained of the pygmy's physical presence, Enlenea felt the warm embrace of an old friend. Indeed, she had experienced the particular warmth of its flames before—before she departed for the tower, perhaps before she even met Astot.

Once again, she ascended a spiralling staircase, the one she was certain she had taken before; yet what awaited her at its precipice was not the same den of water but a collapsed platform with only a part of the ceiling it once possessed now exposed to the elements of the murky sky above the lowest clouds. The sting of a flame unseen grew prevalent beyond the numbing as she approached the precarious edge and fixated upon what now lay directly between her feet.

"Are you now keen on those existences down below?" she asked as she struggled to grasp the circumstances.

But the recipient of those words, a crawling mass of black flesh not unlike the feeble tainted supposedly felled by the hands of those two mortals, arched its back as dark fluid began to form a puddle under its belly. Even its tainted form began to exude the shroud of death before Enlenea's senses as she, by its influence, envisioned a dark beast swathed in placid black flames, clasping the frail hand of a trepid little girl before its body dispersed against the breeze as a shapeless gas, having never possessed a form to call its own.

And so it had imitated the form of another.

"Regnal?" Enlenea uttered, speaking the name of the entity who had proven himself so distinct among both the Elegies and tainted in their entirety—and now, perhaps, had somehow conjured a proxy with which he would expand his vision.

Like the little girl deprived of a hand to hold, Enlenea was abandoned to linger in confusion as the body of the pygmy tainted faded away, blending into the colourless swill of the wind. But as the wind whispered, it conjured a coherent parting message.

"I will make claim to all things that be; death be my guide to all things *I* must be," Enlenea recited. "So what must I be to you to have followed me thus, Regnal?"

She gave a parting gesture in the form of a slight bow before returning to the tower's depths. Upon the day she reunited with the Elegies, she would leave both herself and Regnal to their own secrets—unless the Ideal One were to sway her hand before the others, an outcome she desired but lacked the will to invoke by her words alone.

Chapter IX: The Coveted Saviours

Astot awaited her return in a land far away, his presence signalled by his vast influence. An aurora borealis glistened in the starlit sky as Enlenea trod upon the barren dirt in search of the Elegies she had long abandoned. In her absence, her allies had embarked on their own adventures, and she prayed for their greater fortune.

Astot sat in solitude, marvelling at the stars from upon a hilltop. Once Enlenea found him, he ran to her with a child's glee and caught her in an affectionate embrace. "Ah, Enlenea, at last, you return to us!" he exclaimed. "For so long have I awaited this moment."

Enlenea anxiously searched for the other Elegies. "Am I the only one?"

Astot shook his head. "They have already returned. Now, let us summon our family so that we may each share our stories." Astot retrieved a decorated bell from underneath his robe and stood before the precipice of the hill.

From the toll of the bell came Trophykeeper Inguis, who peered below from a rift in the sky, his arrival signalled by the everlasting cries of the victims stacked in his unseen coffer. Then from a distance came Constius, the man-horse draped in black who galloped daintily to the top of the hill. Regnal then spawned from a rock several paces behind Enlenea, taking the shape of a shadowy snake with gleaming blue eyes.

"I greet and thank each of you for serving the will of the Begetter," Astot smiled. "Though we may each differ in habits or desires, it is what we share—the faith we share—which will draw us together always for as long as the Begetter has yet to be known."

"Abandon your stupidity, sycophant," Constius spat. "I act of my own interests and that alone. 'Tis only your destiny to be tossed aside one day, such as I have done with many before you."

Inguis cackled at Constius' words. "Behold this fool who knows not his place, and pray the Begetter may have mercy on his soul," he grumbled.

Constius glared at Inguis. "Sh— shut your cur mouth!"

"Your words soothe my weary heart, Inguis, Constius," Regnal sarcastically added. "Truly, this is the home I have missed for so long."

Nothing had changed among the Elegies. Although threatened and ignored, Astot maintained his welcoming countenance as though none of it mattered. His faith kept him brave but exploitable; Enlenea knew it could one day mean his downfall. Perhaps even Astot knew that his charming words would sustain his influence for only so much longer, but no such concern manifested in his countenance.

Astot raised his palm. "Please, please, 'twas not my wish to be audience to this bickering." At those words alone, Inguis and Constius promptly fell silent. "Now, please, all of you, I wish to hear your stories—I wish to know how you have acted to earn the favour of our Begetter."

The Elegies proceeded to tell tales of their newest exploits. Constius deceived a great kingdom and led it to ruin; Inguis demolished half of an entire continent and conjured a literal sea of blood in its wake; Regnal claimed having consumed a legendary tainted and seizing its power and form as his own, no mention given of his encounter with Enlenea. But it was only when Enlenea spoke of her own experiences, acting as a tenant within the tower of a bygone king consumed by the flames of a powerful tainted—no mention given of its ties to Regnal—and later witnessing its banishment from the tower by the hands of human visitants, that the Elegies all considered their next course of action.

"'Tis not unheard of for a human to vanquish a

tainted," Astot explained. "Enlenea, have you yourself not been vanquished before?"

"I *have* been slain, only as I allowed it."

"But 'tis forsooth a first that humans treat us as game. How times have changed…"

"A mighty civilisation lies far to the North," Inguis informed. "So it seems they possess power enough to stand against us."

"This woman of red eyes and yellow skin you spoke of may be Halian," Regnal added.

"A Halian?" Enlenea asked, recalling her former encounters with those mysterious humans.

"What *is* a Halian? Do I ought to know?" Constius asked.

"Consider them a human race gifted with some manner of sorcery," Astot answered.

"We shall claim her life and do away with her kind."

"Nay, let us use her, for she seems to know not of what she is."

"How so?"

"We shall lead her astray against the Halians which threaten us and learn of where they reside."

"'Tis not unthinkable it could be done. So be it."

"And what of the woman she follows?"

"She is strong."

"Indeed brave is this mere human to have led such a victory against a tainted so mighty."

"Then let us destroy her."

"Such a waste it would be."

"She should be tainted."

"Yes, she should join us."

"Then shall we break her spirit and watch her fall?"

"Yes, yes… she could be a worthy Elegy."

So it seemed they had reached an agreement. With every other Elegy speaking at once, Enlenea could barely recall which of whom spoke what. As Regnal, Constius and Inguis embarked together on a new adventure, Astot remained beside Enlenea for a time.

"Are we to torture them?" Enlenea asked.

Astot gave a slow nod. "Let us pray they will not suffer long."

"They wield a power to stand against us, to vanquish us against our whims. Do we not have aught to learn from this?"

"Their efforts shall prove futile, for although our bodies may die to their hands, our souls shall be ever bound to this world. Humans are but relics of an olden era—feeble animals when compared to us. They stand only to fall as chaff. Such will be the penalty of their own arrogance."

"They strive only for survival, for if not, they may die before they see their wishes fulfilled, be it of old age, illness, or the hand of a murderer," Enlenea argued. "But not us, no—'tis as you say, our lives are everlasting. We *will* see our wishes made true, as time's passing is of little matter to us. We lack adversity and the will to survive it. Imagine that we were mortals—that we, too, knew a sort of adversity, a power that could grind our wishes to dust ere they be. Would we know the courage humanity now possesses? Could we then continue to believe ourselves better... or would we be as but a flock of cowards without faith?"

"To some living creatures, death is liberation," Astot quietly said. "I do not wish to live forever, truthfully said. When finally I know the man who created me, for what purpose would I have left to live, after all? Should my death come, I will not face it a coward; that I promise." He placed his hands on Enlenea's shoulders. "Still, think only of your own wishes, Enlenea—not those of humanity, nor those of myself, even. Beyond all else, you, and the others, too... you are all free spirits in my own eyes."

And she did have a wish her tainted heart held strongly— to give her own life for the sake of all others. Would that one day mean to stand against the other Elegies? Enlenea could only hope she would be forgiven for her acts to follow.

Chapter X: A Veiled Sacrifice

Year 137 B.G.

A red-eyed Halian from a mighty civilisation to the North and a brave heroine who led a small settlement in the wastelands—the two saviours who would be pawns in the Elegies' cruel games. The Elegies swiftly discovered the heroine of the settlement, but they could not so easily reach the Halian, who had returned to the North under great protection. So it was agreed that the settlement's leader would be their first victim, and the Halian would share her fate another day.

Enlenea would spend the following year under the company of the Elegies in their period of rest before enacting their conspiracy. She would bide her time travelling to and fro the tower, studying the numerous records of Halians within its vast archives. The Halians were of Halia, a sacred place upon which, it was written, mankind was born. The Halians were thought to serve as humanity's godly overseers until the day they were cast into the forlorn lands. Others viewed them as malicious keepers who sought to conquer mankind with the power of the Scourge. To many, they had been extinct for countless millennia. The truth, Enlenea would need to discover for herself.

Regnal was greedy, Constius was deceitful, Inguis was powerful, and Astot was wise and faithful. Enlenea was weak and indecisive—she would be of no assistance to them, nor did she desire to be. Whilst her allies mercilessly tortured the vanquishers, Enlenea concerned herself with the presence of the tower's guardians. Aerbith, she soon learned, had already departed, having seemingly forgiven his own folly. Madcow remained the tower's only tenant, eagerly awaiting Enlenea's revisit.

Madcow slumbered in the darkness of his prison. As soon as Enlenea set foot upon his territory, the beast's eyes lit open with excitement. "Enlenea... have you come to scorn my ways?" he asked in a weary murmur.

Enlenea shook her head. "I have already forgiven that we do not think alike. Wayward beast—nay, Madcow—I simply wish to rest here for a spell."

At Enlenea's words, Madcow narrowed his eyes. Had he already begun to doubt her resolve? "Then so be it. Lingering here by oneself is a tiring bore, and with my master's absence, I strain to tolerate it." He let out a prolonged growl. "What of your own master, Enlenea? Do you now show yourself of your own accord?"

"Truthfully spoken, ne'er was he a master of mine," Enlenea replied. Madcow gave her a bemused look. "Should a master of mine not share my own beliefs?"

"What you speak of is a master you have chosen," Madcow said. "A master is of many things. Some choose their own master; others are merely chosen by them. For those who choose, they may seek guidance from one greater than themselves, or perhaps they seek shelter in the form of a living thing. For those that are chosen, they were conquered, powerless, or led astray with words. What is your fate, Enlenea? Are you one who chooses or one who is chosen?"

Enlenea carefully considered her past and Astot's words from that night. Astot was to her both a teacher and a guide, but had she ever truly cared for his plight? She was a compassionate creature; she valued all life beyond her own. But she lacked the power to bring her dreams to fruition since birth. She would have the Elegies to act as her blade if only she could convince them of humanity's worth. They did not choose her—she chose them.

"I go my own way, now and always," came Enlenea's response.

Madcow looked away from Enlenea, perhaps recalling his own past. "In some way, I am one who both chooses and is chosen. I was chosen and soon resigned to my fate; I was truly pleased with how things had become. I, too, can now choose my way; 'tis my own decision to be ever by my master, for such is the boon of my gratitude and all I have to give."

"I see," Enlenea mused. "Yes… perhaps such is my bond with my own master—more a guide than a master. How ever could I thank him without standing by his side?"

"If his way is not your own, do not profess gratitude in servitude, but show you have transcended his guidance—that his words will bear fruit as you part ways. 'Tis a most welcoming outcome for a guide, is it not?"

"Is it?"

As before, Madcow distanced himself within his den until he was no longer visible, concealed before the darkness. "Act, Enlenea, lest you never know, and seek me out again once the time is right. It seems that I indeed have much to learn from you. Beyond that…"

Enlenea remained silent for a moment, awaiting Madcow's words. "Madcow?" But the beast would not respond; she could only assume he returned to his slumber to be awoken another day.

She departed the tower shortly thereafter. She knew in her heart that the vanquisher of Regnal's proxy neared her final moments, tormented and broken by every other Elegy. Inguis destroyed her homeland; Astot led her to question her purpose; Regnal vexed her no matter where she ran, seeking to claim all she was as his own; and finally, with her spirit broken, Constius offered her a sanctuary she no longer had the will to refuse. She would become a tainted and an ally of the Elegies, unaware of all she would lose in turn.

The Elegies saturated the region with corruption. The churned lands gave birth to ebony flora trickling with fetid liquid; dark mist paled the skies and the sunlight; human remains lingered everywhere in sight. It was here that Enlenea would find the woman clinging desperately to the last vestiges of her human will. Alone she leaned against a tall spire before a murky lake about which dim fireflies fluttered, and it was here she would choose to die on her own terms. With her bloodied hand clenched tightly around her weapon, she pressed its muzzle against the side of her head, mumbling to herself her parting words.

"Do you wish to die?" Enlenea asked as she at last emerged from hiding.

The woman gave Enlenea a prolonged stare, her eyes sombre with disinterest and hopelessness. It was only as she began to recognise her face, or lack thereof, that a hint of curiosity became her expression. "Why are you here?" she grumbled.

Enlenea drew closer.

"Y'know what? Just stay the fuck away from me. You've got nothin' to see here."

"I will ask again—do you wish to die here?"

The woman began to laugh. "Oh, I get ya', so that's what this is all about! Here to play the role of my executioner? Think you're the one who decides when I've seen enough? I don't need you; you have no idea how strong I am."

"Is that so?" Enlenea turned to the lake. "Then you do not wish to die in earnest, but to commit a final act of your own volition—to remind yourself of what you are and deny what you now must become. I do commend your resolve, yet so much more could come of it. What do you truly want, human?"

The woman lowered her weapon. "Now, isn't it obvious? I want them all to scream in anguish for what they did to me. I don't even care if it's through my hands or someone else's. I'm blessed to have some friends who got away, at least."

"They, too, will soon know the malice of the Elegies. They will not survive; they are all but fated to join you in death, lest you forfeit your life here." Enlenea extended her hand to the woman. "You and I are more alike than ever you could fathom. With haste, human, I would save your life with all that I am."

The woman promptly pointed her weapon at Enlenea, struggling to stand on her feet. "I'm sick and fucking tired of playing games with you goddamn monsters!"

Enlenea took a step forward. "I do mean you no further harm."

"Fuck off," the woman growled.

Enlenea took several paces forward still. "I would welcome my death... if 'twere only a possibility."

"I'll kill you!" the woman screamed, her hand trembling.

"You are already tainted. 'Tis not I who stand to lose aught should you—"

A deafening sound brought Enlenea to silence. A sudden impact along the centre of her chest rattled her lucidity. She lurched backward, landing softly in the grass as her sight wavered. What she last saw was the woman's unrecognisably placid gaze, as if under a trance, before she pointed her weapon downward, taking aim at the centre of Enlenea's forehead.

Another burst ensued; silence and darkness followed.

"What will you do? What *have I done?*" were Enlenea's passing thoughts, and a small glimpse of a rift dilating beside the silvery moon preceded her death.

Chapter XI: The Other One

Year 133 B.G.

A silvery coin reflected the cerulean lustre of a sky flushed with innumerable city lights, even from the height of the skyrise apartment. A woman with long crimson hair wore a bathrobe as half of her body sat precariously against the edge of the balcony's railing, currency clinking from her fingers as she flipped it repetitiously. Her eyes wandered about the bustling night—the flying traffic lines entwining the skyscrapers, the underworld of gridlock in the highways some hundred metres below, and the hovering, bulky automations hauling steel around the roof of a nearby commercial building. The boundless metropolis provided a respite from the dead wastes and the abominations roaming them—the constant fear of the unknown as every moving man and creature sought her mortal blood.

Not to say she was any more welcome here than there.

As she lifted her right arm—bringing within view a firearm clasped within her other hand—she froze. A familiar but untraceable fear engulfed her as she stared down its barrel. For a fraction of a second after her heart began to strain dangerously close to its limits, a flash blinded her; a bullet had darted from the chamber without so much as a twitch from her finger. Light gradually faded from her eyes as blood rushed down the bridge of her nose from the freshly dug cavity adorning the middle of her crown.

Her eyes, wild with shock, were engulfed in darkness before she sealed them shut, but her anticipated death never greeted her. She opened them again, cold sweat flushing under her brows, her firearm breathless as though nothing had come from it. Her cowardice died off as suddenly as it came, for it was never hers at all.

Or perhaps she killed herself and was reborn as someone else, but what was she even suggesting? Before she could delve into a trove of repressed memories, her handheld communicator vibrated against a glass table beside her, and she promptly brought it to her ear, composing herself before speaking, "What's up, Cyg?"

"I'm all set. I'm heading to your apartment right now. What about you?"

She twirled her firearm around her finger before placing it on the table and retreating into the darkness of her apartment bedroom, hand on her hip as she began to steel herself for the coming battle. "Well, you sure know how to keep me at the height of suspense."

Her partner, 'Cyg,' chuckled faintly. "Does that mean you're ready?"

The crimson-haired woman slid open the bifold doors to her sparsely occupied closet. "Sure. Just tell me when you're close by, and I'll be on the porch." She dressed modestly before strapping on her gear—a dagger around her right boot, two pouches around the thighs of her jeans, and a shoulder holster around her v-cut white shirt. She returned to the porch, grabbing her gun before leaning over the railing. "Cygna, what's your ETA?"

"Nearing your position. Keep an eye on your nine."

"And you keep an eye on your back."

"Are we doing this like before?"

"We're doing this like before."

The crimson-haired woman stashed her phone, exposing the coin she kept in her palm. As a bulky, open-top transport came hovering towards her left, she flicked the coin in the air, swiftly bringing her gun in front of her and sending the coin cutting through the air like a shooting star with a well-aimed bullet. Once the transport came close enough that she could spot the waving hand of her partner below her wild mane of blonde hair, she lurched backward, jumping to plant one foot on the railing before launching herself from the building, traversing the several-dozen-metre drop and landing shoulder-first into the transport's third row of cushioned passenger seats.

"Ow," she groaned before sitting upright.

Cygna glanced over her shoulder to grin. "That sounded less enthusiastic than last time. You're getting better at this!"

The crimson-haired woman twirled her gun before holstering it in one swift motion. "Sarcasm from you? Hah! Are you getting nervous?"

"Well... no." Cygna's neck shifted towards the passing buildings from left to right in a moment of silence. "I guess... maybe I'm a little envious of you."

"What do you mean?"

"How you can be so carefree, even at a time like this. And just look at me, doing nothing but potentially flying my only friend to her death when I, a Halian, should be capable of so much more than that by now. It's pathetic."

The crimson-haired woman vaulted over the front passenger seat to join Cygna. "Look, maybe he won't even turn up tonight or any other night in Proto-Golem. Even if he does, he won't kill me—he never has."

Cygna furrowed her eyebrows as her tone turned grim. "He only needs to kill you once to win; you can kill him once—you can try to kill him as many times as you want, but you'll never win, no matter what."

"Regnal can restore his body all he wants, but he'll never regain his ego, and that's something he will miss no matter how much he wants to pretend it doesn't exist." She felt a pang in her chest as a small, insect-like creature coated in Regnal's black flames appeared vividly in her mind—another memory she was certain was not her own. "Hey, Cygna?"

"Oh, no, she called me by my full name in front of me! That must mean she wants to ask a difficult question."

The crimson-haired woman rolled her eyes. "There you go again. I was thinking... do you ever feel like you're not quite yourself sometimes?"

Cygna turned to give her a blank stare, narrowly evading the foundation of a holographic billboard in her absence of mind. "What are you saying?"

The crimson-haired woman diverted her attention to a bustling balcony with a velvet carpet contrasting the gloom of the surrounding buildings. It was an upscale restaurant in a giant mall; mechanical waiters, patrons in fancy clothing, and theatre screens affixed to both walls presented a wealthy, yet cozy vibe.

Let's stop by there one day, she thought before shaking her head, realising those thoughts had gone awry. "Just try to answer the question."

"Okay, um... there are many times I feel that way; when I'm tired, angry, scared—moments like that. What about you?"

"I don't sleep, I'm too cool to lose my temper, and if I doubt myself, I'm dead. Still, it feels like I've been trying to reclaim a part of me that died long ago, ever since I woke up with that giant cur staring down at me. Or maybe it was someone else entirely whom I inherited something from, and she's still here, waiting for me to return it. I haven't yet figured out if she's trying to help or control me." She gazed into her palm. "And for everything she's done to try and earn my acknowledgement, I don't even know her name."

Cygna fixated on the sky ahead as a smile gradually extended upon her face. "You remind me of a partner I haven't seen in a long time. She always seemed so modest until she really expressed herself to me."

"You're not trying to call me crazy, are you?" the crimson-haired woman asked half-jokingly.

"Crazies like you bring out the best in me. I guess that makes me somewhat crazy, too."

The crimson-haired woman shrugged before reclining in her seat and kicking her legs over the front of the transport, entertaining her crazy thoughts in the welcoming company of her only friend. The transport ascended further until it was aligned with the deck of a sausage-shaped aircraft carrier, built like a ship sailing through the air. She could spot several formations of heavily armed troops at the ready, surrounded by flying patrols of armoured vehicles with manned weaponry.

"I don't think they've seen Regnal yet," Cygna remarked, squinting as she surveyed the area.

"It looks like Aerbith is running late, too," the crimson-haired woman added. "Did you show him the front door?"

A ring of dust extended outward from the transport as it abruptly stopped slightly above the carrier. Cygna took her rifle and disembarked before the crimson-haired woman's eyes, bringing her face-to-face with a long row of passengers and the carrier's captain, an older but slender man who acknowledged Cygna's bowing with a quick nod before turning his attention to the crimson-haired woman, his sharp cheekbones accentuating the gravitas of his spiteful glare.

Cygna turned to her as well. "Unless he's using Inguis to carry him here, Regnal is just like any other tainted—he can't just appear where he pleases in areas with lower DEAS prominence. He has no choice but to physically chase us here."

The crimson-haired woman jumped from her seat, landing beside Cygna and flashing the captain a smirk. "That's why we're doing this here at all, right? I know that much, but what about Aerbith?"

"He never guaranteed anything. Honestly, given who we're working with right now, I wouldn't blame him if he never showed up." She waved her hand in the air, signalling the transport to activate its autopilot controls and take off in the direction it had arrived.

The captain arched an eyebrow at Cygna before confronting the crimson-haired woman with another glare. Ultimately, he furrowed his eyebrows and nodded, a gesture she took to mean that he was willing to ignore their difference to accomplish a common goal—the extermination of their greatest adversary.

"My name is Gingern," he began, stepping forward,

revealing his long, dark ponytail as it swayed. "Let me be clear here—our objective is not the *indefinite* elimination of Regnal, for we have all learned the hard way that his kind will always return."

"Intimidation—that's the name of the game," the crimson-haired woman added, folding her arms while looking wayward. "We bash his balls in enough times that he grows the wit to never trifle with our ilk again."

The crimson-haired woman widened her eyes as a large canine's silhouette ascended, eclipsing the moon. A long, furry tail brushed against her cheek as the entity darted past her with unnatural impetus, landing weightily onto the deck.

"Aerbith!" Cygna shouted.

The crimson-haired woman faced the other direction to be met by the golden gaze of the three-tailed silver hound. "You sure know how to make a heart-pumping entrance," she smiled. "Try not to startle me next time, why don't you?"

As Gingern stared him down with the same disdain he imposed upon the crimson-haired woman, Aerbith let out a low-tone growl. "Apologies," he responded in a deceptively calm tone. "I have come for Regnal."

"Not here yet." The crimson-haired woman waved at Gingern to divert his attention. "Anyway, this is Aerbith. Let's say he and I have had more than our fair share of 'disagreements.' He's a pretty good doggo."

Aerbith glanced at her with a slight look of indignation.

"A feisty doggo."

"Well, I hope you're pretty damn good with his leash," Gingern spat. "The only reason we of Reverentia tolerate your presence here is that Regnal is directly impeding our mutual hunt for Halia, and I don't mind dusting off this old carrier and enlisting just a couple of unlikely allies if it means bringing him down."

"So, what's our plan?" Cygna asked.

Gingern drew closer and formed a tight circle with the other three. "We need intel—all the info you've acquired of what that bastard can and will do when you've lured him here."

"He's a politely passive-aggressive fellow when he opens his mouth," the crimson-haired woman commented. "Kind of annoying. Don't let it bother you, though. Anyway, he has this thing for me, so he'll probably ignore the rest of you until you attack him directly."

"Regnal is a tempest of dark flame unshaped," Aerbith added. "At his purest, he is mutable and passable, beyond the reach of your weapons and mine. But, he cannot remain this way eternally, for this 'form' will then fade into the flow of the Scourge—or DEAS, as your people name it—a fate akin to a slumber from which he cannot awaken at a whim."

"Basically, he's put on a fixed timer before he can respawn at the nearest checkpoint," the crimson-haired woman clarified. "Just think of it as a video game."

"So it's just like 'killing' him," Gingern remarked. "And where is this 'checkpoint?'"

"The Halians taught me a lot about the tainted," Cygna stated. "A tainted can only be 'killed' by two means: Either through the power of the Halians or the power of DEAS itself, in other words, something else tainted by DEAS. When a tainted dies, its body returns to the stream of DEAS. After a certain amount of time has passed, the tainted is revived near its 'link'— something it is most drawn to—which can be an object, a place, or even a living person. It all depends on everything that was most significant in its human life. If this link is destroyed, the tainted could reappear potentially anywhere in the world, as long as there's enough DEAS to sustain it."

"Regnal's been stalking me ever since I woke up, but he always runs away before one of us kills the other," the crimson-haired woman recalled. "Supposing we do kill him, we can use the allotted time to not only find Halia but figure out what he's linked to and destroy it. If his link is nearby, that will keep him out of my sight for a long time."

"Any plans on how to find that link?"

The crimson-haired woman shrugged. "Not yet, but I'll

come up with one like I always do."

"So, to summarise, we can kill Regnal by either blasting him apart with DEAS equipment or tricking him into killing himself by forcing him to remain shapeless."

The crimson-haired woman looked directly into Gingern's eyes, her expression turning grim. "One thing I should warn you about, though: There's more than one Regnal."

"What?"

"Regnal grows stronger by devouring other tainted and stealing their forms and memories. With all the bodies he's claimed, he's capable of dividing any number of them into several separate entities that share his mind. There could be three, five... nay, even more of him wandering around at any time. Worse, we have no way of knowing which one is the real Regnal, or if we've ever encountered the real Regnal."

Gingern scoffed. "Are you serious? Why are we wasting time trying to lure him here when he could just throw us off with a decoy?"

The crimson-haired woman placed her hand on his shoulder. "Look, I know this is a risk, but what alternatives do we have? Besides, the fact that Regnal has been so cautious about staying alive against me suggests that he's been sending out his main body. Let's not forget that my intuition has got me this far on my own."

Gingern spent a moment in silence until his face scrunched with resolve. "I'm putting this fleet's lives at stake for this chance. We know our roles in this fight; you had better understand yours."

"Sure." The crimson-haired woman abandoned the debriefing circle to overlook the edge of the carrier. "By the way, little Cyggy over there may have recently discovered that she's a Halian, but she's still inexperienced, so don't expect her to sprout wings any time soon."

As Gingern left to address his men, Cygna approached the crimson-haired woman. "Watcher, about Regnal..."

The crimson-haired woman, 'Watcher,' sighed. "It's about

time for a new nickname, don't you think?" She tapped the gun holstered over her shoulder. "That's just the name of this damn gun I woke up with, remember?"

"Do you want me to call you 'Blade of Humanity' instead? That's what Reverentia called an old companion of mine after she and I saved a nearby colony from a DEAS structure by ourselves, and now they're starting to call you that, too."

Watcher glared at Cygna, eagerly awaiting her to announce that she was joking. "Please, *anything* but that. Watcher it is, then."

Cygna flashed a smile. "Anyway, what you just said about Regnal might not be accurate. What if the real reason he keeps running from you is because he needs you alive?"

Watcher shrugged. "That doesn't make much sense, does it?"

"It does when you think about what we're after—the origin of DEAS, Halia. The Halians are risking exposing Halia by harassing us. If we die, Halia becomes that much more difficult to find."

"Then why bother going after me at all? Why not pull up a seat and watch the show from afar?"

Cygna ignored Watcher, her eyes dilating as they trailed an object in the sky. As Watcher attempted to follow her, a gust of darkness balked her moonlit view—silent lashes of phantasmal flames ascending from the unseeable below, amassing in the sky until they formed a virulent vortex above the carrier.

"REGNAL!" Cygna shouted in unison with several crew members, lifting her rifle only to strain as she apparently recalled Aerbith's words.

Watcher waved towards the alarmed crew, who had already ceased a brief fusillade to no avail. "You panic, you die! Can't harm him until he goes solid!"

The entire carrier began to tremor under the influence of a deafening screech. Watcher slammed her palms into her ears, squinting at the sight of the crew members. Many began to aim their weapons at one another as several of them clutched their heads in an apparent display of rapidly-spreading hysteria.

"Spread out!" Gingern shouted while retreating closer to Aerbith.

But by the time Gingern escaped to relative safety, the crew had already begun to trade bullets with one another. The bodies of the distraught crew members turned their weapons against their former allies as passive dark flame coated every inch of them, and their eyes gleamed like sapphires. Those who had failed to gain a sufficient distance relinquished their weapons and clamoured as the flames began to spread onto them from the tips of their fingers, dooming them to the same fate.

"Cyg, get off the carrier!" Watcher commanded while pointing to a weapon-mounted vehicle stationed next to her.

While Cygna moved to operate the vehicle, Aerbith directed Gingern's attention to where the vortex once stood, the flames now condensing into a tenuous silhouette of a blue-eyed avian giant over half the size of the carrier. Only then did the fleet prevailing the skies open fire, innumerable bullets splashing into Regnal's solid form from every angle as he folded his wings, turned sideways, and began a slow dive below the carrier like an unsinkable ship plunging down the watery depths in defiance, engulfing several hovercars in fiery explosions in the process.

Watcher glanced at Regnal's left wing the split second before he disappeared below, barely noticing Aerbith clinging to his inflamed plumes by his own teeth—a gambit to prevent Regnal from shifting again and to buy the others time.

Gingern briefly fired his rifle towards the ongoing melee between the insane and lucid crew members before approaching Watcher. "Plans?" he asked with some distress evident in his expression.

"He's going to crash into the carrier!" Watcher shouted while looking intently at the chaos amongst their own people.

Cygna circled back towards the carrier in her new hovercar, coming to a stop behind Watcher and Gingern.

"Gingern, get in!"

As Gingern obeyed Cygna's order without question, Watcher drew her pistol and charged forward, confronting the corrupted crewmen with her limbs and armaments. One of them, distracted by the gunfire of a former companion crouched against a disabled hovercar, met his end with a sharp kick to the back of his neck. The next one exposed himself to retaliation after Watcher erred from the path of his knife thrust, driving a single bullet into the centre of his chest as she was crouched under his extended arm. She sprang to the side with the leverage of her right leg, narrowly avoiding another crewman who attempted to pin her to the ground before he was shot dead by several others.

She was caught in a bear hug from behind as her attention lay towards an insane crewman readying his pistol to shoot a lucid one down. She pivoted her midsection to deliver an elbow to her captive's temple with her free arm before whipping her pistol around to save her companion by delivering a bullet into his assailant's head. She swung her leg backwards to disable her own assailant with a roundhouse kick to the face before grounding him permanently with another headshot.

While the above fleet remained mostly occupied with Regnal, who circled the carrier a small distance below in an apparent struggle to shake Aerbith off him, several of them broke formation to retrieve the surviving crewmen stranded on the transport.

One of them approached Watcher. "Let's go!" the driver shouted.

Watcher shook her head, a bluish glint beginning to emanate from her flesh. "It's me he's after. You'll be safer on your own."

The driver nodded before taking off. "It's your funeral, kid!"

Watcher looked to the right; no sight of Regnal there. She pivoted towards the left; only the circling fleet greeted her. She twirled around; no imminent threat approached from behind.

The Ideal One lingered directly beneath, ready to collide with the carrier at any moment, and only she had yet to escape the deck. The power of all tainted thrived upon the flow of the Scourge; without a sufficient flow, most tainted would suffer no insignificant loss of their might. Watcher was no exception, for, though she did not understand how, she was a human capable of harnessing the power of the Scourge—she could materialise and project her will in a variety of forms and dematerialise her body from one spot to rematerialise it in another in an instant as any tainted could, reducing her velocity in the process. Try as she did to realise her vision of escaping safely into the skies above, her powers could not keep pace with her imagination.

And so she would need to grasp her new limitations. She sprinted towards the bow of the carrier, counting each second she remained stranded as her flesh gleamed more intensely with each step she took.

One second. A screeching roar emitted from beneath the carrier.

Two seconds. The fleet fired another volley of ammunition beneath the carrier.

Three seconds. Her vision rippled, and her heart began to race—the profound influence of an impending menace she was all too familiar with.

Four seconds. An explosive crash buckled the carrier's steel underfoot, throwing her into the air as the bow abruptly bent downwards.

Five seconds. She was high in the air above the carrier, safe and far away from the ensuing chaos. Regnal soared above her, emerging through the fiery pit of the carrier's severed midsection. Aerbith, thrown from his grip, spiralled in disarray alongside the black avian, several plumes stabbed into his lower jaw. As Watcher freely plummeted towards the elevated highway, along with the bifurcated carrier and all its contents, Regnal turned his back towards her at the beginning of a backwards loop, apparently intent on colliding with her from behind before she landed.

"It'll be a close one," she muttered, counting one second as she neared the height of the tallest buildings in the sector, her flesh radiating blue as she focused only upon the position of every hover car she could sense beneath her.

Two seconds. She descended below the height of the tallest buildings.

Three seconds. The giant avian Regnal commanded had vanished overhead; in its place, a cloud of hovering black flame formed a blockade along the elevated highway a considerable distance away, leaving every hover car that passed through untouched.

Four seconds.

Five seconds. With several metres between her and an upper row of hover cars trailing the highway, Watcher transported herself into the front passenger seat of an open-top model driving directly towards Regnal's unshaped mass.

"What in the—?"

Watcher huffed as a craggy voice at the wheel distracted her. She looked from the corner of her eye at a haggish, dishevelled woman with a cigarette clasped between her fingers staring at her with similar anxiety in her expression. Watcher approached her with a quiet but urgent tone. "You're with Reverentia, right? *Right?*"

"Are you?"

"I'll take that as a no," Watcher groaned, slapping her palm upon her face, silently lamenting Reverentia's failure to clear the sector of civilians. "Look, if you don't do precisely as I say, you can consider us both dead. Now give me the wheel."

The driver snuffed out her cigarette on the dashboard before flicking it aside. "Says who, kid?"

Watcher pointed to the approaching blockade comprised of Regnal's flames. "You see that harmless-looking black circle on the highway? Avoid it, now."

"What, you want me to manually enter into a no-fly zone and go 'round the highway? No, thanks. If I got a silver for every traffic violation reprimand I've got already, my thousand-crease plebeian ass sure wouldn't still be stuck slaving in a fast-food joint!"

Watcher whipped her head around and winced as the destroyed carrier behind them impacted the ground like a series of comets, inflicting a cascade of fiery destruction upon the elevated highway and the surrounding buildings from above and below, along with any civilian unfortunate enough to have noticed its descent in time. The driver had silently observed it all from the rear-view camera on her dashboard, expressionless as if pausing to comprehend her predicament.

Neither Watcher nor she was keen to the movement of Regnal, who, by the time Watcher turned around, was already rushing towards them as a black-flame torrent.

"Buckle up, dumbass!" the driver roared before slamming her fist into a button on the dashboard to hold Watcher in place at the waist with a curved metal belt extending from an opening at the base of her seat. With a sharp vertical ascent, she narrowly manoeuvred her car over the torrent, stroking her eyes with her finger as she experienced the blinding sensation of Regnal's influence. "Shit, my eyes are killin' me!"

"He's still on us. Go forward!"

"He?" The driver fixed her vehicle horizontally and diverted from the highway, her altitude comfortably above most of the surrounding buildings. "Are we dealin' with a tainted or what?"

"Well, it seems Reverentia isn't keeping any secrets around here." Watcher pulled out her pistol, pivoting her midsection as much as she could to aim at what had now shifted into another avian, albeit smaller and slower than the last. "Just keep driving while I shoot!"

The driver proceeded to zigzag throughout the sector as Watcher pelted Regnal with bullets—until he became mutable again.

"So monotonous," Watcher sighed, pulling out her phone while continuing to aim with anticipation. "Cyg, where are you?"

"Engaging Regnal now!"

Watcher promptly put her phone away as she vaguely spotted the fleet emerging from the giant dust cloud in the distance inflicted by the fallen carrier. She looked to the driver, a mischievous grin on her face. "Hey, stranger! Let's see if he follows us when you circle back."

The driver gave Watcher an unamused glance. "Sure, let me just charge us straight into the crossfire and pray to my ancestors our heads stay intact!" Before Watcher could complain, the driver did just that, taking a wide turn-around before speeding up towards the approaching fleet at a slightly higher altitude. "But who in the shit am I trying to kid? I'm just an expired git with nothin' to lose anyway!"

Retreat into the city or die trying to devour her—Regnal was liable to do one or the other. Watcher gambled on the former, and she was more than prepared to pursue him from one city block to the next on foot and finish off what was likely his true body.

But where she expected to see a dense stream of black flame descending into the city, she saw another flame-shrouded avian, even smaller and slower than the one before—so slow, so feeble, that it could not hope to reach the car that had now gained a considerable distance between them.

Why? Watcher thought, furrowing her eyebrows, as contemplative as she was pitying. Why was her rival chasing his inevitable death after giving it his all to survive time and time again during each and every one of their previous encounters? Did he not dare show weakness before her?

Did he have nothing to lose at all?

"Regnal, you damn mongrel," Watcher muttered under her breath before the car passed above the fleet, leaving her to watch as Regnal was thrown to and fro from one artillery assault after another before he turned mutable yet again, descending slowly into the city as a pitiful wisp of what formerly comprised an avian as massive as a ship.

Watcher pointed to the wisp before it disappeared behind a building. "He's over there! Go park somewhere, and I'll finish this."

The driver nodded before descending into the streets, parking beside a curb several blocks from the building. "Good luck to you because I ain't gettin' any closer than this," she said before releasing Watcher's seatbelt.

Watcher leapt from her seat and rushed upon the overcrowded pavement, weaving through the density of confused and panicked onlookers on her way to a quiet, trash-ridden alleyway with lampposts emitting blue light. In the middle of the alleyway, within a fetid puddle of something Watcher dared not stain the soles of her shoes with, was a dark raven, its wings sprawled on either side in surrender, the colour of its eyes blending with that of its surroundings.

"You do not know it, yet it knows you," the raven spoke, its pitched voice emerging from a source unseen. "It has no form to call its own, and so it takes yours or another's of its choosing; it does not stagnate." It looked directly into Watcher's eyes. "Where it watches you, never will you know."

The sound of a blast bounced against the walls—Watcher had pulled the trigger without so much as a pause of grace, reducing the raven to a fading cloud of dark smoke. Her hand trembled against the grip of her pistol before she managed to relax and return it to its holster, leaning against the wall and folding her arms as she awaited the arrival of her friends.

First came Aerbith, who shambled into the alleyway with a trail of dark blood from the gaping wound where his lower jaw once was.

"Hey, Aerbith," Watcher languidly greeted, her eyes dilating as she turned her head to look at him. "Wow, he got you in the jaw *again*? Is there some reason he's so obsessed with doing that to you?"

Aerbith remained silent, swaying his head slowly.

"Oh, come on. We're buddies, remember? You can talk to me about anything you—"

"Regnal yet lives, does he not?" Aerbith interrupted.

Watcher shrugged, managing a jovial grin. "Well, of

course he does. He's a tainted, remember? You can kill him, but you sure can't *kill* him." She exhaled a sigh before speaking in earnest. "To think he would send nothing but a clone after me, now of all times."

Aerbith drew closer, slamming his paw into the puddle Regnal's effigy formerly lay. "Now, shall we combine our powers and vanquish this gloomy cloud looming from above you?"

Watcher briefly diverted her gaze before attempting to change the subject. "Come on, Aerbith, don't put your paw there. It's filthy!"

"Watcher! Aerbith!" Cygna shouted from one end of the alleyway, running closer with Gingern alongside her.

"So, what's our situation?" Gingern asked. "Did you manage to stop that thing?"

"We have ended the reign over the skies of an entity born of Regnal's deception," Aerbith answered. "Alas, Regnal is not here in the flesh, nor was he ever. And thus are we left to mourn the passing of those who have given their lives without meaning."

Watcher allowed Aerbith to speak on her behalf, as hopeless to do so herself as she was helpless against the might of Trophykeeper Inguis the day the only life she knew began—the day which linked her to an unending chain of hollow victories and unanswered questions. Never did she despair against any foe, no matter what insurmountable challenge they presented; never did she surrender her life or sanity, even knowing her every victory only delayed the inevitable.

She was content with the prospect of fighting and dying for nothing. She would continue to survive if only to spite her foes and forfeit her life on her own terms, both without having accomplished a single thing. Meeting Cygna and Aerbith—the only friends she trusted to survive alongside her, whom she would proudly give anything to protect and serve—did little to waver her death-seeking ambition. They were no less destined to fail than she was, but their journey together would be marked with jovial moments alongside the storm of strife.

That was before she discovered she could have everything and give nothing, for the Scourge itself indeed had a beginning, and anything that began was fated to end. She would journey to the land of its origin and defeat it at its source, ending the chaos wrought by the Elegies and saving countless humans, herself, and above all else, her friends.

But Regnal, her trial to prove she could defeat even the greatest of tainted, had toyed with her all along. He was her rogue shadow, mirroring her steps until he was ready to lunge upon her, only to flee before their battle reached its climax time and time again. He nurtured her hatred and inspired in her a desire to outlive him, and for that, she would lead him to Halia so that he could see to his own desires. What that desire was, she would never know. Never did he desire to kill her, for he was powerful enough to do that at a whim—for as possible as it was to stop the Scourge, she would never possess the means to do so herself.

But if death by the Scourge was to be her fate, then so be it. She would enjoy her eccentric life to the last breath, in the charming company of her red-eyed blonde and feisty magic cur.

"What did you just say about my father?" Gingern growled in front of Aerbith, dragging Watcher from her trance to observe an ongoing argument between the two.

She stamped her foot to draw the attention of both. "Just calm your tails, Aerbith. We won, Regnal-lite lost, and we get to live another day. Isn't that all that matters in the end?"

Aerbith smacked the ground with his tails. "But I was not first to blather."

Gingern lifted his fist at Aerbith. "You don't get to tell me I sent my men to die for nothing. You are missing a jaw; why don't you start acting like it and shut up?"

Aerbith stepped forward but apparently caught himself before he could lunge at Gingern. He pointed to Watcher with his middle tail. "Were that woman not standing behind me, I would mince your meat where *you* stand, you powerless simian!"

Watcher sighed. "All right, Cygna, you're better at mediating than I am, so maybe you should start speaking up. I'll leave this to—"

Her throat abruptly constricted before she could finish. She collapsed to her knees as a stream of black fluid erupted from her mouth, taking her clarity of mind with it.

"Watcher! What's wrong?"

"Shit, she's losing it again!"

"To her side, Cygna!"

She collapsed on her belly, her hair soaking in her filth, having only vaguely heard the cries of her companions. But before her vision abandoned her to darkness and she no longer heard anything, she basked in the joy of the peaceful present instead of obsessing over the tragic future awaiting her.

If only she knew the name of the other one within her, could she perhaps redesign that future?

Chapter XII: An Eternal Venture

"What about you? You weren't hurt, were you?"

"I thought I was, but I guess I was just panicking."

"Understandable. It looks like your partner might be out of commission for a while, so hopefully, you weren't planning on leaving right after Regnal."

"It's happened before. We have all the time in the world anyway, right?"

Watcher opened her eyes halfway, recognising the voices of Gingern and Cygna. A crude blanket of wool enveloped her lower body with warmth; a device bound to her wrist relayed her vitals to a nearby monitor; the morning rays stung at her eyes from a distance past her feet. Her jumbled memories of the day prior gradually returned to her like puzzle pieces resonating and joining with one another of their own accord. She had collapsed the night before with her bickering companions beside her, gurgling on her own bile and drifting in and out of consciousness as Gingern carried her on his back, transporting her to a militarised zone beyond Proto-Golem's border.

It's happened before. Cygna's words clung to her like a rope of thorny vines. *It won't happen again,* she told herself the last time it happened, despite its having happened twice prior to that. She was a fearless fighter able to stand against any living foe, but she lived ever in denial of her impending death, for it represented her greatest fear of all—facing a threat no amount of strength would help her overcome. She knew she would die as all living creatures must, but she never foretold the despair that would come with knowing how close she stood before her own death.

Cygna noticed Watcher's lively expression and responded with one of her own. "Watcher? Gingern, she's awake!"

Watcher waved at Cygna with a limp arm, groaning.

Gingern jolted up from his chair. "Are you all right? Can you hear us?"

She nodded slowly. "Loud and clear, captain. Sorry about… last night?"

"I don't need any apology from you. At least the three of us are all in one piece after that mess."

"Three?" Watcher abruptly sat up, ignoring her light-headedness. "Aerbith! Where'd he go?"

Gingern scoffed. "I didn't know mutts counted as people, but you'll find your pet wandering off in the base somewhere."

"I'm sure he appreciates the hospitality." She flicked her wrist, drawing attention to her armband. "If my clothes are still on me, I take it my condition wasn't all that dire? Am I free to walk?"

"You're not planning on leaving Proto-Golem already, are you?" Cygna asked, briefly looking over Watcher's body.

Watcher's thoughts fell upon the destruction of the city and the countless deaths indirectly wrought by her presence as she answered, "Well, yeah. I think it's best for all of us if you and I get away from here as soon as possible."

"Watcher, I think all of us could use a rest."

"Regnal won't be waiting for us to recover before he comes after us again, and I don't want to be in a crowded city when he does."

"Just one day. Aerbith was still missing his jaw last I saw him."

"And I'm missing my patience."

"Watcher, I know—"

"If my dead men are leaving a bitter taste in your mouth, suck it up," Gingern sternly interrupted. "I'm as eager to crash the Halians' party as you are, but no soldier's worth a damn without the morale to back them up."

"We can just go for a walk around the base," Cygna added.

"There's a lot to do around here, and we won't have to worry about endangering civilians."

"Well, I..." Watcher trailed off before throwing her arms in the air in surrender. "All right, have it your way. As long as I'm off my butt, I'm good."

Watcher silently parted ways with Gingern as she and Cygna stepped outside into the gigantic, transparent dome encompassing the base. Soldiers strapped with bulky firearms patrolled the dense encampment amid a clearing in the sparse woods, some accompanied by vaguely humanoid automatons with bent legs, four stubby fingers and skeletal facial features. The field was laden with foreign equipment and several-metre-high dark pillars with glowing blue crevices marking every medical tent. Military vehicles swarmed the dome's air space. With the peace of mind to do as she pleased, Watcher had only begun to realise how spectacular a utopia Proto-Golem was.

"You're from Proto-Golem, aren't you?" Watcher asked while strolling slightly behind Cygna.

"I was born and raised here by my mother—my adoptive mother, I mean. I was a soldier here, too, before I found you and... you know, the Halian business and whatnot."

"Yeah." Watcher looked about her surroundings erratically while struggling to make small talk in peace—this suffocating peace she had yet to grow accustomed to. "Do you remember that day we first met?"

Cygna chuckled. "How could I forget? That was well over a year ago now, wasn't it? My team was deployed to investigate some anomalous activity in Outerzone Section Fifteen, a couple of sections from the same area where I was trapped in that giant tower." She pointed skyward. "That's when I met you and Inguis."

"By all accounts, our little adventure should have ended before it even began. He could have killed us easily." Watcher inflected her voice to be as booming as Inguis' as she quoted, "'I come to behold the birth of Acantelieth's herald.' Didn't he say something like that?"

"And we still never learned who Acantelieth is or was."

"But I get it now—I'm just a sacrifice."

Cygna paused, turning to look at Watcher with a woeful expression. "What are you talking about?"

Watcher averted Cygna's eyes. "You said Regnal probably needs me alive; I'm beginning to think you were right. A dead woman would make a poor sacrifice."

"That wasn't what I meant."

"Cyg, that was all you could have meant. Regnal is toying with us. Isn't it obvious by now?" She chuckled bitterly. "He can end this and me as he damn well pleases, and I'm sure it feels damned good to have that much power over another. I'll never get the chance to experience it myself because I was born and will die a woman in shackles."

Cygna fervently shook her head as their discussion drew the attention of several soldiers. "If we find Old Halia, we can stop the Scourge—"

"And that's exactly what he's waiting on, isn't it? Yeah, let's go and spare him the trouble of finding Halia himself so he can dispose of us and show us just how foolish we were to think we ever had a chance to win."

"He can't control our future—*your* future. He can't control that."

"Nor is he required to," Watcher added almost before Cygna had finished speaking, her tone elevated with lingering frustration. "No need to control what was already beholden to your whims since day one."

"You're not giving up, are you?" Cygna asked, elevating her own tone.

"I'm just accepting reality and all of its willingness to set my backside on fire regardless."

"So, you *are* giving up." She drew closer to Watcher, glowering at her. "What about me? What about Aerbith?"

Watcher shrugged. "Should have picked a better babysitter, but thanks ahead of time for dying with me."

Cygna gazed at Watcher with unblinking eyes, her face

turning incredulous. "Look, you didn't give yourself much time to rest. Let's go back, and we'll—"

"Cygna." Watcher her friend at ease with an endearing tone before resting her hands on her shoulders. "Cygna... this is fine. I've known it since day one—I can't win. I just want to spite them all as long as possible before I die, that's all. Whether or not you join me in the grave is up to you. You're not just a tagalong to me—you and Aerbith are the only people I care about in this harsh reality, and I want you both to live your lives to their fullest, with or without me."

Cygna lowered her head. "You're not going to die," she whispered.

Watcher tightened her grip around Cygna's shoulders, smiling warmly. "Yes, Cygna, I am going to die. Just accept it now and spare yourself the heartache."

"No."

"Everyone dies anyway, right? What does it matter if my death comes a few years off-schedule? Maybe, someday, Regnal will get what's coming to him; but that'll be by the hand of someone made of tougher stuff than me, and certainly long after our time. Cygna..."

Watcher lowered her head while recollecting her past, marred by the mental scars of unending strife. Every day of her life was made by a fight for her right to keep it; some days even began with her at the cusp of death and ended with her confronting a threat greater than those that came before it. Despite the curse of unending hardship until death, her path was sparse with moments of joy that meant everything to her. Those cherished moments she and her companions spent side-by-side, trading tales with Cygna and bickering with Aerbith only to embrace him with love hours thereafter, she would trade for nothing—not even a chance to start life anew as an ordinary socialite.

Those moments alone made a life even such as hers worth suffering through.

"Cygna," Watcher softly repeated, "let's just... breathe

for now, all right? I mean, let's forget everything—forget the Halians, forget the Scourge, forget Regnal. Let's just, you know... pretend to be ordinary people for once. Let's spend the rest of today having fun like there's no tomorrow."

Watcher looked over Cygna's shoulder as the sound of something crashing into the ground drew the attention of the surrounding soldiers. Panicked as the soldiers were, she quickly drew a smirk to assure her beloved friend that his presence was welcomed—especially with his jaw in place. "Aerbith! Good morning."

Aerbith shook his head as if to clean out his ears. His eyes quickly shifted both directions to glance at every bystander before he addressed Watcher with a casual tone. "What now do you intend to do?"

"What do I intend to do?" Watcher chuckled, releasing Cygna and spinning behind her with her arms outstretched. "Look at this place! Have you seen anything like it? I say we go back to city and have Cyg give us a nice tour."

As Aerbith's eyes widened with incredulity, Cygna turned to face Watcher, smiling faintly. "How will we hide him? Aerbith, I mean."

Watcher shrugged. "Should be easy enough to convince everyone he's some kind of chatty robot. If not, let's just put a blanket over him or something."

Aerbith growled as he slammed his tails into the ground. "Inconceivable! I never thought you the sort to languish away your time while we've still enemies upon every corner of this land vying for our heads!"

"And if they come here, we'll just..." Watcher planted her fist into her palm. "... beat them back, same as we always have."

Aerbith stamped closer to Watcher. "Have you gone mad, woman? Have you forgotten to whom you speak? I am an ancient immortal, survivor and conqueror of battles and wars from long before the nadir of your diminutive existence. I will *not* be merely strutting alongside you with my form degraded by the embrace of a simian's shroud! My claws—these fangs and these claws which I bear—have rent too many lives to be put—"

"Hey, I just thought of something," Watcher interrupted. "You can put things in your mouth and swallow, can't you? If you're a tainted lacking any normal bodily functions, then what happens to what you eat?"

Aerbith stood silently, his tails no less motionless with what Watcher assumed was annoyance.

"Fine, I'll take that as an 'I have no clue, ma'am,'" Watcher continued. "Let's go get you something to eat, then. I'm sure you'll like what I have in mind."

"Where to?" Cygna asked, stifling her laughter.

"I saw a fancy-looking restaurant down below when you drove me around the city. Let's go back there."

Cygna nodded. "Sure! I parked my cruiser just straight ahead. Come with me."

Aerbith let out a quiet growl before walking closely behind Cygna, with Watcher following the two from a greater distance.

"I can only hope I need not curl myself to fit your machine," Aerbith grumbled.

Cygna glanced at Aerbith's face. "Don't get upset with me. It's not like this was my idea."

"But you did agree to it."

"I didn't!"

"Then *why* are we walking, child!?"

"Watcher isn't going to take no for an answer. I'm just following orders."

Watcher admired the two from where they could not see her uncontrollable grin nor the tears swelling in her eyes. Beyond living the remainder of her days to their fullest, her greatest wish was that her friends would survive without her and remain together long after she died—that they would stay strong and carve out their own purposes amid the unending strife awaiting them.

And were that not possible, she could only hope they were willing and able to wait—until a true saviour emerged who could look after them and fulfil her dreams in her stead.

Chapter XIII: To Live Forever

Year 132 B.G.

To die by the hand of a human and be whisked away into ephemeral bliss... What she had experienced many times before suddenly felt more profound than ever before. Whether from grief or a sense of unfulfilled duty, Enlenea was for once thankful that she would live forever. She would one day see her desires fulfilled, for the passage of time held little meaning to her. And she knew by heart that her journey neared its end.

A bell tolled beyond the abyss of nothingness, and she regained her senses. She awoke within the vastness of a colourless desert in the bright of day, soothed by the caress of the placid winds. She was cradled and carried away by a dark mass in the shape of a towering man, the silhouette of a familiar tower far behind him.

Enlenea spoke the name of the entity that came to mind as she gazed upon a familiar pair of gleaming blue eyes. "Regnal?"

"My condolences to you, Enlenea... but you have yet to exhaust your worth." Regnal did not so much as glance at Enlenea as he spoke, and the faceless woman could sense he now bore a heavy burden.

"I have not forgotten my everlasting existence. Much time has passed since my death, has it not?"

"Indeed." Regnal fell silent as a tumultuous breeze swept by, dust amassing in the air from the churned lands. "For where Inguis and Constius may now be, I do not know. Now, only I remain by Astot's side."

The Elegies' bond was fickle indeed; they acted as one only for Astot's kindness and wisdom. Alas, they held to their own desires, and it was inevitable that their bond would waver —Regnal's words only affirmed what Enlenea suspected. What aroused her curiosity was why Regnal, for all his greed, would remain as the final link in the chain Astot forged in the pursuit of the Begetter.

"Ah, Astot... I have so much to say," Enlenea lamented, minding the consequences of her actions. "Please, Regnal, I wish to see him."

"Why not stay for but a little hunt?" Regnal requested, excitement subtle in his tone. As the duststorm settled as suddenly as it came, Regnal looked towards the horizon, where Enlenea could see a row of figures journeying through the desert. "Yea, it seems my greed ever decides my own needs... as of this moment."

Enlenea grew tense. "Regnal? I do not understand."

"Answer me this, O painted woman: Is it more your wish to unendingly live than to die without purpose?"

"I do wish to die," Enlenea hesitated to answer. "Do we not all desire the same?"

"Not I."

Before long, the trio in the distance took notice of the pair. As Regnal began his delighted stroll in their direction, Enlenea could gradually make out their faces. One was none other than the red-eyed Halian from the tower; another was Aerbith, the missing guardian; and the last was a woman Enlenea saw well in her dreams, one with long crimson hair and a strapping figure. But as the woman drew closer, visions of that night in the tainted grasslands flashed vividly in Enlenea's subconsciousness.

"O Painted Woman, that I wish I were by your side that day to see with my own eyes the beginnings of the 'Blade of Humanity.' Fate and great fortune have smiled always upon you."

Standing close enough to reach the trio with a few paces more, Regnal gently set Enlenea aside and waited. Cygna, Aerbith, and Watcher did the same, pausing momentarily to acknowledge the two tainted in their own ways. The fiery glare of Watcher fell upon Regnal alone; Cygna stood in awe at the sight of Enlenea, having clearly recalled their former meeting; Aerbith was less welcoming of their reunion, growling in a low tone while poised as if ready to pounce upon her at any moment.

"Always right ahead of me, always in my way," Watcher murmured at Regnal with a half-hearted grin. "Well, at least you've brought a buddy with you, so maybe that'll help refrain the monotony a bit."

"Aerbith, is that you?" Enlenea asked, leaving Regnal to his own affairs.

Aerbith settled down at the sound of her troubled voice. "Enlenea... I do remember you well. What now do you seek by impeding our path?"

"Is that her name?" the Halian asked. "You were part of the Elegies all along?"

Enlenea nodded. "But 'twas only after a long slumber I suddenly awoke here; 'tis not my own wish to stand in your way."

"An ex-buddy of yours over there, I presume?" Watcher asked Cygna.

Cygna sighed. "What's done is done. It doesn't matter anymore."

"Then let us concern ourselves with the outcome which has yet to be decided upon our actions," Aerbith interjected, taking a step forward. "Begone from here, Regnal—you and the no-face—and do not again impede nor think of us."

"Pay no mind to this 'buddy' of mine," Regnal responded. "O guardian hound, I pray your forgiveness if my humble curiosity so troubles you; but no matter your choice to bare just forgiveness or a vicious maw, I will act, as always, for naught but what pleases me. And 'tis only in claiming you, and everything that is, that I may derive my greatest pleasure."

"That's fair enough for me," Watcher replied as a volatile blue aura began to emanate from her like a flickering candle. "It's only in killing you and denying everything you are, or want to be, that I derive my own pleasure."

A pair of saturated black wings spouted forth from Regnal's back in an eruption of fluid and miasmata, after which the Elegy extended his palm to stop Aerbith before he could instinctively lunge at him. "I had near forgotten my words for you, Enlenea. Indeed, I have never wished to die. 'Twas not for Astot's beliefs that I lent him my power, for I always understood how opposite we were. Astot would speak of an existence beyond our own, yet never have *I* considered a being greater than myself. Astot would prattle of enlightenment and such as a thing held only by the advocates of our Begetter...

"... yet in my world, there is no Begetter. Astot knows not of my place upon this world, for with but a look in my face, he stares upon the eyes of his greater self—ignorance, at present, you all vilely share, along with humanity whole."

Before concluding his speech, Regnal stepped forward, goading the trio to approach if they dared. "There is no ideal more desirable than this creature you see before you, and it will never die. Now, please come forth—exchange your blood for a pardon of your heresy. Sleep eternally under the blessing of one who will never share such an abysmal fate, and pass blessings of your own to all who will live to bear witness as one oversteps what you were or ever would have been, 'till one is all and all is one—'till comes the era in which we are all the One Ideal."

"You seem to enjoy grandstanding before it even means anything," Watcher scoffed. "I'll pay for my heresy in *your* blood if anything, so, by all means, indulge in your deluded fantasies of a world you could never make a reality in your last moments."

But before the tension could mount any further, Astot's voice echoed in the wind, "Enough, enough," with an exasperated sigh. The leader of the Elegies made his presence apparent by taking shape behind an isolated duststorm not far from the space the group currently occupied. He glanced at his fellow Elegies with different expressions—a smile for Enlenea and a look of pity for Regnal. "Pardon my... unwelcome intrusion, all of you, but, Enlenea, we have much to discuss."

"Do with her as you please," Regnal calmly responded, "but leave be me and my own affairs."

"I agree with that," Watcher murmured, staring expectantly at Regnal and Astot. "At least I'd have a little less on my plate that way."

"I'll not allow even that, I assure you." Astot turned to Regnal. "Regnal, if you would kindly leave them be for now and let us properly continue our pursuit for the favour of the Begetter..."

"Your flavoured animosity bitters my resolve," Regnal replied in a monotone before turning away from Astot and distancing himself slowly. "Then it will be as you wish, and they will live for but a few days more. But heed well these words, Astot: Your progress grows stagnant, and my patience grows thin. Before long, you may find any desire you hold of gaping before your Begetter become but a fantasy forever untrue."

Regnal assumed his avian form before flying away, and the trio silently observed the last two Elegies momentarily before continuing their journey through the desert. Enlenea was left at a loss for words until Astot assured her with a warm smile to express her doubts.

"What will become of the Elegies?" she asked.

"Dear Enlenea, you have naught to fear," Astot responded. "Do not fear Regnal, do not fear your future, and most of all, please believe in my words." He let out a wry chuckle. "Thank the Begetter for Regnal's absence, for what I will shortly say is not for his ears. Come, Enlenea, let us reunite with the others."

Chapter XIV: To the Ruins of Old Halia

With a snap of his fingers, Astot transported himself and Enlenea to a dimly lit hallway of a tall temple with a tiled marble floor and stone walls engraved with crude depictions of a familiar man-horse warring against humans armed with spears and swords, leading a following of empty-handed believers with their heads lowered. Not immediately would Enlenea begin to question where she was, for her thoughts remained of Inguis and Constius. Had the Elegies begun to hide themselves from Regnal in her absence?

Two lit candles stood upon respective plinths on opposite sides. Astot delicately held one candle and illuminated the path as he continued forward, with Enlenea following closely behind him. "We have Constius to thank for such a fitting abode," he smiled. "'Twas his mercy and convincing tongue that earned us the service of this... prospering human dwelling."

"You hid amongst humanity all this time?" Enlenea asked.

"Forsooth, we have done so for many a reason; but let us say that the citizens of this city have proven worthy of our study so that we may better understand how humanity resists us. But I will spare you the details, unnecessary when weighed against our predicament at present."

The hallway opened in what seemed to be a wide ceremonial space illuminated with torches of blue flame against the walls. On the opposite side, a single window cast the full moon's light, shining upon a great blood-red pentagram surrounded with four pillars in the centre of the space.

"I have not been ignorant of Regnal's disloyalty," Astot spoke as he stepped in the middle of the pentagram to behold the sunlight. "He is a valuable Elegy I would not wish to lose, but as well, I could not allow him to act as he pleases. Inguis, Constius and I—perhaps you as well—we were all prepared for the moment of his betrayal."

Whilst Enlenea was yet undecided as to what should have become of Regnal—and indeed, she knew well he placed his own affairs before the Elegies'—she doubtfully pondered what they would stand to gain in opposing him. No matter how long the Elegies could war amongst one another, they were all undying and always would be.

"I wonder, Enlenea, are you the slightest aware of Regnal's powers?" Astot asked as though he had read Enlenea's mind. "Regnal is a creature with no form to call his own, and so he imitates things of his interest."

"He consumes them," Enlenea added, recalling Regnal's story of consuming another tainted.

Astot nodded. "Without consuming them, he cannot perfectly imitate them. Living creatures he consumes become ever part of him in both mind and body, and it seems he needn't fear losing his own mind as a consequence. In a way... the unfortunate creatures die, no matter what they may be. Regnal, I once feared, was the only tainted capable of killing another."

"And it is Regnal's belief that an 'ideal being' is one which embodies every living thing," Enlenea concluded from Regnal's speech.

Astot placed a finger on his chin. "If this is true, I do not understand him," he murmured. "Life will continue no matter his growth, and he will always find new things to consume. Is it his intention to consume everything there is until he is all that remains? No, perhaps..."

As he fell silent, Astot lowered his head in deep contemplation. Suddenly, his laughter echoed throughout the hall. "I see, I see!" he exclaimed. "Truly, he *does* believe! 'Tis Regnal's belief that the Begetter will appear to conquer a being of greater power, and Regnal desires to become that being. So what he seeks is the power of the Begetter, which means he must not truly doubt his existence. He will still be of some use to us yet."

Astot clenched the candle in his hand tightly, scattering its form as particles of light. He conjured a bell within that same hand and rang it until a four-legged black figure seated in the corner stepped forward by its sound—Constius. Soon afterwards, Inguis emerged in the sky beyond the window, eclipsing the moon and tinting the space red with the glow of his six eyes.

"Regnal would tell you these two are gone from the Elegies, but he has been deceived," Astot continued. "Among the Elegies, Regnal yet has Inguis to fear, and so I hid him away to test Regnal's loyalty and observe his actions with no one left to defy him. Whilst Inguis was hidden, Constius assisted me with tasks no less important, one of which I have already explained. Enlenea, you have studied Halians before, have you not?"

Enlenea nodded. "You spoke of them as humans gifted with strange power."

"The Halians are strange forsooth. We knew what they are but not what they seek, nor how they came to be; but in your absence, we have sought to learn. They seem to know something of the origins of the Scourge, which we do not. The Halians have warred against the Elegies from the beginning, and their powers have proven enough to banish us from this world, albeit for a brief passing of time unique to every tainted. They have grown more restless in the days of your slumber, and it would seem they defy the 'Blade of Humanity' as well, the woman whose existence we have you to thank for."

Following an uncertain moment of silence, Enlenea turned away from Astot. "So, it is true, then," she mused quietly. "I knew from that look in her eyes we had met before. Forgive me, 'twas not my wish to trouble the Elegies so with my actions."

Astot faced Enlenea with a smile. "You have not troubled us at all, dear Enlenea. Perhaps this, too, was the will of our Begetter."

"So I am responsible for all that has happened? Tell me, Astot, what have I done?"

"I spoke before of Regnal's power, that I once believed with it, he was the only tainted who could kill another. But it would seem, Enlenea, that you might possess such a power as well."

"The 'Blade of Humanity' is so titled because she is a human who wields the Scourge against the tainted; her spirit does not waver to it," Inguis cackled. "To conquer us with the very power which birthed us—such is her own task."

"The power of the Scourge—that and the light of the Halians only—can vanquish even the tainted, although always we are fated to reawaken thereafter," Astot added. "The Scourge is a power humans have unwittingly harnessed in times past, and such folly would oft demand a great price. And so they built weapons derived from the Scourge, but for that, too, many sacrifices were made.

"Then came the Blade of Humanity, a human who wields the Scourge as a power of their own and does not yield to it. In exchange for her own identity, she had claimed this great power from none other than you, Enlenea. Thus explains your true power—to take the identity of another as your own, no different than Regnal, or to grant power to others, much like Constius. You merely lack the means of controlling your power."

"Do you know this for certain?" Enlenea asked.

"Astot knows only what I have told him," Inguis answered. "'Twas I who witnessed your death by her hands; as well, her rebirth as the Blade of Humanity."

"Beyond that, I can feel your presence within her," Astot added, "but that presence is fading—your union is fickle, and she will soon become a tainted. If you wish to save her, we must act quickly."

"Now, let us be done with this wearisome exposition!" Constius clamoured, stamping his foot. "The ruins of Old Halia, once home to the Halians, contain the answers we all seek. To discover this land is the design of us, Regnal, and the sycophants of the Blade of Humanity alike."

"Old... Halia?" Enlenea asked.

Astot nodded. "In the centre of a vast meadow lies a great lake upon which stands Old Halia, so a legend tells," Astot said. "It is there the Halians might await us as well. That only we knew where this meadow resides..."

But Enlenea knew well this meadow of which Astot spoke —none other than her birthplace. Perhaps it was there that she would further understand her own origins as well. It was the first time since meeting with Astot that she felt some semblance of excitement. "I know the meadow you speak of, as do I know where to find it."

"Then fortune does smile upon us forsooth!" Astot exclaimed. "Inguis, Constius, we shall follow Enlenea's lead. Let us be first to step foot upon Old Halia!"

"Regnal and Humanity's Blade might win this race nonetheless," Inguis laughed. "What then if we encounter them?"

"If Regnal is there, we will make him kneel before Enlenea's power. I leave the Blade of Humanity's fate in her hands as well."

"If it is her fate to die, then I wish to save her," Enlenea answered. "Once we have discovered the Begetter, the Scourge must be destroyed. The Blade of Humanity may hold the power to do just that."

Astot smiled. "As may you, Enlenea. Perhaps one day, you, too, will be renowned as Blade of Humanity. But let us be concerned with the Scourge another day. Enlenea, Constius, Inguis... let us depart immediately."

Enlenea's final trial awaited her in the ruins of Old Halia. And she foretold the coming of a great battle. One task yet remained before her journey to the sacred ruins: To revisit the home of her old friend and finally earn his aid.

Chapter XV: A Master and His Subjects

Much time had passed since Enlenea last set foot upon the tower. Nothing had changed beyond the corridors, more silent than before. As Enlenea stepped into Madcow's lair, she was first greeted by resounding groans.

"Madcow?" Enlenea whispered in front of the creature's prison.

And by the sound of her voice, the groaning ceased. A pair of gleaming red eyes opened from beyond the darkness of the prison and drew closer until the face of the weary yet familiar beast could be seen. At the sight of Enlenea, Madcow briefly inclined his head, his nose tilting as he scented the air.

"Enlenea? Do my eyes fool me?"

Enlenea answered his question by resting her hand atop his snout.

"Ah, my only friend, that I so yearned for the sight of you all these years," the beast whimpered in response.

Enlenea affectionately stroked his nose. "I had only slept for so long; 'twas not at all my wish to abandon you so."

"And so, you at last return to me. I am ever grateful to be treated with such kindness. Aerbith is gone, and my master still has yet to return to me. I do not take pleasure in being alone, not with only my musings for company. I have done little than prostrate my life in the hollowness of this forgotten structure. Is this the meaning of a life without purpose? Is this my fate for the remainder of eternity?"

"Aerbith has gone, as you have said already. Why will you

not do the same?"

Madcow shook his head. "'Tis because I cannot," he murmured.

"Yet there is no master to keep you here," Enlenea retorted.

"Oh, but there is, if only you could see. My master remains —along with his teachings—engraved in my spirit and in the walls of his tower. Until he commands something more of me shall I remain as well, for how else could he know my earnest gratitude?"

"What then if your master is never to return?" Enlenea asked in an elevated tone. "Would you obey the word of a master with naught a care for your own needs?"

"My master still knows me; his teachings tell me this much. I do not fault him as I fault my own ignorance—my own inability to understand his judgement. Perhaps this is the design of his trial, one I must overcome to prove my loyalty, for 'tis only then may I be with him once more."

"Madcow..." Enlenea paused to consider her words carefully. "'Twas your own words that set me free from subordination, and for that, I am grateful. My plight was one which now you know well. 'Tis for our similarities and my own debt to you that I wish to be of aid to you in any way I can."

"In some ways, we are alike; in others, different," Madcow retorted. "You were lost in that you did not know what a master is to his subjects, nor a subject to his master. From my own words did you come to understand the man you once called master as but a guide, chosen by your own whim. My master is my master, for the beast I once was had been rightly conquered by his might, abandoning arrogance and finding wisdom in turn. 'Tis because I am wise that I may acknowledge a greater being; 'tis because I am in the presence of a greater being that I remain ever by his side, proud and loyal. And although we may be separated with naught a say of mine, I will go forever the way of my faith in him."

"Faith and loyalty... I know those words well," Enlenea solemnly mused. "'Twas in my faith to take Astot's hand, and 'twas for my loyalty that I remained by his side no matter my own wishes. Your meaningful words are why I followed my heart, to help me see that he believed in my will above all else. 'Twas following your heart, not heeding your master's words, that shaped your comprehension of his ambitions in regards to you. You were conquered by his might and soon set free from the cravings of a ravenous beast because, in your den of humiliation, you began to see something more within yourself."

Enlenea's frantic tone softened with each word she spoke thereafter. "Madcow, I am not your master, and so I can only lecture my own understandings, not speak in his place. And what I understand is that your master seeks not your subordination but a sign you have learned all he has to teach—a sign you can now pursue wisdom on your own, free from the shackles of both a servant and a beast. Can you one last time follow your heart to understand his teachings?"

Enlenea anxiously watched as the troubled beast bowed his head. "It would seem you, as well, hold wisdom beyond my own. Despite my efforts—my centuries committed to solitary prostration—I remain but a poor lost lamb without the guidance of another. Can you not say what I am to do were I to leave on my own?"

"Experiencing new things, however heedless you may be of the outcome, is part of learning. I, too, am left with much to learn. I would not ask you to serve me to repay my guidance; all I ask of you is to lend me your power."

Madcow's eyes widened with curiosity. "And to what end would my power be used?"

"Whereas you seek wisdom, I seek knowledge. I seek to know the beginnings of the Scourge which birthed us and with that, a means to destroy it at last."

Madcow chuckled. "After all this time, your misguided spirit has yet to fall. You have yet to convince me of any merit in your ways, but I do hold interest in witnessing the outcome of such a journey with my own eyes." Madcow stood tall before the boundary of his prison. "Then so be it. For my own interests, not mere servitude, I grant you my power for as long as it is needed."

Enlenea extended her hand beyond the bars. "Then come with us to Old Halia, my friend; the Elegies welcome you with open arms. Take my hand, and I will lead you to them."

Madcow placed his nose in Enlenea's palm. "I look forward to meeting these so-called Elegies."

And before Enlenea could set off for Old Halia, the master of the tower finally came to her in a vision for a fleeting moment before leaving without a word. But Enlenea knew by heart what he had entrusted to her: His last faithful servant along with his own blessing.

Chapter XVI: The Betrayer's Stand

Nimbus clouds darkened the skies above a barren plateau with crumbling snags and rustic grass. Astot took each step forward with intrigue and caution alike, closely followed by Enlenea and Madcow. The familiar scent of the once sacred lands gently graced the air. The meadow was but a few paces farther.

Astot looked at Enlenea with a smile. "Do you feel regret having left these lands to oblivion?" he asked with a moment of hesitation.

"Had I not left, I would not have come this far," Enlenea murmured, silently mourning the withered meadow over what little remained of its scent. "I have no regrets."

"To be reunited with the air beyond the tower is truly such a pleasant sensation," Madcow mused. "And with all I have learned, I may prowl the fields under a greater perspective. You have opened my eyes to the wonders of freedom, and for that, Enlenea, I am ever grateful." Madcow looked at Astot. "We are but strangers to one another, but you have naught to fear from me; you need not hide your companions from me."

"Oh, dear; if my actions seemed suspicious in any way, I apologise," Astot hastily responded. "But, truly, I have hidden naught from you. Constius journeyed ahead of us whilst Enlenea sought your aid; I can only pray he has found the meadow. Inguis departed elsewhere with naught an explanation, but I was assured he would return to me in the meadow. Regnal, I pray, does *not* find us."

"So it seems one hound ventures far from his leash,"

Madcow quipped.

Astot laughed. "Forsooth, forsooth!"

At the precipice of the plateau was a plain of brown grass spanning far and wide, untouched by all but the weather and the Scourge. The great lake could be seen before the horizon, and the vague ruins of Old Halia stood beyond a fog.

"How pleasant to see we are among the first upon the meadow as it is now," Astot smirked while gazing longingly ahead before promptly turning his attention to a man dressed in white and a woman in a black coat standing a short distance ahead. The woman was unmistakably the Halian fighting alongside the Blade of Humanity; the man, Enlenea was certain she had not met before.

"Who's there!?" Cygna shouted while turning frantically, facing Astot with a meek expression as he greeted her with a smile.

The man observed the trio over his shoulder as though their arrival had been long anticipated. "History repeats itself in curious ways," he mused with a gritty tone, greeting the tainted with a smile of his own. "From upon the day we hid from mankind, our fear has persisted unwavering throughout the ages. Oh yes, we knew, however we denied it. 'Twas only a matter of time ere a new scourge would come—that of revenge, that of destructive inquisition—to churn the wounds which had yet to heal. But nevertheless, I welcome you proudly. Welcome to the Garden of Mercy, once a beautiful meadow about our humble home, now a reminder of forgotten misdeeds."

Astot furrowed his eyebrows, glaring at the man with a fierceness Enlenea had never before observed in him. "So you, too, are Halian," he muttered. "For what purpose have you come?"

The man's eyes shifted towards the horizon. "Have you not guessed already? Be it Old Halia or New Halia, you will not be permitted upon our sacred lands."

"Assuming you speak in earnest, that is fair enough," Astot sighed. "But surely you do not intend to best us with your power alone?"

The man drew closer, his arms outstretched. "So I am to die here. What of it? I am but a calm before the tumultuous storm, an eminent preacher who would only observe the coming reckoning. To smite me would be to lay bare your cowardice. I permit my death, I welcome it... for soon shall you all wish you could die as well. No matter your struggles—your efforts to seek truth—you will find those efforts thwarted time and time again. You will live eternally wallowing in your own helplessness, trembling afore our cleansing light in wake and in slumber."

Enlenea stepped forward. "What would you know of our determination? Ne'er will we cower whilst in trying we lose naught. You Halians will be the ones who learn to curse your own mortality 'till the day comes when not one of you remains."

"And, of course, I must also consider the possibility that you wish to stall us," Astot added. "Let us be done with this trifling; you may die now."

But just as Astot raised his hand to personally execute him, the man lurched forward into the ground, the moment heralded by a deafening sound. Blood pooled underneath his buried face from a wound at the back of his head. The assailant standing behind his lifeless body was none other than Cygna.

"Is this what you wanted?" Astot asked after a pause, suspending his look of bewilderment.

Cygna lowered the weapon held in her trembling arm. "My mother... she took me somewhere far away to be raised by a human family," she thoughtfully murmured. "I loved my family; I didn't know what I was before I decided to try to save the world, just like the man I always thought of as a father. If that means taking a stand against my entire race, then that's okay to me because I never was one of them as far as I was concerned." She turned to face the horizon. "And I'm not here to listen to anything they have to say. There's something here for me, and I'm taking it by force."

Astot drew closer until he stood beside her. "I will confess that I had wished to use you to slaughter the Halians from the beginning. I did not foresee you willingly committing to such a task alone. Would you not consider us your enemies as well, nevertheless?"

"I've experienced enough to know that not all of you are enemies. In fact, maybe we could even work together. What do you think?"

As Enlenea and Madcow walked towards the precipice alongside him and the Halian woman, Astot smiled assuredly. "Though one day we may truly be as enemies, mayhap we had best be concerned with that another time. You may call me Astot, wayward Halian."

Cygna gave Astot a wry smile. "My name is Cygna."

Madcow proceeded to introduce himself. "I am Madcow, an adherent of wisdom."

And with some hesitation, Enlenea stated her own name. "And I am Enlenea, a tainted birthed within this very meadow."

"Enlenea and I, as do all of the Elegies, seek only to understand the truth of our existence," Astot explained. "Old Halia was the seat upon which everything began—of that, I am certain."

Cygna's eyes widened. "So if I follow you there, I could find a way to stop the Scourge forever. And you're really okay with that?"

Astot nodded. "That is what I wish, yes, so long as I am given a chance to meet with my Begetter before embracing death eternal. If only you would grant me this, will I see your own desires fulfilled."

"But how?" Cygna worriedly asked.

"To speak frankly... do not destroy the Scourge before the moment I deem it fitting."

Cygna narrowed her eyes. "Can I trust you?"

Astot raised an eyebrow. "Can *you* be trusted?"

"We have not the time to argue trust amongst one another," Enlenea interjected.

"Oh, how could I argue with that?" Astot sighed before looking wayward. "Ah, Cygna... has the Blade of Humanity not come along with you?"

"Yeah. She's the one I'm trying to save. Maybe her life is more important than mine, but that's not why I've come this far. I'm just trying to save a friend, that's all."

"I want to save her, too," Enlenea declared before looking into Cygna's eyes for a lasting moment. The Halian woman gazed sharply upon her featureless face as though making a futile attempt to read into her thoughts. In the end, Cygna acknowledged her with a slow nod before looking away, the two having silently agreed to express themselves through actions rather than words.

A pillar of black miasma spewed upward into the sky from a higher plane standing a small distance to the West. The lands tremored before its gargantuan influence, and Astot faced its direction with a frantic look. "Constius!" he shouted. "Let us go with haste ere the Halians vanquish him."

As Enlenea and Astot rode the winds on the way to the presumed onslaught, Cygna rode atop Madcow's back, and the two followed closely behind them. Though the strife settled by the time they arrived, they found Constius as Astot predicted, standing alongside Aerbith, the guardian hound. Hovering above them in opposition was a sizeable creature shrouded in black flames, its shape mirroring that of a long-winged avian whose form swayed with the wind—a phoenix shrouded in darkness.

"Regnal?" Enlenea whispered.

And by the sound of Enlenea's voice, the creature, or rather the entity that had claimed its form as his own, glanced carelessly upon her with unmistakable blue eyes before descending ceremoniously to the earth like a higher being ready to pass judgement upon mortals. Regnal drew closer to Constius and Aerbith, his every step followed by a resounding tremor, and he spoke first to Constius. "Sight the faces of those who pay audience to your abasement ere aught else, Lord Constius. Abandon your pride; bask in humiliation; know humility and enlightenment thenceforth.

"And claim my words as your own blanket of comfort should ever you look back fondly upon your glorious days: I alone—now and eternally so—shall smile upon you who was destined as an ornament in the mausoleum of amity. To embrace one's fate is such a beautiful thing."

Constius stamped the ground in defiance and valour, his sword arm trembling with anger. "Oh, you would smile upon me nevertheless?" he growled in a low tone. "Then hearken my words, traitorous caitiff: I would be so beholden as to carve painstakingly every letter of my name into your defiled skull once I have mounted it upon the tip of my *blade!*"

"To think I would die alongside this many of my foes," Aerbith cackled as he poised himself to lunge.

"What's going on?" Cygna whispered to Enlenea.

But Astot would be the first to respond with a slow clap, and all three of the battling tainted turned to face him. "You should be praised for having found this place afore me, Regnal," he began with a wary expression. "Now, pray tell, why are you here?"

"To emboss your path with the bodies of your foes, Astot," Regnal languidly answered. "I knew you would come, as did I know the Halians would await you,"

Astot furrowed his eyebrows. "Constius is not my foe. I will speak my mind forsooth—what has he done so deserving of your wrath?"

"Heed not one word this traitor speaks; he is gone beneath all reason," Constius hissed.

Regnal ignored Astot and Constius as he spoke to Cygna, "If you, Halian, would seek your 'Watcher,' then look to the garden and think naught of my own presence; you do not concern me." He looked up into the cloud-blotted sky. "Yea, the Elegies have returned, yet Inguis has not come... or have my senses been so cruelly deceived?"

Astot let out a heavy breath as if to brace himself for what was to come. "I take no comfort in being left without Inguis... but 'tis as you say."

Astot had barely finished speaking as Regnal outstretched his powerful wings, sending torrents of errant flames and volatile winds forth. "Oh, yes... I *am* fortunate." He looked into the faces of his distraught spectators in respective moments of pause as he called out their names. "Herald Astot, Enlenea the Painted, Lord Constius, Guardian Aerbith, nameless beast I newly meet... I shall walk the path to Old Halia alone with the existences of each of you cast unto my own, along with the burdens of your impossible fantasies, which I will so proudly bear in remembrance of you. Is it not that we all would wish to be free from our own wants?"

"Enough!" Enlenea shouted as she finally stepped forward, facing Regnal directly. "Regnal, what of your own fantasies— your own existence? Or are you naught more than what you design to imitate?"

Regnal lowered his head as he gazed before Enlenea, his narrowed eyes reflecting a longing for resolution. "You, Enlenea, whose own spirit is as the recompense of mockery, hold not the right to cast judgement upon me."

Astot frowned. "Few could know of her power. I did not think to count you among them."

"And you did well to stay from me your knowledge, Astot," Regnal added. "But of what little you knew that she and I are as opposites. And opposites are ever drawn to one another."

And so began the conflict between the Elegies and their betrayer.

Chapter XVII: The Cleansing Canvas

Aerbith made the first move, lunging upon Regnal and driving his own fangs into the inflamed flesh of the Ideal One's left wing.

Then followed Madcow with a gallant charge from the front, pressing his head against Regnal's belly and forcing him aback with his own might.

Last was Constius, in all his fury, brandishing his ornate, elongated broadsword and severing Regnal's head and right wing from behind in one swift motion.

Astot had observed it all with a look of anxiety, knowing perhaps as well as Enlenea that Regnal could never be so easily slain. And indeed, all efforts proved meaningless as Regnal's body, along with his severed head and wing, erupted into an expanding vortex of sentient black flames, disintegrating the ground where Regnal once stood and threatening to do the same to the trio that had dared a preemptive assault.

Constius, having already stood a distance afar, took a prompt step backward and eluded the danger.

Madcow, acting purely of instinct, so it seemed, retreated a moment before the flames emerged and observed the spectacle unharmed.

But Aerbith would not be so fortunate, for by the time he had loosed himself from Regnal's wing and gained a safe distance away, the flames had already claimed his lower jaw, foreleg, and left eye.

"Regnal!" Enlenea shouted in protest as the flames

condensed into a gentle orb hovering overhead.

"So by your hand be it," Regnal's scathing, disembodied voice echoed through the winds as the orb began to reshape. First from its sides spouted the shape of a delicate pair of arms; then, from its crown, formed the shape of a human skull; finally, from beneath fell a woven fabric like the skirt of a ballgown, long enough to reach the cratered ground. And so hovered the shade of a skull-faced woman in a long dress, her right eye blue and her left eye golden like Aerbith's own.

Enlenea stood pondering Regnal's uncanny facial expression from a moment prior. She had never observed something more than hatred in his eyes until he responded to her words. As a being with uncountable faces and forms, did Regnal seek to claim all power as his own, or was his own power but a veil of his true identity? Perhaps he could see reason if only she knew how.

If only she knew the identity of the child who caught his hand.

The dirt of the land, beckoned by Regnal's influence, returned as it was to the crater beneath his feet before he descended upon the earth, his form now an amalgam all his own. He—or rather, it—glanced at Aerbith with its mutated eye as if taunting the maimed guardian before turning its attention to Enlenea. In the midst of it all, Constius flailed his blade savagely upon Regnal, his every attempt at cutting the Ideal One thwarted by an unseen obstruction that responded with a clanging noise as though one blade were clashing with another.

Astot stood between Regnal and Enlenea. "So be it if we are to become as enemies," he muttered, "but I pray you cease this bloodletting until you have answered me this: Do you stand willingly in our way to Old Halia?"

"I will cast all you are and desire unto my own being; you know this already," Regnal replied, its voice now inhumanly hoarse and untraceable like a wind's whisper. "We will venture to Halia as one and the same."

Astot gave Regnal a threatening glare. "Do with us as you

please, but you will not have Enlenea."

"You were ever a being subordinate to his faith in others, Astot," Regnal mentioned slowly. "Your final moments will be in condemnation of that very faith."

"Aerbith is to me a partner and a brother," Madcow said as he stepped between Astot and Regnal. "I will raise your head on account of his suffering. And Enlenea, I consider my salvation embodied; ne'er could I allow the ruination of your greed befall her. Though I bear no grudge against you for our differences—and you do not care to even hear my name—if by your hand my friends are to perish here, then I would wish to join them in their final resistance."

With Enlenea and himself concealed behind Madcow's leg, Astot gave Enlenea a prolonged stare as if to speak to her through his stern expression alone; but Enlenea could only speculate his expectations. Was it to say all fell upon her to stop Regnal here and now? Was she expected to run and abandon everyone to their deaths so that she alone may live to challenge Regnal another day?

"Tis not that I wish not to know your name," Regnal responded to Madcow, "but that I would choose to know it first as one of my own. I can offer for your bravery no recompense greater than a promise that you will be first to forfeit your existence and be spared the grief of playing witness to the slaughter of those so admired and beloved by you."

As Regnal finished its speech, Constius' blade finally cut into the ground as far as Enlenea could hear, her vision still obscured by Madcow's standing. Panic spread amongst the Elegies and their allies before Enlenea could so much as look behind, beckoned by both Astot's and Cygna's frantic glaring in that direction. And there the Ideal One now stood, black flames rippling through the ground from beneath its feet.

"Run, Enlenea!" Astot finally shouted.

But the time to act had already come and gone, and Enlenea only managed to grasp Cygna's arm before the Ideal One's power was upon them again. A deafening explosion flung her violently through the air. She felt no pain—she had survived unscathed. But with her senses thrown into disarray, she could not tell where Regnal had gone nor if it had already killed her companions. She was left confused and frightened with only the comfort of Cygna's flesh against the palm of her hand as she fell to the ground. But she could not even tell if she still grasped a living being.

Enlenea had landed soundly on her back, engulfed beneath a vast bed of tall grass. She had fallen upon the Garden of Mercy. From a distance away, a cloud of dust coated the plateau where she once stood, a giant portion of it having been rent apart.

A woman's scream sounded closely alongside her. Enlenea quietly crawled in that direction until she stood in front of where Cygna lay, her body under the shroud of a brilliant glow. So it seemed her own powers had saved her life.

"Cynga?" Enlenea whispered.

But Cygna responded with only an anguished cry.

Enlenea stood up to examine her closely. "Cygna!" she shouted frantically. The Halian had lost both legs and blood already drenched the soil beneath Enlenea's feet.

"Leave us be, Enlenea," a wavering voice called out to her in another direction. "Save your life, and leave us be."

From the distance Enlenea stood, the source appeared as an oddly shaped rock. With each step closer could she gradually recognise its true form. "No," she whimpered. "Not you too."

All that remained of Madcow was his head. Enlenea waited anxiously to hear his voice once more, but the beast would not respond, his eyes idling beneath their lids.

"Madcow? Madcow!" Enlenea shouted.

And miraculously, Madcow answered her desperate cries, forcing his eyes open with his little strength remaining. "Why live at all if we are to die?" he murmured. "To die would be to forfeit the meaning of my existence, to cast myself aside into an everlasting void. I know it well—I have died before, only to be reborn. 'Twas such a lonely, empty state I found myself in...

so why would I condemn myself to it for time eternal?" He looked at Enlenea with a complacent countenance. "But finally —now that I am to die eternally such as any mortal could— I finally understand. Though I may die, it is as such I find more appreciation for having lived at all and having learned all I have... and knowing a friend whom I could pass unto my wisdom. Though I may die, I will not be forgotten."

An ominous black cloud collected in the distance, within which emerged the form of Madcow's headless body, comprised of the Ideal One's black flames.

"Live, Enlenea, lest my words be wasted," Madcow pleaded as his own stolen body pressed its leg against his head. "And should you one day find the might to stand against your foes... please, save my soul."

Enlenea could only watch as Madcow's head crumbled unto dust in the fair wind.

"Farewell, Madcow, O advocate of wisdom," Regnal spoke through its completed effigy of Madcow, its blue eyes gleaming through the head it claimed from him. "For you, I now declare a promise anew, that I will be all-knowing in honour of you."

Now Enlenea knew hatred and fear—fear that she could do nothing to save her friends and hatred of the betrayer who would become their executioner. But she could not run; she could not fight. All she could manage was to stare into Regnal's eyes and pray for an end to its madness. She was no less powerless than a human against a tainted.

"Do you feel disdain for all I have done?" Regnal asked quietly. "Rejoice that I have spared from him a fate far worse. What that fate holds for all of us tainted deviants, I leave you to discover beyond the cradle of your ignorance. Know the truth with your own body." It lowered its head closely in front of Enlenea. "Forget not the cries of your fallen brethren as you venture to surmount my overcast shadow. And when comes that day you may stand against your foes... I will stand before you to proclaim my greatest prize."

An abrupt surge of Regnal's flames incinerated its

surroundings, but Enlenea, having already lost the will to resist, noticed Regnal's deceit only too late. The flames engulfed her, throwing her to and fro like a speck in the wind before leaving her on the sundered ground with wounds of despair.

"Until then, I claim this arm as my token," Regnal continued as its flames condensed upon its body, revealing Madcow's form with the addition of a pale arm protruding atop its forehead.

Enlenea looked down where her right arm once existed, now but a gaping wound seeping dark blood and miasmata. "Regnal... stop," she pled feebly.

Regnal gave her a blank stare. "Share in me my ideal, Enlenea; then, we may beg for mercy together."

A familiar sword came soaring through the air, impaling Regnal's back and pressing him against the ground. A triumphant roar ensured far behind Enlenea. She turned to see Constius alive and well, the wounded Aerbith held in his hand.

"You will not be rid of me so easily!" Constius declared while stamping to Regnal's location.

"Forgive my knowing not how to die by your hand, Constius," Regnal spoke behind Enlenea, slithering past her uninjured as a gargantuan serpent before she could turn to face it.

"You are an Elegy by my decree," Astot spoke in a muttering tone, his voice resounding from all directions. Constius and Regnal promptly halted in acknowledgement. "'Regnal' may be a name of your own choosing, but mayhap my lack of guidance is to blame for your unquelled wickedness. I alone will annul this living fault of my foolishness." Astot's form finally appeared before Regnal. "I am Astot, leader of all Elegies! I will prove with fitting might my *right* to your reverence!"

"I declare this on behalf of all Elegies, Astot: We do not serve you; we do not care for you," Regnal retorted before lunging upon Astot.

So continued the brutal battle without Enlenea's participation. She observed the duo of Constius and Astot in their gallant struggle for survival, keeping Regnal at bay in an even bout as Astot distracted Regnal's senses with transient dreams conjured from the toll of his bell, allowing Constius to carve his enmity upon the black flames solidified, however futile it was to harm the ideal in command of them. The opportunity had come to escape to Old Halia as Astot required of her, but she would not go alone.

"Let us journey to Old Halia, together," she quietly urged in front of Cygna.

"There's nothing I can do," Cygna groaned.

Enlenea glanced at Cygna's legs, noticing she had managed to stanch her own bleeding. "You will not survive here." She extended her hand to Cygna. "Please, I wish to help you."

As Cygna took her hand reluctantly, Enlenea held her body in her remaining arm and carried her along as she hovered above the meadow towards the lake of Old Halia without looking back. Their journey was silent and more lasting than Enlenea could recall, and she was lost in thought until its end, disgusted in Regnal as well as herself.

The lake beyond the meadow, as expansive as a sea, hummed gently before the sway of the quiet winds. A persistent fog loomed above its space, but Enlenea could see a ruined city beyond it, a hodgepodge of half-sunken, dilapidated buildings and domes tinted rustic white.

Enlenea gently laid Cygna before the shore and gazed resolutely at the source of every answer she sought. She could faintly sense the presence of a tainted amid the Halians' light. The Blade of Humanity was still alive. "What do they seek of the Blade of Humanity?" she asked.

"I was only told the answer would be made clear to me if I could reach her," Cygna replied. "I guess I'll have a chance after all. I can't believe I really made it this far."

"In some way, perhaps... nor did I," Enlenea murmured, contemplating her past. "Ne'er did I fully believe I would live forever—that I would live to be the one to destroy the Scourge."

She solemnly planted her hand against her chest at the thought of Astot's wishes. "And discover the Begetter foremost." She raised her hand to halt Cygna's speech. "Come, let us act quickly."

As Enlenea traversed the density of sunken buildings, bundles of light grew apparent in the air, centred above a circular space left afloat over the lake amid the rubble. A closer look revealed Halians with wings of light, observing what appeared to be the well-maintained ground of a giant stone altar, along with a single woman kneeling at its centre—the Blade of Humanity. The Halians did little more before Enlenea's arrival than to quietly observe her descent onto the altar.

Watcher lifted her head. "You finally made it," she spoke in a gloomy tone. "I see you made it out with a bit more than just a scratch."

"Sorry," Cygna laughed wryly.

Enlenea drew closer to Watcher, noticing no obvious signs of mortal injury. But as she drew close, she met with a chilling cold—the Scourge within the nameless woman had grown frighteningly unsettled.

"Where's Aerbith?" Watcher asked. "Don't tell me these fanatics got to him."

"He is—"

Cygna interrupted Enlenea. "He's just staying behind to keep the Halians at bay. We wouldn't have made it here without him."

Watcher glared at Enlenea. "And what brings you here, O faceless one? It's a little too late to have a change of heart. Just look at me; I'm already done for."

"We were waiting for you," a Halian woman spoke as she descended to the altar directly behind Watcher, a glint of curiosity in her emerald eyes as she lay them upon Enlenea and Cygna.

Watcher strained to grin. "Oh, great. Well, you could have at least left me *something* to be hopeful for."

"Do you refer to me?" Enlenea asked, examining the Halian woman carefully. Aside from wearing an identical robe to the other Halians, the woman clearly presented herself as a figure of authority, standing tall, well-postured, and with kempt white hair framing a softly aged visage.

"I am Caevin," the woman introduced. "If you seek to forever rid the world of the Scourge, then fear not, tainted one, we are not your enemies. We have awaited this moment for so very long—awaited the day you would return to us to fulfil your destiny as designed by your creator."

"What do you know of my creator?" Enlenea sternly asked.

"Do you believe your creator, this 'Begetter,' to be a god? He was but a human with a gift worth more than the man himself. Alas, he has long parted from this world, and much of his past is unknown to me." Caevin narrowed her eyes. "Now pray tell, why have you come? Have you come on behalf of this tainted in front of me? Is it merely the destruction of the Scourge you seek?"

"I will save her and destroy the Scourge," Enlenea declared.

Caevin chuckled. "'Tis funny of you to say. There is naught to suggest that with the death of the Scourge, all tainted will not soon perish along with it. Surely you have pondered this, have you not?"

"Yes, I have. The Scourge must be destroyed, that we may all finally rest for eternity."

"Such is your purpose—to bring forth that change. The question is, what will you sacrifice to that end?" She pointed to Watcher. "Tell me, what is this creature before my pointed finger —a human or a tainted?"

"She is a human who will lose her identity and become a tainted."

"Are you to save her as a human or a tainted?"

"She is an innocent who has suffered from circumstances beyond her control. She does not wish to be as a tainted, and so I wish to uphold her humanity."

A slight smile crept upon Caevin's lips. "Well and just, tainted one; but surely you are now aware that some tainted, such as you, do oppose the Scourge, and some may even share similarities with humans. What is to say it is wrong to live as a tainted with the power to cling to one's own goodwill?"

"Yet not all tainted are so fortunate and wise, and I will abide by her own wishes."

"Does your respect of human will—the desire to save humanity—precede the wishes of your own friends?"

"Should I destroy the Scourge, my friends will accept their fate."

"But first, a meeting with their 'Begetter,' no? As I have said, your creator lived and died a man—never will you chance upon this meeting you desire."

"Could a mere man create a being such as I?" Enlenea retorted. "Even so, is it wrong to believe that such a man, in death, could prosper as a tainted?"

"If he is a tainted, you may yet find him; but who can say how long you must wait? How many more sacrifices must be made to appeal to his favour and earn his audience?"

Enlenea shook her head. "Ne'er have I taken a life in his name."

Caevin folded her arms. "And yet you do naught to stay all slaughter by the hands of your companions; you are no less guilty than they. Constius has led many humans to their deaths with the act of deception; Inguis alone has killed tens of millions in the name of your so-called Begetter, to say naught of the many more lives he had claimed afore that. Even the hands of Astot have been stained with human blood. And the bloodshed will go unhindered for as long as they remain unknown to their Begetter. I ask you, when will enough be enough? Will you allow them to be as they are for eternity, ever in pursuit of an entity which may well not exist?"

"But I..." Enlenea spoke timidly before lowering her head, struggling to ponder her response.

"Don't listen to a single word she says," Cygna growled.

Caevin glared at Cygna. "And what of you, exile? Is your own life so precious that you would do naught before humanity's downfall to sustain it?"

"You haggish bitch!" Cygna roared, struggling to free

herself from Enlenea's grasp. "Everything I've done was to *save* mankind! I would have given my life away at any point for their sake!"

Watcher sighed. "Give it up, Cyg. None of it matters at this point."

Caevin breathed deeply. "Yes... for once, this woman speaks true," she spoke placidly. "At any rate, you come to us for three purposes, tainted one: To destroy the Scourge, to seek out your creator, and to save this one tainted woman. We cannot provide you with the answers you desire, and killing us will not stay the spread of the Scourge. Knowing this, how are you to act?"

Enlenea lifted her head. "If you cannot stop the Scourge, then so be it—I will save these two and be on my way."

"Do you hope we could simply leave them be? Cygna is the daughter of an arrant rogue and must be put to death in retribution for her mother's sins. The Blade of Humanity possesses power beyond our comprehension, and should she lose control of it, we may face a calamity far greater than the Scourge alone. And try as you may to restore her humanity, you cannot take that power away."

"I will *not* allow you to claim their lives," Enlenea boldly declared.

"Are these two lives more worthy of your salvation than humanity whole?"

"I will save them because they are the future of humanity."

"All the while leaving other mortals to their deaths? If they are our future, then you are to be their greatest foe. To save them is to forgo the pursuit of the Begetter. Even your own Regnal is well aware of this. So, you must decide what you find more important: Enlightenment or heroism—your creator or our humanity. There is no standing amidst good and evil—you cannot but confront your own moral chaos." Caevin lifted her hand over her head, gathering countless specks of glistening dust to cluster above her grasp in an elaborate shape before solidifying into an engraved blade bearing a subtle glow.

"Is that the regalia?" Cygna asked, fear prominent in her eyes.

Caevin flashed Cygna a murderous glare before returning her attention to Enlenea. "Make your choice, Enlenea. You will free these women from our grasp and dirty your hands with our innocent blood, unite with us to stand against the Scourge and the Elegies... or leave us be in the name of your creator."

"I will *not* leave them."

"Then will you slay us?" Caevin asked.

"No."

"Will you stand with us against the Elegies? Will you abandon your creator and his deluded followers?"

"No!"

"I'll kill them all myself and make it easier for both of us!" Cygna declared.

"*No*, Cygna!"

"Make your choice, or I will make it for you," Caevin growled. "I will put these defilers to death and enslave you, I swear it."

"You've done all you can," Watcher murmured. "Just forget about me, all right?"

Enlenea froze, visions of her whole life flashing before her. She cherished nature; she valued all life beyond her own. She sought a means to end her undying existence for mankind to reclaim this decaying world. But she had long become an individual with selfish desires—she shared Astot's yearning to understand her own existence before casting it aside. And beyond that, Astot had proven himself as her friend, a guide that without, she would never know what it meant to dream. She would have strongly condemned her existence had she foreseen the trial of this very moment, but there would be no escape from her accursed life. A decision had to be made, no matter the outcome.

Enlenea gently lowered Cygna to the ground and extended her hand to Watcher, forcing her own words with what little remained of her, "Please, take my hand."

Watcher widened her eyes. "What are you going to do?"

"My decision is made—I will save your humanity. But I choose to do so in the name of the Begetter. And by your hand will I accept my punishment, not only for the sins of my fellow Elegies but for the sins I will soon commit myself."

Watcher grasped her hand without hesitation.

"For now, let us exist as one," Enlenea continued. "Allow me to bear the burden of your corruption; I will conquer it. And when I am pure, I will pass unto you your humanity—an existence to call your own. You will one day be reborn anew."

Watcher smiled. "Sounds good. I could use a rest if you ask me. And, who knows, maybe we won't need to be enemies in the future?"

Enlenea kneeled in front of her. "What is your true name, Blade of Humanity?"

"Yours is Enlenea, right? I'd be glad to know the name of that woman in my head, at least."

Alas, the deed was done before Enlenea could answer. Watcher faded away, and nothing remained of her but the will she passed on.

"I know it now—your hands, as well, are stained with the blood of innocents," Enlenea grumbled with her head lowered. "Madcow gave his life on behalf of my ambition; I cannot hope to walk away and pardon your misdeeds."

"Enlenea?" Cygna called out.

Enlenea stood up and lifted her head, revealing tears flowing from a pair of silvery eyes, a face wrought with guilt and anger.

"I must kill you all. Forgive me."

So began her retribution. Decayed branches spouted upward from the centre of the altar, high as the clouds and burning bright with flame. From that flame emerged innumerable fireflies. From within the waters around the altar spawned grotesque and gargantuan branches and roots lashing in every direction. In mere seconds, everything had become smothered beneath insects and rotted wood.

"Use the Annulling Clasp!" Enlenea heard from one of the Halians. Before long, they could let out only screams. Many Halians died by impalement of the shifting branches; others were torn apart by the rancid roots or set aflame by the ravenous fireflies. Enlenea soon grew deaf to the uncountable cries.

She was Enlenea, the Painted Woman—a name gifted to her by Astot of the Elegies. She sought enlightenment and aspired to save humanity.

Caevin calmly observed the events unfold from afar, having gained a safe distance from the isolated onslaught. But Enlenea had not been oblivious to her survival, and with a pointed finger, she directed a sunken branch through the Halian leader's torso before her entire body was incinerated unto ash.

She was Enlenea—a name gifted to her by a man known as Astot. She sought enlightenment.

"We must retreat!" One of the Halians managed to announce. He, too, was quickly silenced by impalement.

She was Enlenea—a name whose origins she could not quite place. What did she seek? Why did she exist?

"Enlenea?" called out a woman lying next to her. And although she did not recognise her voice, Enlenea could not bring herself to kill her as she flew away.

Enlenea? Why had that name been mentioned?

What was it? Did it exist?

Unplaced hatred. Uncontrolled power.

Blackness, and nothing.

Chapter XVIII:
My Gift to You

Fluttering butterflies and singing birds gathered before the backyard of a grand stone temple on a sunlit day. One man alone bode his time within its garden, wearing a modest apron over his ornate robes. He hummed complacently, singing along with nature as he tended to the abundance of flowers with a watering can.

"Greetings, Astot," my relaxed voice spoke from the shadow of a tree behind the man. "Have you summoned me?"

Astot smiled as my voice reached his ears, turning to greet his long-departed friend. "Oh, dear Vaharja, how I have longed to see you!"

I rewarded Astot's smile with one of my own. My long, silky raven hair framed the dark complexion of my delicate face; an intricate shell of gilded marble obscured my eyebrows and sealed my eyes shut, perpetually crumbling as luminescent dust with every pace I took. Despite the presence of two engraved black horns protruding from my head, I aspired to maintain an air of wisdom and solitude. I had chosen my own name —Recordkeeper Vaharja, revered by Astot for my wisdom and might. I declared it was my belief that only in death could the Elegies unite with their Begetter, and so I had retired to a solitary life, awaiting an end to my undying existence.

"How fares the other Elegies, my old friend?" I asked.

Astot's smile had briefly lowered at the mention of the Elegies. "They are quite well," he answered with another smile. "Rather, I should say it is all as you foretold."

I chuckled with a wide grin. "Then Regnal has at last betrayed you as well?"

"So he has; so he has. 'Tis why I was meaning to summon you sooner."

Astot followed me as I strolled to the back of a fountain in the middle of the yard to observe the sky. "So, then... where has he gone?" I asked.

"Rest assured, he is dealt with for now, but 'tis not to say my summons were wasted on you. I welcome you to what I pray you will see as your new home. Welcome, Vaharja, to the land of Yeon, now home to the Elegies."

The land of Yeon, once a nation untouched by the Scourge long ago, had become home to the Elegies and the humans who worshipped them as gods. In the days before the arrival of Constius, Yeon's inhabitants delved into arcane research, seeking a means to command the power of the Scourge. The Elegies had made good use of the pentagram in their temple of worship, a device laden with the Scourge that could amplify a tainted's power. Astot, in particular, had used it to widen his influence, and with that, he had attempted to summon my faraway self along with the other Elegies. He could only lament that I had not arrived sooner. His link to the city would allow him to return to it within an instant, no matter his distance, as he had done after his final meeting with the Blade of Humanity.

Yeon, founded upon an arid landmass with few resources to spare, was forgotten in this war-torn era of four monarchies scattered in the cardinal directions. Its people, destitute and oblivious as they were, enjoyed a peaceful and simplistic existence before the Scourge spilled onto their territory. The four kings, whose territories had long been saturated with the Scourge by the time their first bricks were laid, had Constius to thank for their prosperity in spite of the odds, even if they were left unaware.

Betwixt the four nations lay the uncharted, perilous wastes prowled by tainted beasts with a pittance of settlements populated by outcasts who learned to wield the Scourge and survive against the odds. Skirmishes were frequent as the kingdoms warred for scarce resources, but most deaths were the result of the Scourge, and no human could hope to venture too far from their homeland and survive. Every king would draw the same conclusion—to ascend their nation, they would need to harness the power of the Scourge for themselves, a practice outlawed for their common folk. All of them would bear the weight of their conceitedness as the Scourge swallowed them whole and their nations soon followed, bringing an end to the Era of Kings.

Proto-Golem was an outlier, a nation beyond the wastes the kings could not hope to oppose, and the only one that had emerged without the trickery of Constius; but Proto-Golem was content to leave the kings be, for their war was with the Halians and the Scourge in its entirety. The kingdoms and settlements beyond would nevertheless make liberal use of the Golemians' seized technology whenever their battleships came crashing into the land from either tainted or Halian intervention in an event that would be known as *Godsrain*. Perhaps, I thought, the era to follow would be that of three new warring nations— Proto-Golem, the bastion of the humans; New Halia, the land of the Halians; and Yeon, the bed of the tainted gods.

"Do the humans serve you?" I asked. "'Twould explain why the Yeonese do not fear my presence."

"I now have many reasons to be grateful for Constius," Astot expressed. "I pray he will not leave us after all that has happened. Speaking of which... you may both come forward, Aerbith, Cygna." Astot peered over the fountain and waved at the two new arrivals.

Cygna acknowledged Astot with a slow nod. She wore an eyepatch over her left eye, underneath which was a curious black marking reminiscent of a leafy vine extending to her chin. Her long, buttoned black vest concealed all but the boots of her restored legs.

"How fares Aerbith?" Astot asked.

Cygna drew attention to a large hound standing behind

her. Gentle black flames comprised his body, leaving only his glowing yellow eyes to distinguish him as a living being. Aerbith stepped forward with a prominent limp, having yet to grow accustomed to his new body. "To think I would step foot upon this city once more," he bemoaned.

"Aznia, the capital of Yeon, has seen many a tainted afore the Elegies," Astot informed, taking a moment to scrutinise Aerbith's form. "Might this be the place you, too, once called home?"

"Madcow and I were alike—I was once but a beast who relished the hunt. I sought a greater purpose, and soon I learned the virtue of friendship. You know my story well, do you not?"

Astot gave a solemn nod while recalling bitter memories of a period in which he beckoned a particular tainted to join the Elegies, a visionary with kind sentiments towards humanity— a visionary we would be forced to seal away, for that kindness would betray him and he would lose his sanity forevermore. His madness would gorge him to the breadth of a burg, and far be it from the outcome he envisioned that he was left to wander alone in the vastness of nowhere.

Like the woman clinging to Astot's mind, Eldather envisioned a world in which Humans and enlightened tainted could co-exist. We were all naïve to the reality of our damnation, for even we, having been claimed by the Scourge as humans, would be claimed again as tainted were we to deviate from the desires to which our existences were obliged, and we would be rent anew, reborn as calamitous abominations beyond all reckoning.

Another tainted had learned this with her own body. I could only hope that with the Halians' success at survival, they had spared us Elegies the misfortune of facing such a threat a second time.

"I have not forgotten, and as well know I have yet to earn your forgiveness," Astot answered as I ruminated. "Alas, it pains me to so much as mention Eldather as I stand before you."

"To trust in Regnal, that shapeless wretch... Your

115

imprudent indulgence surmounts his greed."

"I knew from the beginning of what Regnal would try upon me as he tried upon Eldather before me, and I swore to steer his power as best I could until that day. I am not a fool, Aerbith."

"Eldather was no more foolish than you, yet he has fallen, and Regnal remains. Do not vaunt victory when he is yet to be finished with you."

"Aerbith looks like Regnal, does he not?" I remarked with a frown.

"That he does," Astot added, "but 'tis pleasing to see he has regained his form. 'Tis thanks to him we had conquered Regnal."

I tilted my head at Astot. "You nigh speak as though Regnal has died."

"We have much to discuss in regards to Regnal. Constius and I, along with Aerbith, battled with him in a land known as the Garden of Mercy. Aerbith was wounded and later consumed by him. Constius and I did our best to survive, but 'twas a battle which may well have lasted eternally were it not for the miracle of Aerbith's spirit. Though Regnal claimed his body, he strangely could not void his will. What you see before you is Aerbith in command of Regnal's body and power."

"I cannot contain him forever," Aerbith said. "I cannot even manage to free my own brother."

"But you did manage to cease the spread of Regnal's corruption within Cygna with Regnal's own power once she had returned to us," Astot assured. "She would now be as a tainted had you not consumed her eye."

"I can still feel the power of the Scourge inside me," Cygna sighed. "Regnal's power is all there is keeping me human. I guess I can't really say I'm much different from all of you now."

Astot laughed. "But rejoice, for you have gained immortality and awakened as a Halian! And has a being both a Halian and a tainted ever existed before this day?" He gave Cygna a more serious expression. "But even so, what will you do now?"

"The Yeonese don't seem to like Halians too much in

general, and I can't just return home with this body of mine. I'll travel the world alone under a new perspective."

Astot smiled kindly upon her. "'Tis a shame. You would have made a worthy Elegy."

"Would you object to my joining you Elegies?" Aerbith asked.

Astot gave Aerbith a wide-eyed stare. "You would wish to aid us in spite of all I have wrought upon you? Aerbith, you need only answer this one question if so: How do you propose we earn the audience of the Begetter?"

Aerbith growled. "Do you jape? We need only look for him."

Astot lifted an eyebrow. "Can a divine entity be sought as any mortal man?"

Aerbith responded after a moment of silence, "Divinity —'tis as naught without the eyes of its witness. And if we may bear witness to it with worldly eyes, surely can we venture to it with worldly bodies."

"Who are you to propose such incongruity?"

Aerbith blinked slowly before solemnly responding, "I am Aerbith, a mere wayfarer then and now. I do not await an answer —I seek it out, believing naught to be beyond my reach."

"You would set aside such freedom to serve the will of the Begetter?"

"I would agree only to honour a small favour. I am bound by naught but the shackles I place upon myself, for myself."

Astot nodded in respect of those words, not alike that which he preached to his fellow Elegies. "You do not cease to amuse me, hound. Very well, I name you on behalf of your spirit alone. You will henceforth be as Aerbith, the Defiant Guardian."

"I welcome you as an Elegy, my brother in arms!" Constius announced from the height of the temple.

"'Tis pleasing to hear such ardent words from you, Constius," Astot smiled. "Can I take them to mean you will not abandon us?"

"You will learn to refrain your tongue," Constius spat. "I

will watch over Aerbith 'till the day of Regnal's resurrection, and I will dominate Regnal for having stamped upon my pride. Your so-called Begetter is of no concern to me. That is all."

I turned to Astot as Constius disappeared behind the roof with his head lowered. "What did you seek?" I asked.

"We sought enlightenment from the ruined city of the Halian's forefathers, Old Halia. 'Twas there the Halians held captive a human with the power of the Scourge; she was known as the Blade of Humanity. Alas, I was hindered by Regnal's betrayal and could not make the journey there myself in time. I had arrived to see naught remaining of Old Halia or the Blade of Humanity. Ne'er will I know what the Halians truly sought, nor their purpose of protecting their homeland of old. Mayhap, we had all played our parts in their plot all along."

"If Regnal was so bold and presented such a threat, then has Inguis abandoned us as well?"

"To be spoken of by you leaves Inguis very blithe indeed," the voice of Inguis resounded in the sky. "So much so that he wishes you look upon him in all his cravenly glory."

A void parted the skies in front of the sun, shrouding the yard underneath its shadow, and the head of Inguis peered down from its opening, the quaint sounds of nature obscured before the screams of his human trophies.

"I am pleased you have at last returned, Inguis," Astot spoke in a lower tone. "Have you come with tales of your tumultuous journey?"

As Astot and Inguis glared upon one another, Inguis broke the tension with a muffled laugh. "Have I come timely enough to hear tales of your own journey? No, you need not answer; I had witnessed every moment of it in the safety of my sanctuary."

"As you could not—or rather, did not wish—to aid us, I cannot say what has become of our dear friend." No matter his effort, Astot could not bring himself to speak her name. "Is this what you had wanted all along?"

"'Twas only to maintain a fair count of Halians in this world. To compare our knowledge of the Scourge to their own is to compare a newborn infant to an eminent sage. Why not, for now, leave the Halians be and ascertain our Begetter through observation?"

Astot managed a subtle smile of amusement. "What irony that such words slip the tongue of the mightiest destroyer. Would it be within reason to suspect you know aught more than even I had predicted?"

Inguis leaned further from his void. "I wonder..."

"I did think it strange you would merely happen to witness the birth of the Blade of Humanity," Astot added. "And how unlike the destroyer I know to propose we leave the Halians be, having played spectator to their cruelty. And how curious that the Halians did not respond to your presence—a good Halian can sense a tainted in hiding. You were there in the Blade of Humanity's final moments, were you not? Pray tell, then, why was she of such great interest to you and the Halians?"

"The Blade of Humanity was but an unforeseen precursor —what the Halians considered as a threat, I considered as a mere woman of no consequence to me. With her conception, nevertheless, the Painted Woman's power had been revealed to us both."

"Was it all ordained by fate?" Astot breathed, his face wrought with bitterness. "Surely... you do not mean she heralds the birth of the 'Elegy of the End'?"

"There is another verse of the Begetter's fable, one I would be offered to read by the Halians as part of our contract. Its writing had mentioned the conception of the Elegy of the End by the sacrifice of a kind tainted fallen to madness and the touch of the Annulling Clasp to soothe that madness. But this 'Annulling Clasp' is a key which the Halians have yet to reclaim. Lest her madness destroy this world, the Painted Woman must be contained until the time is right. The power of the Painted Woman, upon completion, will unite all tainted as Architect Acantelieth and usher the enlightened era everlasting.

"The Annulling Clasp will serve as her eternal guiding light from the madness whence she came. We had long pondered a means to nurture such madness within the Painted Woman. Caevin played her part well, and the Blade of Humanity did have her use." Inguis relaxed in his void, peering at Astot and the rest of us with some semblance of sympathy in his eyes. "This was all, Astot, for that we could all die upon witnessing the Begetter—not by the hand of Regnal with all his greed, but by the hand of she who will vanquish all tainted, of then, of now, and of later.

"I have fulfilled my contract in regards to the Halians— now, I serve you and you alone. Will you not forgive that I did not save her?"

"You have done naught to require my forgiveness, my old friend. I cast blame upon my own impotence. Mayhap all I should do... is express my gratitude for having one such as you by my side." Astot approached a small stone monument standing in front of the fountain amid a gathering of flora, engraved on both sides with a depiction of a flower with petals fanning down its stem—the lyaphend, the very flower she once touched to awaken to the world and its immortal cruelty. "I do not believe she is fated to be sacrificed to Acantelieth, Inguis."

"Then what will become of her?" Inguis asked.

Astot kneeled before the monument erected in her honour. "I want to believe she will become Acantelieth. She cherished mankind unlike any other tainted. And I do swear there will be no human slain in the name of our Begetter for as long as we are apart. 'Tis my greatest offering in honour of your memory, Enlenea."

"If I may, Astot... who is Enlenea?" I carefully asked.

"Ah, yes; never once had I spoken that name in your presence. Enlenea was a tainted I likened to a painting, and so I regarded her as the Painted Woman. She, as I now know, was the precursor to Architect Acantelieth, and, beyond that, she was—"

But Astot suddenly found himself choking on his words. His vision blurred as warm liquid trickled from his eyes and down his cheeks and finally onto the flowers beneath him.

"What is this?" he murmured while running a finger down

his cheek. And upon his realisation, he lifted his head, looking deadpan at the sky. "To think the Scourge had not reaped from me, of all tainted, this blight of emotion. How unsightly."

As he hopelessly sank his head before the monument, Cygna and Aerbith approached him in silence. I stood in my place, pitying the long-lived man who had never longed for the company of a departed companion before now.

"My faith... keep me strong," he cried.

Enlenea would not return in the passing of many centuries. But not once would Astot abandon his faith in the day they would meet once more.

And even I, blessed—and cursed—as I was with the power to strip bare the minds of others, was not the clairvoyant sort who could predict the state of affairs a millennium forward. Indeed, *four* great nations would tread upon the ashes of the kings: Proto-Golem, Halia, Yeon, and...

Chapter XIX: New Golem

Mohrens 24th Reign, Year 988 I.G.R.

A delicate blanket of dark haze shrouded a flat desert expanse under the twilight sky. Tall snags dotted throughout the land testified its fertility from long ago; the repetitive sound from the creaking of their rotted branches accompanied that of the harsh winds. Olden remains of ill-fortuned human travellers and unidentifiable animals accentuated the land with a grim ambiance. The stench of death lingered in the air.

A cadence of creaking came from a lone dilapidated horse-driven carriage, its contents cloaked with a tattered grey sheet. Eight travellers walked in tow, each barefoot and cloaked beneath black robes. Three, in particular, stood out from the rest —a woman with straight brown hair, an old man with a rough grey beard, and a short boy clearly the youngest of the gathering. The travellers, far away from home on an errand of importance, tread with caution and haste, surveying their surroundings with unblinking eyes. The long-winded journey had left them weary and parched, their exhaustion only exacerbated by the knowledge that they were on their own, at the mercy of the land itself.

The wary old man walked slightly ahead, wiping sweat from his brow as he stopped and turned to face the rest of the travellers, who all stopped in tandem. As the old man nodded, he turned to face the setting sun, kicking away an adjacent human skull beneath him with his callused foot before carefully sitting down upon the dirt in a cross-legged position. Acknowledging the old man's gesture, six others promptly sat alongside him.

Several minutes passed as seven of the eight individuals

silently sat close together in contemplation of their journey—the young man stood away from the others as he fed the battered carriage horse the remainder of their forage. After tending to the horse with food and attention, the young man went to his travelling companions, standing behind them as he surveyed the land. A strange sight, a small shallow pond, quickly caught the boy's attention. A body of water in a land otherwise destitute of life surely could not have been real—one of his companions must certainly have already noticed such a peculiar sight.

The young man quietly walked up to his eldest companion and pointed to the pond; the remaining travellers were quick to take notice thereafter. Standing on their feet once more, they exchanged expressions of confusion and relief before, overwhelmed with questions and driven by thirst, they forwent their better judgement and rushed to the pond with renewed enthusiasm, leaving the carriage behind in their haste.

There was no mistaking the crystal-clear pond, a surreal blemish upon an otherwise dry land. Upon approaching the pond, the travellers paused, trading glances amongst one another, wary of their enervated minds. Disbelief had frozen all but the woman, who knelt before the pond in admiration. Clasping her hands together and dipping them into the pond, she collected a handful of water and took a sip, prompting eager stares from her companion onlookers. Standing to her feet, the woman turned to her companions and let out a cry of glee. Five of the travellers joined the woman immediately afterwards; the old man, though initially hesitant, succumbed to temptation and drank from the pond as well. Yet again, the young man observed his companions from a distance, crossing his arms and frowning in woe.

When his companions were finished, the young man again became the centre of their fixation as they circled about him with deadpan stares. The young man lowered his head with trepidation, waiting for someone to say something amid the unbearable silence—anything. The old man quietly walked up to the troubled child and solemnly placed a hand on his shoulder as their eyes met. The old man's reassuring nod brought a wry smile to the young man's lips as he approached the pond whilst the others left for the carriage.

The young man knelt before the pond, staring into his own reflection, before he too could quench his thirst, the water rippled. As he raised himself and lowered his hood to reveal shaggy, pale hair and round, hazel eyes, a single drop of rain collided with the centre of his forehead, prompting him to place a finger between his eyebrows. As the droplet slipped between his fingers, his complexion grew pale as the ground, and his resultant yelp perplexed his companions as they halted their stroll.

The young man raced towards his companions with arms outstretched, calling out to them in between bated breaths, but it was too late. Within an instant, a downpour of rain doused the entire land, descending from the cloudless sky and thickening the dark haze; this was no handiwork of nature, a truth even the travellers, ignorant as they were, could fathom. In helplessness, the travellers huddled together as the haze trapped them within a cold, swirling embrace, stripping away all light and sound. Before long, the travellers were deaf even to one another. Trapped alone in the abyss and separated from their companions as far as they could tell, each traveller pondered to themselves in solitude; whether or not they had died, not a single one could say.

No one dared to take a step, for no one knew where to step, and no one dared to call out to their companions, for no one knew if such a cry would fall on the ears of a friend in chaos or a foe in hiding. All were helpless to act but the old man, who carefully brought his hands together with his eyes closed in meditation as a radiant white light illuminated from within them in the shape of a wisp. As the wisp lifted itself above the old man, its radiance expanded beyond the nearby travellers and revealed a long corridor. As his companions huddled together once more in relief that they were not alone, the young man stood back, barely within the radius of the wisp's light, and surveyed his surroundings. He let out a small yelp once he lowered his head and noticed tiny black maggot-like creatures crawling up and down the crevices of the beige stone floor. As he looked to his left, rusted sconces hung from the dark stone walls and evenly spaced by around three meters caught his attention. Finally, as he fixated on his companions, a more dire realisation came to mind—someone appeared to be missing.

The young man alerted his remaining six companions by gesturing in front of the old man as before, following which a man's blood-curdling scream echoed throughout the corridor. Trembling in fear but concerned for their companion, every traveller save for the eldest and the youngest briefly exchanged looks and ran off down the corridor without a second thought, the wisp following alongside them. Now in total darkness once more, the old man clenched his fist and raised it in the air, producing another wisp. With a reassuring smile, the old man placed his hands on the shoulders of his youngest companion before pointing towards the others. His eyes burning with resolve, the young man nodded and rushed for his other companions under the company of the wisp's strong effulgence. By the time he realised that his eldest companion did not follow, it was already too late to turn back.

Indeed, the young man knew of his responsibilities—he knew that only one of the travellers would need to survive this portentous dimension to fulfil the objective they all shared; he knew that if only one of them was to survive, no one would be more unfitting than him. He was more prepared to die than ever before; all that was left was to become the stepping stone for the ones with the strength to persevere.

With a bottomless well of stamina, he travelled a significant distance, or so it seemed; he had become so indulged in his thoughts that even the passage of time eluded him. How long had he been running? Should he not have already located his companions by now? Was it too late to save his distressed companion, who had already stopped screaming? Before he could take notice of the path ahead, he collided face-first into the back of a stationary individual.

And relieved, the young man was, at the familiar look of the aghast woman in robes standing before him! As the woman tenderly helped him to his feet, the young man turned his attention to three of his companions who stood ahead, unmoving and silent. Unnerved by his companions' trance, he gently pushed the woman aside, revealing to him the girth of the square room before him—the end of the hallway, the seat of an ongoing execution, for the unconscious figure hanging above the gaping pit between the room's centre, arms and neck enshrouded by rusted chains extending from the ceiling and the walls, was indeed the man who had vanished before. The numerous sconces lining the crumbling walls would allow all to see the ensuing carnage under a blazing luminescence. And the orchestrator backstage would obey no naysaying of the spectators, as one of them, inclined to flee, turned to see but a wall in place of the hallway.

Having taken notice of the isolation himself, the young man silently counted those within the room. Five? What had happened to the man who had gone missing earlier? He could not then inquire his other companions, who pondered a means to defy the orchestrator and save the man kept alive by his burdened arms alone. With not a single word spoken, the travellers, sans the young man who only stood dumbfounded, acted in tandem— first, the woman, who, conjuring a similar power as the old man, clenched a single fist as a magnificent light emanated from within; then, the remaining three travellers, who, in preparation for the woman's spell, approached the bottomless pit in a triangular formation and held hands. The woman outstretched her arm in the direction of the imprisoned man and opened her palm, letting loose a giant cluster of sparkling dust that compressed to form tiny, innumerable needles. Organising themselves as three separate wisps of light, the needles proceeded to onslaught respective chains, maintaining formation throughout. As the chains plummeted in shambles, the needles of dust scattered and dissipated, and the three travellers ahead secured their companion with sorcery of their own—a telekinetic force that stayed his fall before the pit could claim him, sending him safely into the arms of the woman. With their task complete, the collaborators huddled together, eager to ensure their companion's safety.

But as the woman fixated on her liberated companion, she gasped—a face of rotted eyes and emaciated flesh protruded from the hood of his robe. From tissue to bone and bone to nothingness, a profound force had dissolved his remains into airborne grain, a feed for the condemned structure itself. In an orderly fashion, the grain layered itself upon the room's walls and adopted a similar form, filling the crevices and restoring the walls anew. No longer could any traveller question the nature of the structure they had defiled with their living presence, nor the purpose they were to serve within it.

The woman frantically discarded the abandoned robe in her arms before rejoining the others. The sound of condemning titters filled the room with dark glee as the walls and sconces mutated into a tapestry of glowing blood-red mingled faces; soon, their laughter diminished, replaced with hateful glares directed upon the travellers. With their mouths open inhumanly wide, the cascade of faces above the pit in the centre of the room regurgitated a dark red liquid, the abysmal stench of which permeated the air and nauseated the travellers. The putrid fluid spluttered and trickled below the pit, and a deafening crackle disrupted the room with a subtle tremor before what occurred was an eerie silence as the faces ceased, motionless as stone. A pool of the fluid slithered up from the pit and took the shape of a hand that stood upon the tips of its ivory claws with the height of several men.

Before any traveller could properly react, the hand drove its claws deeply into the ground, and from the cracks emerged another pool of dark fluid which once again moved of its own accord—this time, in the young man's direction. He could only lift his arm before his body was swallowed whole, isolating him from the cries of his companions. Blinded, deafened, speechless, and powerless, he closed his eyes and eased his body. Such a painless and abrupt death could father no terror, and no one would need him for their own survival.

His breathing did not cease. The young man reopened his eyes, which reflected nothing but darkness—no wisp was at his side. Whether he had died or lay in darkness, he could not immediately say. In a jaded attempt to uncover the truth, the young man would do what he had previously never attempted —conjuration. Mirroring the old man's posture and focus, the young man raised a clenched fist and paused, asking himself a single question: Could any being capable of such movement be dead? He cleared his thoughts and closed his eyes, envisioning the miracle he would conjure from within. A bright light illuminated a hallway—a bright light emerging from the young man's fist. As he opened his eyes to marvel at his success, the young man opened his hand, and from which escaped a small wisp that hovered above his head, emitting a dimmer light compared to the wisp of his elder companion.

The young man stroked beneath his nostrils with a single finger as a warm fluid trickled from his chin. Blood? Had such a simplistic spell taxed him to such an extent? He struggled to his feet, knowing that with his survival came a chance for redemption if only he could reunite with his companions. He had already died and become numb to any sort of crippling fear. All that remained was courage—a will to act despite all fear. And so he acted, dashing through the hallway with little else on his mind.

With the passage of time evident only in his own exhaustion, the young man stopped and leaned against the wall, his face saturated with perspiration. With the abruptness the young man had come to expect from the rotting structure, a familiar stench—the putrid stench of death—flooded his nostrils. Placing his hand firmly upon his chest, he took a deep breath before gazing upward at the source of the stench, squinting his eyes to perceive the ceiling beyond the light of the wisp.

Splat! Leaving the young man only enough time to shut his eyes, raw viscera amassed on his face, alive with gluttonous maggots. Taken too far aback to cry out, he planted his feet and stood straight up, allowing the filth to slide off his body before, with nonchalance, brushing aside the maggots remaining, leaving only the blood which masked his visage beyond recognition.

The young man opened his eyes halfway as he pondered a single question: Could that decayed mess have been the remains of his missing companion? He would soon have his answer from the very blood beneath him—the blood which, before his eyes, coalesced into the shape of a familiar face painted upon the ground. And even more familiar was the tone of its deafening scream.

A cold breeze flew past the young man, and the face was gone. The young man, stripped of the courage he once held, could not face forward, for the breeze carried an ill presence that loomed in that direction. He quivered as the blood below him once again moved of its own accord, slithering towards the omen he dared not face. As his eyes instinctively trailed the blood-soaked path, however, he could not elude the sight of a pair of feet so white as to emit a faint glow contrasting the black miasma behind them. The blood slid between the feet and vanished under what appeared to be a tattered black robe not unlike that of the travellers, the young man, intrigued as he was terrified, opposed the entity only to immediately consider his act a grave mistake.

With a face obscured by miasma and a left hand clenching a freshly severed head of one of the travellers the young man had last seen in the room, this entity was certainly no visitant of circumstance, yet it did little but observe him in silence. The young man, numb to the passage of time, knelt before the entity as a submitting gesture; his fate, at the very moment this being confronted him, was writ in stone, for what could he ever hope to achieve by resisting as the others had attempted?

The entity brought its arm forward as if to point its trophy in the young man's direction, its pulsating red veins apparent with its sleeveless garb. The entity loosened its grip and relieved its hand of the severed head, dissolving it to cinders as it fell to the ground. It pointed to its right, and a portion of the wall beside the young man's left, as if bowing to the entity's will, disintegrated to a tepid black fluid, revealing a room with an ascending spiral staircase. The young man who had given up hope not minutes before had begun to reclaim it, and he rushed for the new pathway without questioning his own actions—his final fortuity for redemption.

As the young man tirelessly scaled the steps, the wisp that had followed gradually dimmed, disappearing and leaving him alone in pitch-black darkness once more; but it no longer mattered, for the way had already been made clear, and the growing sound of ferocious winds indicated an imminent escape. Upon reaching the top of the ascending steps, the young man found himself in a wide space with lit candles lining the walls and a black gate accentuated with two one-armed skeletons bearing white candles facing opposite sides of the gate. Beyond the bars of the gate, the young man could clearly see a massive circular space surrounded with impenetrable black haze obscuring all scenery, even the sky. The space illuminated with an unnatural glow, sparing it the darkness from within the unidentified construct. Had he reached the precipice of a castle?

As he approached the barred gate to peek at the centre of the open space, he could clearly see a group of three standing together in a triangle near the edge; but from such a distance, he could not identify any familiar faces, and with such a distraction as the sound of the wind, no cry could alert them of his presence. As he pressed his hands against the gate, he did not need to wait long before the latch burst apart with such intensity to knock the young man off his feet, and the gate opened with a grating creak; even the group of three in the distance could not disregard such disrupting noise.

As the group drew closer, the young man responded with a weary smile. From the distance, he could recognise the woman he had journeyed alongside, yet the old man was absent. With a weighted breath, the young man drew upon his last reserves of strength and rushed forward, reuniting with his surviving companions at the centre of the open space as the woman greeted him with a caring embrace. With tears streaming down his face, all the young man could think of was the fond life they had all cast aside for a greater cause—a thought they had strove to suppress throughout their entire journey.

Alas, the damned would be given no reprieve. The woman, the first to identify the calamitous presence looming behind them, shoved the young man aside before the flying debris smashed heavily into her skull, and her disfigured body was sent flying over the edge and into the abyss. Emerging from a surge of miasma behind the gate was the woman's executioner, the same entity the young man had first encountered. As before, the miasma shrouded the entity's visage as it approached the remaining travellers with slow, deliberate steps. The young man backed himself towards the edge while his final companions stepped aside; it had become all too clear whom the next victim would be.

As the entity stood before the young man, the other two travellers, powerless to do nothing but await their own reckoning, did not intervene, expressing themselves only in trembling bodies and wide-eyed stares. The entity clenched the neckline of the young man's robe and lifted him off his feet with a single arm, an overwhelming chill burrowing into his chest and settling his galloping heart before spreading throughout his entire body. With a body barely able to sustain his consciousness, the young man closed his eyes as his thoughts crossed over, and a deep voice quietly spoke to him from the nexus of hither and thither.

"Go home," the young man last heard as the entity flung him over the edge, and his consciousness finally gave out.

Quietus...

Taciturnity...

Obscurity...

... And land? Regaining his consciousness, the young man, now clean of blood, clenched his fist to sample the dirt he lay upon. Flipping himself over on his back, he opened his eyes to glistening sunlight in the sky of dawn. The young man stood up, his strength restored, and turned to his left, gasping in shock at the sight ahead of him—the very carriage the group of travellers had escorted! How, he wondered, could the horse have located him on its own? More importantly, where was he? With few snags and no carcasses present, was this area truly of the path he had trod before?

As the young man spun around to familiarise himself with the environment, a single tear ran down his eye—his destination was within reach. No more than several kilometres ahead lay a towering silver wall so vast that it appeared to span endlessly across the land. A few tall buildings could clearly be seen a distance behind the wall. Lined across both sides of what appeared to be a gate in the centre of the wall were towering humanoids nearly the height of the gate yet too far away to discern with certainty. Automatons, perhaps? The young man knew of this utopia only what he had been told by the old man. He had made it without a doubt, yet his glee was short-lived as he recalled the sacrifices to make it this far. The weakest of the flock had become the sole survivor.

Before the young man could sulk, what seemed to be two massive bestial animals drawing closer from the direction of the magnificent wall caught his attention. Squinting his eyes for a closer inspection, he could clearly identify the nature of these beasts. With metallic skin reflecting the sunlight and dim yellow eyes of glass, these panther-shaped creatures were certainly creations of man.

Upon reaching the vicinity of the blank-faced young man, the machines stood before him at opposite ends, towering over him by about eight metres, before sitting down and shifting their heads towards one another as if silently communicating.

When the machines were finished, the cranial compartment of the one to the left lifted open to reveal a male pilot wearing only torn jeans and slick black shoes, and the young man's eyes lit with newfound resolve.

"Creed," worriedly called the machine to the right with a male voice amplified through some sort of speaker. The exposed pilot, Creed, evidently quite young himself, excitedly jumped from his machine and pampered his well-trimmed neck-length brown hair as he approached the remaining traveller for the sake of but a single question.

"You got a name, kid?" he asked, placing a hand on the young man's shoulder.

The young man lifted his head and gazed into the pilot's sky-blue eyes. "Argen," came his monotone response.

Chapter XX: The Reverent Fortress

Mohrens 25th Reign, Year 988 I.G.R.

Argen opened his eyes to find himself sprawled within a rocking carriage, comforted underneath a thin, tattered green blanket. So familiar to him was the carriage's dilapidated wooden exterior, yet more familiar was the wooden crate lying beside him, containing the very object he and his companions had been instructed to deliver at any cost. Gazing mellowly at the crate and recalling the horrors of that last twilight, he pondered but a single question—was their objective worth more than their lives? He had never been told the nature of what he was to deliver, but he could patiently await the moment of revelation—the moment he would set foot beyond the towering wall and into this foreign metropolis in front of him.

The sound of curious banter from outside the carriage drew Argen's attention. As he peered his head through the grey blanket and looked both ways, he could see the gargantuan panther-shaped machines travelling alongside the carriage. He would eavesdrop on their discussion with a keen ear as he had little time to familiarise himself with these men before falling asleep. Indeed, in such little time, he had only presented them with two questions—who were they, and what did they intend to do with him? Both questions were met with vague answers; they had assured him that all would be made clear upon reaching their destination.

"Also, are you sure we should be turning back right now?" the man in the machine, who had not yet introduced himself to Argen, asked Creed. "What about the DEAS residue we picked up just before?"

"Dude, we'll worry about that later," Creed replied in a comparatively casual tone. "Let's focus on getting the kid to someplace safe first."

"Where? To Golem? Shouldn't we have at least asked which colony he came from?"

"We've still got a lot of questions to ask."

"Exactly."

Argen pushed an arm outside the carriage and meekly waved it around to catch the pilots' attention. "I am awake!" he shouted. Both machines turned their sights on him.

"We suspected," the unnamed man murmured. "Now, since you're aware, there are a few questions we'll need to ask you before we arrive at our destination. We'll answer a few of your questions right away as well, but don't worry about who we are or what we do, all right? That's all a long story if we don't know exactly what you know."

"Right now?" Creed asked with a slightly elevated tone.

"There are some things he needs to know now, as you should be aware."

Argen exhaled a sigh as he crawled out of the carriage and sat astride on the old horse, preparing himself for a lengthy interrogation. Why, he wondered, was he being regarded with suspicion?

"By the way," the unnamed man spoke following an unnerving silence, "my name is Wesley. I apologise for not introducing myself earlier. How about you tell us something about yourself?"

Argen groaned as he considered his words, knowing any wrong answer could compromise his objective and perhaps even his life. "I am from a land far away from here. I am here because there is something that I need to deliver."

"Are you from any neighbouring colony?" Wesley asked.

"Colony? What do you mean?"

Creed guffawed with exaggerated enthusiasm, adding a hint of levity to the conversation. "So, we go chasing after a DEAS signal, and it turns out to be a delivery boy. Explaining this one's going to be interesting."

"Oh, I can hardly wait," Welsey sarcastically added. "If you aren't from any nearby colony, Argen, then where did you come from?"

"Probably from a faraway land," Creed interjected as Argen opened his mouth to reply.

"That's not what I meant, but whatever; it's not important. I'd say what is more important is that you tell us what you're trying to deliver."

"I was told not to open the crate until we had reached our destination," Argen sternly answered, glancing at the object from within the carriage.

"By whom?" Wesley asked. "And if others were with you, where are they now?"

His mind deluged with once-repressed memories, Argen silently sunk his head within the silvery mane of the old horse, withholding the sight of his weeping expression. Throughout the remainder of the stroll, neither pilot would speak a word.

Upon reaching the gargantuan steel gate, the pilots, having moved slightly ahead of Argen, paused and sat their machines on either side of him as before. Argen approached the gate and halted the carriage, lifting his head to marvel at the gilded architecture of the gate and the mechanical sentinels lined across the walls, segregated by concrete pillars. An orb embedded in the centre of the gate caught his most immediate attention with its glistening beauty. The sentinels, structured with components of black iron and shaped like bald human males, stood proudly holding their massive claymores—rusted and battle-worn as they were—before them with both hands. The mouthpieces and gleaming-red left eyes of these sentinels presented them with an ambiance of mystery. These sentinels, Argen thought, had amassed numerous victories battling for the sanctity of their homeland, the history of which he could now confidently determine.

Wesley loudly cleared his throat from within his machine, partly diverting Argen's attention. "It's not every day we have some kid wandering off on his own out here. This probably goes without saying, but no one will trust you right away. Answer all questions presented to you, and don't wander off. "

"Will that gate open on its own?" Argen asked in a deliberate attempt to ignore Wesley. "Are the both of you waiting for something?"

"So what if he's telling the truth and he's not from any neighbouring colony?" Creed asked Wesley before the latter could reply to Argen.

"Fortitude will be sending him back to wherever he came from," Wesley replied. "If that's not possible, he's going to need to earn his citizenship here, which obviously begins with making himself known and gaining the trust of the dictators."

"And if I fail?" Argen asked, his tone plagued with unease.

"Then you'll be detained for life, or at least until you can be deported back to wherever you came from, but rest assured, we're getting that package one way or the other."

"I understand," said Argen as he lowered his head. Now more than ever, he would need strength for his survival—a strength he could pull only in remembrance of his martyr allies. No longer could retrospect hinder his confidence with nary an undoing, for the time to move on had come sooner than he would be prepared.

In an instant, the gate's orb illuminated brightly, deterring Argen's gaze. "Are they scanning us?" Wesley asked, addressing Creed.

"Yeah," Creed replied. "Don't worry; it'll be opening soon."

After a moment's passing, the gate gradually lifted from its foundation, Argen shielding his ears from the resultant roar. Beyond the gateway, a massive gathering of identically dressed individuals could be seen, as well as a few panther-shaped rovers. Argen stood at too great a distance to make out any significant details. The time for his final trial had come, and he, eager for closure, made the first step towards the opening; but this did not go unnoticed.

"Stay behind us, Argen," Wesley warned as he and Creed

proceeded to traverse beyond the gateway, quickly passing Argen with their larger mounts. Upon passing through the gateway, the duo strafed to respective sides, drawing full attention to their find. Even with all eyes aimed at him in wonder and fascination—or so it had seemed to him—Argen remained stout in action and expression, halting his carriage in the middle of the two pilots before assuming a rigid posture. If fortune favoured him, this would be a marvel in the eyes of his spectators.

As the gate shut behind him, Argen responded to the ensuing momentary silence not with a change in continence but with a deft surveying of his surroundings as his eyes began to wander. The 'pilots' gathered together wore garbs of several variations—most had outfitted themselves with tight jumpsuits matching the colours of the machines scattered indiscriminately upon the grounds; others cloaked their figures with long, hooded black trenchcoats worn over varying white tee-shirts, jeans, and sleek shoes; the few others, who retreated back near two aligned black tents upon losing interest, simply wore varying mundane attire of the colony, lacking the distinctive round badge worn by the others. Upon closer inspection of the casually dressed foreigners' activities, Argen shifted his attention to the usage of tools he had never before witnessed—small boxed-shaped contraptions with windows which projected perplexing imagery; oddly shaped armaments with which the foreigners prodded deconstructed machines; and hand-held circular devices with image-projecting windows at which the foreigners gazed endlessly as they paced back and forth.

With his interest further piqued, Argen once again centred his attention on the remaining spectators before him, who stood aside upon the arrival of a seemingly important man. Although this man was plainly dressed, Argen was not so naïve to mistake an important figure hiding within the flock. Indeed, the time for both sides to be enlightened had come, and as the man drew closer, Argen abandoned his carriage and placed a hand on the neck of his horse, diverting some attention to the carriage itself.

As the two stood within arm's reach of one another, Argen squinted his eyes at the imposing height of this older gentleman before him. Given his own minute stature despite his age, it was as if he had always been outcast by the world. He once yearned for a body to reflect the boundless strength he had always wanted—fear did not overcome his envy. Why was it, then, that the sight of this gargantuan man, tall not unlike that which he had already seen many times before, brought to him even a slight feeling of unease? Perhaps it was, in fact, his powerlessness in the eyes of these people that he had truly come to understand and loathe.

By the time Argen regained his focus, he had noticed the man's hazel eyes scanning him from head to toe. As the man finished, his lips sank upon his hardened face, and there was silence. Before Argen could utter a word, the man had already placed his hands on Argen's shoulders.

"I'm betting you came a long way," the man spoke gruffly before glancing at the carriage. "You got something in there for us?"

"Something heavy," Argen responded with a forced cackle.

"We've got it. Don't worry; we'll be taking good care of you." The man smiled from ear to ear as he patted Argen's shoulders, alleviating him of some trepidation. With his well-trimmed grey hair cut short and an imposing figure which betrayed his true nature, this older man had begun to remind Argen of the mentor he held so dear.

"We've scouted the location of the DEAS signal, sir," Wesley informed. "No eldritch hearts sighted. The signal seems to have vanished as well."

The commander groaned. "No shit? You two, get your asses out of those rovers and I'll deal with you later."

"It was fun while it lasted!" Creed bellowed through his laughter. As he and Wesley disembarked, a party of casually dressed mechanics encircled the abandoned machinery for maintenance; another group of individuals, wearing specialised protective equipment, detached the carriage and began rummaging inside, quickly extracting the crate. As the men carrying the crate headed into the sparse woods yonder, Argen lent his ears to their curious banter.

"This shit's heavy!"

"Let's hope there isn't a bomb inside or anything."

"BOOM!"

"This for me? Ain't even my birthday."

The crowd gradually dispersed, tending to their own duties. The commander once again placed a hand on Argen's shoulder. "As for you, you look damn tired. We'll have some food and a tent prepared for you ASAP."

Argen shook his head, more eager than hungry. "Sir, to be curt, I do not know what is inside of that crate, but I risked my life to bring it here."

The commander gazed at Argen with a contorted look. "That explains the DEAS spike, but what in the blazes are you talking about besides that? Are you some delivery boy sent from some faraway don't-know-shit colony?"

Perhaps, Argen thought, some disinformation would be necessary. "That is one way of saying it, yes."

The commander rubbed his temples. "Okay, we're gonna need that tent. You're gonna have to fill me in with all the details —your side of the story. Walk with me."

Forgoing all formalities, Argen stood closely behind the commander as the two proceeded to tour the field, during which Argen would be enlightened to the nature of the utopia beyond the inner gate—Golem, as it was called, an ancient and massive colony whose origin was a fortress meant to protect its inhabitants from the world outside. Golem had been constructed nearly a thousand years prior, marking the era known as I.G.R—In Golem's Reign. Among the first of its kind and most technologically proficient, Golem would quickly develop into a beacon of hope and protection for its neighbouring brethren. It was a colony so well-protected that its civilians, like Argen himself, knew little of the perilous beyond; such knowledge was reserved only for those involved in Golem's perseverance. Even Argen could trace the pride the commander exuded as he spoke of this supposedly impenetrable shelter, yet a hint of doubt loomed over Argen's mind. Was this man before him a prideful hero, a prideful liar to behold, or a puppet with thin strings whose master Argen could never hope to trace? It remained to be seen if this man could become a beacon of hope in Argen's jaded eyes. As for himself, the eventful tour left him little time to tell the tale of his own homeland, let alone his name. Perhaps the commander's intention was to put him at ease first and foremost.

As the sun began to descend, the commander kept true to his word and escorted Argen to a tent reserved for him alone, isolated in a small clearing surrounded by tall trees and other greenery, away from the other tents. Following this, the commander left to tend to more pressing business, promising to shortly return. Argen was left to his own chaotic thoughts, with his only asylum being Amdis, the mare of the carriage that followed him even to his camp. Together, the two sat before a campfire beside the tent where not a single word was spoken by Argen, who had long grown fond of conversing with Amdis in solitude.

Argen longingly gazed at the campfire before the sunset. As weary as he had become in his restless travel, business left unfinished kept his mind alert. Despite having fulfilled his courier's duty, his mother and mentor would have wished something other than for him to disappear and die. Argen could not help but draw comparisons to his discorded homeland, where he at least had companions who shared his woes and sheltered him from conflict, and this new land he could not yet be certain of in many ways; this land where he would spend the remainder of his days in isolation. If he was never to see his homeland again, then so be it. He would move on with his life by foregoing his old ways and adopting Golem's ways as his own, no matter how painful a transition it would be. He would undergo drastic changes as an individual, for better or worse, and much sooner than any child could be expected to bear. He would become a man solely by refusing to let the world topple his spirit; his future thereafter mattered little to him. After all, he had already died in that castle, or so he kept reminding himself. Perhaps it was his own fear of conforming to this new world that resigned him to his fate as he had seen it back then. Change was of little significance to him in his homeland, a world which would never soon change its course and betray the child he hoped he could remain forever. Not so would this ever-changing world as he understood it accept a lost child if he remained so stagnant. Flowing along as the world evolved around him was a challenge he cringed at the thought of. Was it even worth trying?

Argen fell asleep within his daydream, and the moonlit sky greeted him once he awoke. The flickering campfire and the crickets hidden in the shade were all that was there to break the silence of the night. The familiar sight of the old mare lying beside him relieved him of the stress from his horrific nightmare within which he relived his fight for survival; there was no escape from the weight of his incompetence, only small comfort in the fact that a piece of his homeland yet remained alongside him, and what a beautiful sight she was, the sleeping old mare of the carriage. A warm smile graced Argen's lips as he gently ran a hand through her bony muzzle to put himself at ease.

"Having fun over there?" a familiar voice spoke from behind Argen. The startled boy acted quickly in shielding himself behind Amdis. At this, the man, none other than the commander from before, chuckled heartily. The disturbance awoke the slumbering mare, who quietly observed the approaching commander without standing up. "Well, looks like you still got some life left in you, at least," the commander spoke as he took a seat around the campfire, gesturing for Argen to come out of hiding. "I never introduced myself, did I? My name is Huwerd Bates; you can think of me as the leader of this little field of misfits. What did your parents call you, kid?"

Argen quietly manoeuvred around Amdis and sat beside Huwerd. "My name is Argen." The ease with which he enunciated those words concealed his uncertainty of the situation before him, but as disconcerting as Huwerd's presence was, he had endured worse.

"Well, shit, I was expecting something a tad more unorthodox!" Huwerd remarked with a small bout of laughter to follow. Argen observed the jovial leader with a look of bewilderment. Was this man intending to discuss important matters, or did he simply desire the company of someone to whom he could converse as a fellow individual? When Huwerd's laughter ceased, Argen opened his mouth to speak, but Huwerd continued before he could utter a single word. "Anyway, Creed and Wesley—you were introduced, right?—filled me in with the details, so at least I know for sure that you were brought here to deliver the contents of that package. Can I assume that also means you knew exactly what to expect from us before you showed? That isn't the impression I'm getting from you."

"No," came Argen's blunt reply.

"Do you have any *clue* what's in that crate?"

"No, I do not."

"From what colony were you sent?"

"None as I know."

"You came a really long way, son. Do you at least know anything about the technology used to send you here? Don't hold out on me." Huwerd spoke the last line with some levity, but his very real suspicions were all too clear to the likewise suspicious Argen.

"It was not my—our, rather—doing. Our intention was to find this land with only our bodies to carry us here."

Huwerd cackled. "You've got fancy words for a kid your age. You are a kid, right?"

Argen could not read Huwerd's mind as much as he tried. With some unease in his tone, he spoke, "I suppose I am. What of it?" Hopefully, he thought, asking in such a manner would not be considered hostility.

"Just keeping you on your toes." Huwerd laughed as he nudged Argen's shoulder. "So, others were sent with you, huh? Got any idea where they ran off to?" Argen furrowed his eyebrows. If Huwerd had indeed spoken with the two pilots, then surely he knew of Argen's previous reaction regarding that same question. Nonetheless, he would bear with the man's insolence, for then was no time to sulk.

"They died."

"What?"

"We were attacked, and I was the only one to survive."

"Attacked by what, you think?"

"I cannot say."

Huwerd slowly nodded as he looked away from Argen as if all questions had been answered. At this, Argen breathed a quiet sigh of relief—but what was to happen now? Following an uncertain silence, Huwerd finally spoke, "So, it's all coming together now."

"What do you mean?"

"You're in good hands here, that's what I mean. I can't tell you why one of those things would drag you off all the way here, but at least I can say you aren't one of 'em—you're just a shit-crazy courier, coming from some colony even we don't know shit about as far as our rovers can take us. We've got one sort of case on our hands. I'll say that."

As Argen expressed his relief with strained laughter, Huwerd gave him a prolonged serious look. Once Argen's laughter ceased, Huwerd spoke, "So you really have no way of making it back home, huh? That horse won't carry you very far, that's for sure."

"Actually, I was hoping I could stay here until I do find some way to return," Argen stoutly replied.

"Shit, you'd be stuck here for a while anyway, so why not? If you're staying with Fortitude, make yourself at home right here; we've got plenty of supplies to go around. Golem as a whole won't accept you as easily, though, so if you want rights as a Golem citizen, get ready for some pain."

"I am... not sure I understood that."

"What? Oh, right, you hadn't heard of Fortitude, huh?" As before, Huwerd wore a prideful smile as he began his explanation. "You can thank Fortitude for getting you back to safety; that's us. Fortitude is the organisation tasked with ensuring the safety of Golem and its people, and it's been around for just about the same amount of time. Sometimes we're required to aid outsiders like yourself, but that's usually by request from some other colony; we don't get many chances to wander off very far from these walls, and I'm guessing even your colony never gave you much of a chance until recently. Every haven has its ups and downs; we still get plenty of action even within the walls, and Fortitude has continued to expand to meet Golem's demands. Right now, you could even say we run this colony just the same as the dictators themselves." Huwerd rose to his feet. "You want some advice? If you don't intend to get involved in our dirty work when you become a man, then I suggest forgetting anything you saw out there because we're going to be making sure you never see it again. You got that?"

Argen nodded before asking, "What do I need to become a citizen of Golem?"

Huwerd gave Argen a dumbfounded look, perhaps not having anticipated his decision nor his promptness in coming to that decision. "You got what I said about that, right? It's going to be a shitty struggle convincing the people that matter."

"Then so be it. Living is what my family would have wanted for me, not fighting for a cause that should not concern me."

The moment of silence as the two gazed upon one another ended with Huwerd's laughter. Yet another smile was carved onto his face, but not out of pride. "Boy, I always knew there was something I would like about you. Well, if you're willing to fight for your freedom, we've all got your back. It's going to be a long fight, no doubt, so don't you get too excited until we're both out of the rubble, and you're over at Golem working as a writer with a damn good story to tell." As Argen stood up, Huwerd patted his unkempt hair. If nothing else, he could believe in Huwerd's respect for him. No matter how difficult moving on with his life would be, there would always be comfort in knowing he was not alone. Had he truly died under the entity's snare? As he reflected on his life back home, he considered he was never truly alive at all until the circumstances taught him to fend for himself. With a budding passion he had never felt before, he would soon know the tenacity of his living self—his true self.

"You'd better rest up for tomorrow," said Huwerd, interrupting Argen's contemplation. "In the meantime, I'm gonna make a report in Prime District. No doubt the dictators will think of you as a menace, but someone is going to listen to your story. You'll know what I mean when the time comes. If I have any news for you, I'll personally meet you back here. I suggest getting to know the other children while you wait since you'll be moving in with them tomorrow morning."

As Huwerd turned to leave, Argen hastily pointed to Amdis. "Wait, what about my—"

"Oh, that horse?" Huwerd interrupted as he turned around. "No pets allowed here. We'll be taking it to an appropriate shelter back in Golem tomorrow, so say your goodbyes while you have time. If everything goes well, you'll be getting it back once you've got a reason to be in Golem as well. That's some damn good motivation to give it your all, I'd say."

Argen nodded. "I understand. Please take proper care of her."

Huwerd nodded in acknowledgement, and as he turned and began a stroll, he shouted, "I'd worry more about myself if I were you!"

Argen watched the departing Huwerd until his eyes could no longer follow, and that was that. He felt no yearning for answers—he knew at least what had to be done. The thought of being separated from his horse did not worry him, for they were fated to one day reunite in the colony of Golem—of that, he was certain. Turning towards the towering wall between him and Golem, he pointed a finger, vowing to reach beyond it, before retreating to his tent to rest for tomorrow.

Chapter XXI: A Cherished Novelty

Sahn 12ᵗʰ Reign, Year 988 I.G.R.

How long had it been since that night spent under Huwerd's company? How many days had gone by since he no longer counted them? The newly awoken Argen sat up from a sleeping bag within his miniature tent, greeted by the rays of dawn from behind the sheet.

In the days following Argen's arrival, Huwerd kept to his word and saw to Amdis' transfer to the capital city of Golem while relocating Argen to a different encampment, promising that once he returned, he would have permission to do the same with Argen. Argen would only need to wait quietly in the meantime—far easier said than done.

Argen bode most of his time secluding himself in his tent, rarely venturing beyond it and drifting back asleep the moment he knew Huwerd was nowhere to be found. And today would be no exception in his mind—he would peek through his tent and gaze into the sky while reflecting on his experiences before retiring to his slumber, comforted yet anxious for the day to follow.

As Argen looked outside, the stilled winds of the dim and cloudy day brushed against his face. His tent rested on a small hilltop overlooking the entirety of the encampment populated with children like himself. The encampment was segregated from the militaristic zone by a small woodland concealing all but the towering wall in the distance. As he gazed at the wall, he considered his promise to himself that fateful night. He had at least made some progress in moving on from his losses, but his goal itself felt ever distant. What would he do were he to never see Golem with his own eyes?

As a rustling of tall grass disrupted the silence, Argen looked to his right. A lone little girl knelt before a small flowerbed a short distance away, her back turned before Argen's tent. He quietly observed the girl as she casually picked from the flowerbed, unaware of his presence. Her choice of attire, a somewhat tattered beige dress, was not too peculiar from that worn by some of the other children Argen encountered on his way here; but what truly distinguished her was the presence of a flower ornament worn above her flowing, reddish-brown hair. Indeed, Argen could tell at a glance that he had seen this particular girl a few times before.

It was Argen's decision to seclude himself from the children kept under Fortitude's care from the moment he knew he was to be placed alongside them, at least for as long as he was still in mourning. The children, in turn, seemingly cared little that a foreigner was now among them, or perhaps he had eluded their attention. But every time Argen awoke to peer at the sky, that same girl would be sitting close by his tent, only to flee each time he took notice. She had aroused his curiosity to such an extent that he often found himself thinking of ways to approach her. He was marginally glad to have retained the opportunity after so many uneventful days.

Stepping out of his tent, Argen hurriedly approached the girl without making a sound. "Are you... okay?" he nervously asked.

The girl abruptly lurched forward as Argen began to speak, turning around just enough to fall on her side and catch a glimpse of the boy who had clearly startled her. With the girl's crystalesque blue eyes wide and pointed directly at his face, Argen took a step back and lowered his head, praying he would not scare her away yet again.

"I—I'm sorry, I was just... I mean, I wasn't..." The little girl practically choked on her words as she remained as still as if trapped by a feral animal, calming down somewhat only after Argen outstretched his hand to her.

"Hello, my name is Argen," he softly greeted with a warm smile. "I did not mean to scare you. I should be the one to apologise."

The girl blankly stared into Argen's open palm and, after a moment of silence, stood up on her own, subtly brushing dirt and flower petals off the skirt of her dress. Nevertheless, she remained unresponsive, her eyes darting in every direction but directly in front of her.

"I was... just about to return to my slumber," Argen murmured, becoming somewhat nervous himself. "Forgive me if I disturbed you."

Just as Argen turned away to return to his tent, the girl stepped forward. "Wait a minute," she spoke, prompting Argen to pause. "You... came from another colony, didn't you?"

"I came from a land far away from this one," Argen responded while turning to face the girl, his mellow expression containing his excitement. "I was sent here—rather, I came here —to deliver something to your people. At present... I have yet to know if I succeeded."

"Um... my name is Yeula," the girl greeted. "I'm an orphan, just like everyone else here."

Argen nodded. "Did you come this way to speak with me? I feel I should be honoured, really."

Yeula looked away towards the encampment, her expression concealed behind her long fringe. "I mean, no one has seen you leave that tent since Fortitude abandoned you, so everyone just assumes you want to be left alone."

"I see," Argen murmured, lowering his head. To be left alone by the orphaned children was a foreseeable and desired outcome of his prolonged isolation, but in hearing Yeula's words, he felt guilty. It was clear that these children were left with no one but themselves. Their circumstances were such that Argen could easily understand them, if only he knew that they could understand him. Still, the thought of being inspected like a soulless object of interest was too discouraging to even consider approaching them. And it seemed these children were only beginning to understand how different he was from them.

Argen lifted his head as a warm hand tightened around his own. Having closed the distance before he could take notice, Yeula gleefully smiled as she held his hand, free from the doubt that kept her at bay. "Sooner or later, one of us needs to take the first step. Come on, let's go see the others!"

Argen resisted Yeula as she attempted to run off with him. "Wait, I have... not yet prepared myself for this."

Yeula frowned. "I know how you feel, but you can't be like this forever. You'll be fine with us; just trust me."

"I *do* trust you, but how can you be sure I would belong down there?" Argen retorted. "And I will not be here for much longer; I am sure of that."

"Stop telling yourself that! You're just going to be disappointed."

"No, you lie!" Argen violently pulled his hand away and turned to avoid Yeula's dismayed expression. A long moment of silence followed, but he was certain Yeula remained behind him. "Yeula... how long have you been here?" he finally asked without facing her.

"Since I was four; I'm seven now," she timidly replied.

"Where are your parents? Why are you being kept here?" Argen's voice elevated with each word he spoke.

Yeula huffed. "Why are we even talking? You want to be left alone, don't you?"

As the sound of Yeula's ensuing footsteps became gradually distant, Argen desperately turned around to see her descending from the hilltop. "Yeula? Yeula!" he shouted at the height of his tone, his vision blurring as tears swelled in his eyes. "I did not mean to offend! Please, Yeula!"

But Yeula was shortly joined by a taller, bald young woman making her way up the hilltop. Upon noticing Yeula, the woman hastily stepped in front of her, placing her hands on Yeula's shoulders.

"You okay?" the woman worriedly asked.

Yeula slowly nodded but could not bring herself to glance

at the woman's face. "Good timing."

Before Argen could retreat back into his tent, the woman took notice of his presence and walked towards him, waving both arms in the air. "Hey, you!" she shouted.

Argen warily took a few steps back. He could not decide how to react before the woman drew close in front of him.

"You Argen?" the woman asked, her hazel eyes moving up and down as she looked Argen over with an inquisitive expression. "We've got some Scion Finis rabble down there lookin' to see you."

Argen stared blankly into her eyes with confusion.

"Eh, the Scion Finis? Don't worry much about em'," the woman chuckled.

"Is there something wrong?" Argen asked before the woman could continue.

"Hey, I'm just relayin' a message here; all I was told was to go fetch the foreigner. You comin' or what?"

Argen exhaled a sigh and moved in the direction of the encampment, a cue for the woman to step forward and lead him to the so-called Scion Finis rabble and for Yeula to follow at a distance behind them. His pace was intentionally sluggish and delayed, but the woman would wait patiently for him before continuing on her way. With her back fixed in front of him, Argen focused on her attire. With her white tank top worn under beige cargo pants, she certainly resembled a Fortitude affiliate more than a mere orphan. Either way, he would worry about her later.

The encampment sang with little else than the breeze; most of the children had secluded themselves within tents, whereas those left outside gawked in silence at the small gathering of adults discussing important matters. Two uniformed Fortitude officers stood opposite four individuals with hooded apparel and one black-haired woman between them whose face was more clearly visible. Argen vaguely recalled spotting such individuals in the crowd that had gathered when he first arrived.

"What's your business here?" one of the Fortitude officers sternly asked. "I thought we made it clear you guys would disappear after that DEAS signal investigation."

"Huwerd made that clear, not any of you," the black-haired woman nonchalantly retorted. "And as you can see, he's not here right now. Let me have a word with the outsider, and we'll be on our way, simple as that."

All eyes were fixated on Argen as he approached them. The black-haired woman's gaze felt unsettling in particular, her nigh pitch-black eyes piercing Argen's heart like those of a cold-blooded murderer, but her attire was casual and unassuming. Her short black hair framed her soft-featured face, her fringe fanning towards her left eye. A single beauty mark under her left eye accentuated her maturity.

"Well, here he is," the bald woman announced with a subtle yawn. "I'm I dismissed now?"

"Please go about your business now," one of the Fortitude officers replied.

"Alrighty. Let's go, Yeula."

Before the woman could leave, Yeula frantically grabbed hold of her arm. "Not now!" she griped.

The two proceeded to bicker back and forth for a time before coming to an agreement and staying where they were, but Argen locked eyes with the black-haired woman in the meantime and paid little attention to much else. A familiar sensation loomed in the air.

"Did you call for me?" he asked as he finally looked away.

"Well, it's nice to meet you up close, kiddo," the black-haired woman said, wearing a subtle smile. "I hope you have a minute to talk."

Argen blinked curiously. "And if I do not?"

"Then you're free to return to whatever you were doing beforehand... which I hope you weren't crying over."

Argen promptly brushed the tears from his face with the hood of his robe.

"My name is Yona Igens, or you can just call me Yi," the

black-haired woman continued. "I was there the day Fortitude first laid eyes on you, but I couldn't find the time to speak with you personally. Sorry if I disappoint you, but I have nothing to do with Fortitude, so don't ask me if they plan on setting you free anytime soon." Yona glanced at Yeula and the bald woman. "So... how has Fortitude treated you so far? Made any new friends?"

"Actually, I am more concerned with Golem itself," Argen replied.

"Oh, that's right, you had a delivery for the colony, didn't you?"

Argen nodded.

"It must be frustrating being trapped without any word as to what happened with that package of yours. So... what do you do to pass the time around here?"

"Is there a meaning to that question?" Argen phrased that response more aggressively than he intended. He did not wish to drive Yona away as he did with Yeula, as unsure as he was of her intentions.

"Well, that depends. I would think you plan to do more than just make a home for yourself and live the rest of your life in peace once Fortitude turns you over. Otherwise, you might as well appreciate what you have right now."

Such an ignorant woman, Argen thought. Nothing he had right now could replace everything he lost to make it this far— only what he had yet to rightfully gain. If his lack of appreciation was that of a disrespectful child, then so be it; he would wear that one title proudly. "It is not enough," he rasped. "I will not fade in this abominable prison; I deserve so much more for everything I sacrificed."

"Maybe you do," Yona replied after a moment of silence, maintaining her monotone, "but whining won't get you any candy, not at your age. If you've been left all alone—if you want to *stay* alone—it's time you started thinking like a man."

"And to that end, what must I do? What *can* I do with what little freedom I have, you see?"

Yona's persistent smile finally abandoned her. "Honestly,

there isn't much you can do alone because it's clear you aren't ready to be alone. You're just a poor kid left out in the cold weather having lost his blanket faster than he even thought possible. Not much to do but hope you miraculously find shelter, right?"

Argen gave a disappointed sigh. It seemed their discussion led only to what he had already been doing all along. "I suppose so."

Yona's smile gradually crept back onto her face, prompting Argen to gaze at her perplexedly. "No doubt Huwerd's been babbling about Fortitude like his badge is something to be proud of, but you don't owe him anything just because he found you. Don't think you have any obligation to risk your life to serve Golem's people like a soldier—find your own way to live. Be free. A kid like you is bound to make a name for himself on his own one of these days; I want to admire every minute of that. Until then, take good care of yourself. No matter what you lost out there or what you will lose in the future, just remember that you *are* still alive. Isn't it better to enjoy yourself than to hide somewhere like you'd already died?"

Before Argen could contemplate her words, Yona offered him her hand. Almost unconsciously, he clasped her palm with his as though enticed by his own basic instincts. He felt a gentle pull from the tips of his fingers, a mote of light flashing before his eyes in that same instant. The Fortitude officers immediately took aim with their rifles, but Yona herself remained impartial, as did Argen. Indeed, he had begun to find Yona's composure contagious.

"You wouldn't shoot me in front of all these kids, would you?" Yona calmly asked the officers.

"You've had time to talk, now get the fuck out," one of the officers spat.

Yona sighed. "Well, kiddo, I guess it's time to say goodbye. I didn't hurt you, did I?"

Argen shook his head. "That just felt... strange."

"Did it? You should have felt something similar while you

were stranded out there. That's the power of DEAS, a power my companions have all been granted as a blessing for their devotion to the Scion Finis." Yona spoke quietly, perhaps so neither Yeula nor the bald woman could hear her.

So DEAS was the name of the power wielded by the cloaked entity. Argen vaguely recalled a similar sensation as that entity first clutched his garb. Was that entity, in truth, a mere human?

"Aside from that, it seems you have something special yourself," Yona continued. "Use that power wisely, will you? Certain people would no doubt cage you like a lab rat if they knew how exotic you were."

One of the Fortitude officers angrily grabbed the collar of Yona's vest, violently shoving her aside. The cloaked men next to her flinched as if ready to take action, only to be halted at gunpoint by the other officers.

"Not gonna say it again—get your ass out now!" the officer muttered.

Without saying another word, Yona gestured towards a teenage boy in the distance wearing similar apparel as the other cloaked men. The child proceeded to follow Yona as the officers led the entirety of her group inside the woods. Argen merely stood and stared until they all vanished from view, holding his hand in front of his face.

"Alrighty, looks like the show's all over," the bald woman announced loudly. "Wanna go now, Yeula?"

"Let's just go home," Yeula murmured.

"Might wanna head back pretty soon yourself; got a storm comin'!" the bald woman shouted to Argen.

Argen held his hand out before the two in protest as they departed, yet he found no words to speak.

Yeula glanced at Argen with a sympathetic look in her eyes. "I'll come back tomorrow," she timidly assured. Her words brought a meek smile upon Argen's face, if only for a moment. Yona's influence continued to cling pleasantly to his heart, although he knew he was unlikely to see her again for as long as he remained where he was.

With everyone departed, all Argen was left with was Yona's advice. Even if he had already died within that castle, perhaps he was not too late to be reborn or at the very least, relive his pleasant life alongside his departed friends with the help of new bonds forged in this otherwise abominable prison. He would undergo that process step by step, crawling on his knees before rising to a walk as though he had begun life anew. It would be Yeula who would provide the next step. For the next time they were to meet, he would greet her with open arms. And perhaps, if he were lucky, Huwerd would await him that day as well.

Chapter XXII: Outcast

Sahn 13th Reign, Year 988 I.G.R.

Argen threw himself out of bed at the sound of an outcry from just outside his tent. Sweat seeped intensely from his pores, the sudden disturbance pulling him into a daze, worsened by the phantoms of a haunting nightmare. It was calling to him, goading him into action.

A chipped knife lay on the ground not far from his spot. He stood on his feet with the knife in hand, frantically slipping into a pair of old sandals before rushing outside into the sunlit sky without the slightest hesitation.

Upon stepping outside and immediately noticing his mistake, Argen hastily concealed his weapon behind his back. What stood at a distance before him was simply a pair of bickering children, one of whom he could recognise as Yeula. He quietly stood by his tent, hoping to go unnoticed long enough to observe their banter. He was relieved that Yeula kept to her word, but what of the boy she was conversing with?

"Who cares what they all say?" a rather overweight boy clothed in tatters asked. "There's something outside that wall they aren't talking to us about, and that's why we gotta stay until they let us go."

"I told you, that doesn't have anything to do with us or our families," Yeula retorted.

"Oh yeah? Why would our parents have us rot here, then? I knew my family better than you knew yours, and I know they would never abandon me!"

Yeula took a quick step back as if to run away at any moment. It was surely an argument, but Argen was left to question if they merely pretended to disagree with one another out of pride or false hope. It was hardly his concern regardless. With that in mind, he hid his knife behind him and lowered his head, paying little attention to the ongoing dispute and reflecting on his nightmare. Within that nightmare, he was trapped in a tower, helpless and lone as he was before. His only company was the entity in the robe, the murderer in pursuit from corner to corner. But all of that ended when he was thrown off the tower, beaten and separated from his ill-fated friends. He had met with many such nightmares during his stay in Golem, but this one embittered him more intensely than the others.

By the time Argen lifted his head, Yeula, who then stood alone, waved at him with glee, much to his surprise. After turning around and tossing his knife back into his tent, he took a deep breath and waited for her to approach him.

"Are you okay, Yeula?" he asked as soon as Yeula was within arm's reach.

"Yeah, I'm fine," Yeula replied, her modest tone unchanged by her recent disagreement. As she attempted to peer into Argen's tent, he promptly lowered the sheet. "What about you?"

"I am well; thank you for asking," Argen spoke with uncharacteristic exuberance to put both himself and Yeula at ease.

Yeula gave Argen a warm smile before turning her attention to the encampment in the distance, away from the small hilltop surrounded with shrubbery which Argen's tent stood, prompting him to do the same. The number of children moving to and fro the numerous tents far exceeded that of the tents themselves, yet they shared limited space without so much as a complaint. Even some caregivers from Fortitude stationed around the field could not resist joining these children in harmless recreation. Within that one encampment, child and man alike sought reprieve from their otherwise tenuous lives. It was a wondrous sight, one Argen yet preferred to witness in solitude.

Those children were much like Argen himself, as he

could finally admit. Indeed, like himself, it seemed tragic circumstances brought these children here with a common wish to be reunited with their families and escape back into the only place they ever thought of as a home. In recalling this, Argen realised he had already been one of these children for quite some time. Entire days had come to pass when in his troubled mind, no day was apart from the day he first arrived. Every night in bed had rarely gone without a nightmare. Argen would awake and step outside, hoping that he would be set free into Golem that day, and upon realising that Huwerd did not await him beyond his resting place, he would force himself asleep once more, and the cycle would continue. In some way, he had become the most pathetic child of all, so brooding and helpless that the others would acknowledge him with only sympathy. Only when he met Yeula and her friends did a single day spent here feel any different.

"Sleeping all day isn't going to fix anything, remember?" Yeula spoke as Argen continued to watch the other children. "We're all we have right now, so we need to support each other, right? You lost your parents, too, didn't you? So that makes two of us." Yeula outstretched her hand to Argen. "Come on, let's go meet the others."

"Very well," Argen said after a period of silence. Before he could muster any thought, Yeula took his hand and ran for the gathering of children with him in tow, just as before.

"Not now, I meant!" Argen exclaimed, doubting himself yet again. "I had to retrieve something from my tent first."

"Hiding all the time isn't going to get you anywhere either," Yeula grunted as she hastened her sprint for the other children.

Argen's dismay only worsened upon reaching the territory of the playful children, who all stared at him blankly. He strained to smile as he waved with his free hand, hoping he was not blushing. Yeula released his hand and nudged his shoulder, beckoning him to say something.

"Hello, everyone," he quietly greeted. "My name is Argen,

but I think some of you are already aware of that, so I—"
Before he could finish his sentence, the children had already
surrounded him, speaking to him all in tandem.

"What kinda colony are you from?" one boy asked.

"Well, I believe I am—"

"How old are you?" a little girl asked.

"I believe I am twelve years old."

"Are you really from outside Golem?" another boy asked.

"Yes, I suppose I—"

"What's it like out there?" a smaller boy asked.

"I... would say that it is quite barren, but—"

"Can I have your robe?" another little girl asked.

"My robe? This is all I have to—"

So many questions proceeded to flow all at once that
Argen could no longer make out a single one, and at any
point he did hear enough of a question to respond in kind, he
was quickly silenced with another more loudly spoken. Argen
lowered his head, hoping at least one person would understand
his discomfort and spare him the need to run away or react with
hostility. Only Yeula took notice and stepped in front of him
while attempting to reason with the others, but her quiet speech
went unnoticed in the chaos. Some of the inquisitive children
appeared to sympathise with Argen and respectfully back away,
yet others raised their voices to be heard, and when that proved
to be insufficient, they turned on one another, bickering without
pause. Argen could barely suppress the urge to scream at the
raging crowd for their overwhelming ignorance. Only his self-
control kept him at bay, and hopefully it would last until
someone else spoke up.

"Shut the fuck up!" a familiar teenager approaching from
behind the crowd shouted, but Argen could barely catch a
glimpse at her with so many of the children in his view. It was
under this woman's command that most of the children left for
the tents without saying another word. The few who did remain
were quickly made to accede as the woman pointed a finger at
a group of the fleeing children. Yeula moved aside and looked at

the woman and then Argen apologetically.

The newly arrived teenager, the bald woman from yesterday, briefly looked around to ensure no other child remained before speaking, "Sorry 'bout them. You okay?" Concern was evident in her expression despite her commanding tone.

"Yes," Argen replied with a quick nod. "Thank you."

The bald woman subtly scratched her head as if slightly nervous herself. "Heh, looks like everyone's dying to get to know the newcomer now." She looked sternly into Yeula's eyes. "Didn't I tell you to take it easy?"

"But I just wanted—" Yeula paused mid-speech and turned to Argen. "I—I'm sorry, I didn't mean to—"

"I am fine," he interrupted before turning to the bald woman. "Actually, I think I should be the one to apologise for refusing to speak for myself; but thank you for coming here." Perhaps, he thought, he had more than one reason to be thankful for her arrival, for he remained unaware of her connection to Fortitude.

The bald woman gestured to Yeula to come closer. As soon as she and Yeula were standing alongside one another, she said, "It wasn't your fault at all. Anyway, I'm sure Yeula didn't mean to give you any trouble." she chuckled briefly before continuing, "You should probably run back to your camp before the crazies come to gawk at you again."

Argen outstretched his shaky arm to Yeula and the bald woman as they both turned to leave. "No, please wait."

The bald woman promptly stopped and turned around. "Yes?" she asked uneasily.

"If I may ask, are you affiliated with Fortitude? There is something that I have been waiting to ask."

"'Fraid not; I'm sorry. If you were goin' to ask for a chance to visit Golem, you're probably more out of luck than the rest of us; outsiders don't get much sympathy 'round here, I heard. And most of us are bein' detained so that Fortitude can watch over us until our families return from military duty—that's what I heard. But even if you're here for a totally different reason, I don't think Fortitude'll just abandon you forever."

"I know," Argen replied. While initially certain he would be released within a few days more, some doubt lingered in his tone. "I spoke with Huwerd some time ago. He said he would do whatever he could to help me, and I would only need to await his return. As I said, that was some time ago; that is why I asked."

The bald woman folded her arms. "And that's what you've been waitin' for all this time? Look, I'm not telling you to give up, but you're only twelve years old, right? You could really end up hidin' in that tent for years until you're let loose into Golem."

"And your suggestion is that, in the meantime, I should enjoy my stay here to the best of my abilities? And what for? To befriend those whom I may never see again once I am allowed to leave? All that concerns me is finding a land I can call my home and moving on with my life as soon as I can." Argen's tone elevated with every word he spoke.

"Well, then, Yeula over here seems to have taken a likin' to you," the woman retorted with a raised eyebrow. "I wonder why?"

At this, Argen let out a genuine, almost involuntary chuckle. Silly as it was, at least he could find some humour in irony in the presence of this woman even if his future was still rather uncertain. "Well, that was—rather, I think, it was never my intention because I had intended—..." Before he could finish his sentence, he gave in to his urge to laugh in front of the stranger, although he could not fully understand why and hoped he would not be misunderstood. And to his relief, both Yeula and the stranger soon shared the awkward moment of humour with him, laughing happily for some reason perhaps even they could not understand. Argen had indulged in some semblance of levity for the first time in what felt like forever; with that came acceptance.

Argen spent the remainder of the day alongside these two individuals he would gradually grow fond of. Eyareon, as the stranger was named, explained to Argen that even if the families of the desolate children never returned from their duties, Golem law dictated that children who came of age were to be released from Fortitude's militarised zones regardless of their circumstances, and that right possibly extended to Argen himself as well. Knowing her own time was nearing, Eyareon dedicated herself to alleviating the troubles of her peers as best she could for the remainder of her stay. For this simple deed, she had earned the respect and admiration of the caregivers, and even some of Fortitude's officers who frequented the children's field, and the children themselves were both inspired and comforted within her presence. Argen knew that he, too, would soon become one of these children, for she clearly had something he lacked yet craved—the ability to care for and inspire others despite one's own grievances. And to acquire her strength, he resolved to stay alongside her whenever he could, having made peace with the fact that he would not be permitted into Golem for many years to come. After all, a quiet life was something to be earned and the trials to get to that point would be worth reminiscence.

Several days passed without any trace of Huwerd, but Argen no longer awaited his return; indeed, he had stopped counting the days altogether as he spent them with his new companions. And as he began to act and speak as they would, even the other children began to view him as one of their own, as if they had forgotten he had ever been apart from them. The boy who had once considered himself a hopeless outcast who could never win the favour of these foreign children had finally begun to see how wrong he was. More eager to involve themselves with Argen than ever before, many children approached him with open arms and respect, and soon what was once a simple trio of friends grew into a merry group of over a dozen other children.

On one particular day in the field, Argen sat upon a hilltop among a gathering of his closest friends, one of which was even the boy he had first encountered arguing with Yeula, who had introduced himself as Relt. The group sat in a perfect circle, sharing fond memories and trinkets they had been allowed to keep before they were brought to Golem's outer walls. As he observed the others taking turns parading their favourite items and speaking fondly of their families, Argen considered what he could show them once his turn had come. Although he had thought of these children as nothing less than his friends for some time now, he had forgotten to explain much of anything about himself other than that he was not of Golem. Even his runic powers, assuming they had not faded from lack of use, were not known to anyone else. Argen thought that perhaps he had found a fitting moment to reveal what truly made him special and perhaps learn more of his powers in the process. He had used them only whilst stranded in that ghastly castle, yet he could swear he had never been capable of such sorcery until that point.

Despite watching the children closely, Argen paid little attention to the display of trivial items—stuffed animals, gold coins, defunct machinery parts, and the like. After many children had concluded their show-and-tell and rejoined the circle, Eyareon gave Yeula a nudge on the shoulder, persuading her to stand in the middle of the circle to introduce herself, which she did somewhat meekly. At this, Argen leaned in closer.

"Hello, everyone," Yeula greeted, timidly waving in front of herself. "My name is Yeula—Yeula Nars. I, um..." Yeula lowered her head momentarily before continuing. "Fortitude took me away from my parents three years ago when I was four. My parents loved me unconditionally and supported my decisions even when they didn't agree with them. It was only after I was separated from them that I realised how much they meant to me, and I wish I could thank them for putting up with me for so long when I was so difficult to them. I miss them every day, but I know I'll get to see them again eventually, and I've made plenty of friends here to support me until then. All of you are important to me, and I do my best to make sure everyone stays as hopeful as I still am of the future because I know we'll all see our families again. Thank you."

Yeula promptly returned to her place in the circle without

basking in the accolades that followed her speech. The spirited child's speech was what Argen had come to expect during his time alongside her, yet something was amiss in her words, even frightening in a sense. Argen had long acknowledged that Yeula was as deft a speaker for her age as she was a liar, something he would not dare speak aloud.

As Eyareon stood up and made her way to the middle of the circle, Argen disregarded Yeula and watched with a glint of excitement to hear the speech of his new graven image. Upon circling around to observe each of the children, Eyareon gave Yeula a subtle nod and spoke. "Glad I get to have a chance to speak to all of you at once for a change. My full name is Eyareon Ashta, and I've been stuck here for a good ten years of my life—a while longer than most of you here. I can hardly remember much about mum and dad since they weren't around for very long as I was growing up, but at least I can tell I meant something to them. It sucks living a life without a family, y'know? But I've made plenty of friends around here to fit that role, so I'm not taking any anger out on Fortitude; they probably had a good reason for enlisting my family."

"Eyareon, do you—" Argen paused before he could ask what he considered an ill-suited question when sitting among so many naïve children. Eyareon raised a palm in his direction as though she had read his mind, presumably beckoning him to save his question for a more private discussion.

"Besides," Eyareon continued, "I think I've got my own responsibilities now—you babies need someone who can relate to what you're goin' through while lookin' after you at the same time, and I'm pretty much up to the task for as long as I'm here. And since I don't have much time left, I hope you'll all remember to stay positive even after I'm gone; maybe watch over kids like Argen while you're at it, huh?" Eyareon winked at Argen as she spoke that last line, prompting him to smile nervously as all eyes looked upon him. "And that leaves one more question unanswered—what I plan to do after being released. Well, to be honest, I think I've gotten the hang of this place, and Fortitude seems to like me, so that's a plus. It's been way too long since my last Golem visit, and I've begun to think of this place as where I belong, so I've already decided to join Fortitude when I grow up. I've got unanswered questions just like everyone else, and it looks like the only way I'll get those answers is to stick around with Fortitude for as long as they'll let me. I want to see what it's like beyond Golem's walls, and I definitely want to see what Fortitude is really all about, and why my parents are with 'em."

The children remained largely silent as Eyareon concluded her speech. Argen reasoned that it was a common desire among Golem's civilians to unravel the secrets held by their authorities, and perhaps everyone fell silent because they, too, were beginning to consider one day joining Fortitude and gleaning the answers they sought in their current predicament. Argen himself was not among them, for he had seen more than enough of what lay between Golem and his own homeland to ever consider involving himself with the organisation he gathered existed to combat malevolent creatures akin to the one he first encountered. And that was one encounter he did not wish to ever revisit.

"It's pretty obvious by now," Eyareon continued, "but I didn't get a chance to bring any valuable toys with me. So, who wants to go next?"

"How about you, Argen?" Relt asked. Argen recalled that this boy had been discreetly eyeing him for some time after the meeting began, presumably awaiting his more formal introduction.

"Actually, I was hoping for an opportunity to speak with Eyareon privately," Argen said.

"Hey, it's still an early mornin', isn't it?" Eyareon responded as she placed her hands on her hips at Argen. "Besides, I'll bet most of you kids only came here to get to know that boy hidin' under the robe right where I'm facin'."

Although not a single child spoke a word, the mutual gaze upon Argen more than spoke of their feelings. With grace belying his reluctance, Argen joined with Eyareon in the middle of the gathering, only for her to rejoin the others in the circle. All eyes were upon him yet again, and while uneasy at being observed by so many people at once, he was somewhat excited at the thought of demonstrating his power, although he could only speculate how they would perceive him afterwards. After looking around himself for a suitably sized rock, he stood completely still, narrowing his eyes just enough to allow himself to focus while observing the reactions of the spectators. He silently called upon the rock to gradually rise before him— lifted by a cloud of glowing dust—until it ascended over his head. Looks of disbelief veiled the faces of the older spectators, whereas the young children began to cheer with excitement as to be expected from those with blooming imaginations.

Hearing so many children cheer so fervently at once drew a warm smile upon Argen's face, but he was not yet finished. By extending his right arm in front of him and slowly swaying it to his right, he commanded the dust to crumble the rock into equivalent tiny particles in an instant. The fanfare of praise and wonder turned into a lively debate among the spectators. And while he somewhat pitied these ignorant children, Argen was nevertheless thrilled to have opened their eyes to the reality of powers like his own.

"My name... is Argen," he spoke with some strain in his voice as the particles danced about his raised finger. As difficult as it was to speak with much of his energy spent, it delivered a sense of empowerment he had never before experienced. The ease with which he had conjured such a miracle surprised even himself, for his powers had grown even whilst unused for so long. "I've travelled here from a land far away, and I don't know if I'm ever fated to see it again. With that in mind, all I seek is a new land I can call my home." By throwing his arm above his head, he dispersed the bundle of enchanted and mundane particles to spread upon the hilltop, giving birth to a bed of flora upon the formerly barren soil, enveloping the air with a pleasant aroma.

From the corner of his eye, Argen could see that a few of Fortitude's caregivers had already noticed him and were slowly making their way up the hilltop. The matter was of no emergency given their pacing, so he remained to look upon the faces of the now silent spectators undeterred.

Of all the older children who bore witness to Argen's spectacle, Eyareon was clearly the least surprised; in fact, the faint smile she wore throughout suggested she had always suspected that he was special. "Well, well, that's somethin' I thought I'd never see, to say the least!" she bellowed.

"Yeah, holy shit!" Relt added, promptly shutting his mouth in shame afterwards.

As for the rest of the spectating children, some, including Yeula, remained to vet the fragrant flora blossoming around them, whereas a greater number of children crowded around Argen just as before, deluging him with an incessant storm of questions; but Argen did not fret—he shared in their excitement.

"Hey, I said leave him alone!" shouted a voice that seemed to be Eyareon's from behind the crowd—Argen could barely hear her at all. In fact, it had begun to feel as if he were drifting into a void with the children's voices growing increasingly muffled to his ears. And as if his realm were a dream, his own surroundings grew distorted until he could barely make out a single face in the indiscernible amalgamation. Planting his knees on the fertile soil, Argen presented his arms before his wavering vision and panicked at the sight of his protuberant blood vessels. As his bleeding nose painted his open palms red, Argen barely sighted the presence of the two caregivers urgently approaching from the side, commanding the other children to clear away. It was only a few seconds after the caregivers began to approach him before his vision went completely black and his thoughts faded away.

Chapter XXIII: The Unfolding

Sahn 51ˢᵗ Reign, Year 988 I.G.R.

"Any new word from FOG Central?"

"No, I haven't heard anything."

"Dammit, we need more time. This boy is in no condition to move. Don't they realise that?"

"We'll wait for Sect. Dictator Bates; maybe he can level with them some more. If not, we'll just have to keep doing what we can."

"Is he awake or what? Let us in!"

Resting atop what felt like a regular sleeping bag, Argen peeled his eyes open halfway to the sight of a large tent. On the opposite end of the tent, a plainly dressed bearded old man carefully monitored the readings displayed by a small box-shaped machine Argen now knew as a computer. Standing beside the old man was a similarly dressed younger man. Hoping to catch their attention, Argen attempted to move his battered body, only managing to slightly raise his right arm, bringing to his own attention a bulky device in the shape of a bracelet fitted around his wrist. Perhaps this device was to monitor his health?

As if the readings on the computer he observed indicated that Argen had regained consciousness, the older medic abruptly toppled his chair as he rose in Argen's direction. At the same time, the younger medic scrambled to Argen's side, slowly waving his hand before Argen's face as if to see that his eyes would follow. "Please try not to speak," he whispered. "Your name is... Argen, correct?"

Argen nodded.

"Hello, Argen," the younger medic greeted. "My name is Kal. I'm glad to see that you're okay, Argen. Can you remember where you are?"

Argen nodded.

"That's great. One more thing: Do you remember what happened before you passed out?"

Argen nodded, aware of when he had fallen unconscious but oblivious to the cause. Perhaps he had lacked the strength to bear the weight of his own sorcery, much to his embarrassment.

"You should be good to move now. How does your body feel?"

Argen concerned himself more with the mounting commotion outside. "Is there someone out there?" he asked as he carefully sat up, confirming he could move and speak at the same time.

Kal fixated on the tent's entrance. The older man casually sauntered over to the closed sheets and pulled them back. As he did so, Eyareon and Yeula rushed into the tent with such haste as to nearly knock the old man down before he could back away. "What do you think you two are doing!?" he exclaimed.

Both Eyareon and Yeula ignored the old man as they sat by Argen's bed, worry painted on their faces. Argen welcomed them with a faint smile, grateful they had not been too frightened of what had transpired to approach him out of concern, at least.

"Let them stay, father," Kal quietly spoke to the older man. "This might be their only chance, anyway."

While not voicing his compliance, the older man crossed his arms and stood where he was, presumably agreeing to do nothing.

"Argen!" shouted Eyareon. "Can you see us? You remember anythin'? Are you—"

"I'm fine, Eyareon," Argen interjected. "I seem to have some difficulty moving, but I'm mostly okay."

After some silence, Eyareon smiled playfully at Argen. "Well, don't you seem calm after what happened to you? You've been out of commission all day, in case the medics haven't told ya."

"Did you... know that this would happen?" Yeula asked, almost too quietly for Argen to hear.

Argen rubbed his temples as he struggled to recall every minor detail of their morning gathering. "I don't know. I suppose I thought it was a possibility at first, but then, I..."

"Argen," Kal sternly spoke, "I must inform you that you are to be transported to Golem's Prime District by tomorrow morning for some sort of evaluation. Try to get as much rest in as possible until then."

An evaluation? Argen could only hope that the timing was a mere coincidence, and he was not being regarded with suspicion again. At the very least, the time had come to finally leave the confines of the militarised domain, but this did not leave him as excited as he would have been a few days prior. Whether it was the result of the bonds he had fledged during his stay or an ominous premonition that was slowly seeping into his mind, he could not surely say. "I see. Do you know why?"

"This wasn't our decision to make," Kal replied, partly ignoring Argen's question. "We were hoping to give you a few more days to rest until you had fully recovered, but Fortitude has its orders."

"May I speak with Huwerd, then?" Argen asked, reasoning that Huwerd must have had some involvement in presenting such an order to his sector and had thus returned.

Kal shook his head. "We may not have time to arrange a meeting, I'm afraid. All we can do right now is ensure you can make the trip safely. Can you stand?"

Argen planted his feet on the bed and slowly set his wobbly legs upright. Having managed that much with some discomfort, he attempted to place one foot in front of the other to take a step, only to reel back in front of Eyareon, who timely caught him and gently helped him back onto the bed.

"No way you're gettin' anywhere on foot in your condition," she murmured, her distress all too evident in her expression. "Actually, there's no way I'm lettin' you go anywhere on foot right now."

Argen sat up. "Eyareon, I don't have a choice, and neither do you. What's to say I won't feel better by tomorrow?"

"Is that a bet?" Eyareon murmured before standing up and facing Kal. "Doc, you know what's wrong with him?"

"It's, uh..." Kal stuttered as if trying to think up layman's terms for Argen's condition. "Well, it's some sort of... acute muscle atrophy, from what we know; but his condition seems to have stabilised. It may be hard for Argen to move for a while, but I think he will eventually make a full recovery. With that said, Argen, would you mind explaining the nature of your... powers? Any information you can provide might help us treat you as best as possible with the little time we have available."

"I don't know," Argen replied. "I wasn't even aware I could do those things until recently."

Kal nodded with a stern look on his face. While Argen did sense some suspicion from the doctor, he had far too many other concerns to care; he was more eager to make the most of what little time he had left with Yeula and Eyareon.

"Doc, is he good to go, at least?" Eyareon asked as though she had read Argen's mind. "If we've only got until tomorrow to chat, I don't wanna waste time here."

Kal shrugged. "Sure, I guess. Just remember to report back to us early in the morning if you have the time, and don't strain yourself." Kal turned to his father. "Does that sound good, father?"

Kal's father had glared at Argen the moment he denied knowing the origin of his power, but nevertheless, he gave a quick nod to his son's suggestion.

"I guess it's all settled, then," Kal said as he walked and reached for a small wooden cane leaning against a corner of the tent and offered it to Argen. "Here, you can use this for support until you've recovered a bit. Try it out."

Argen accepted the cane and eagerly attempted to stand with it. With some effort, he managed to straighten his legs. Upon taking a few small steps with added support from the cane as a test, he turned to face Eyareon and Yeula. "I think this could work," he said with a faint smile.

Eyareon patted Argen's shoulder. "Good enough, I guess. Come on, I think we've all seen enough of this place." With her hand lingering on Argen's shoulder, she moved behind him to follow his lead, supporting him with each little step he took. Yeula followed closely behind, and Argen could not help glancing back at her sullen face a couple of times. He noticed she had fallen largely silent since last morning and hoped she had not come to fear him for his power.

"Wait!" Kal shouted before the trio could leave the tent. "Argen, I suggest not using your powers again until we can make sense of all of this. On another note, Eyareon, Argen hasn't been I.D.'d yet, so FOG's transporters won't be able to track him easily. I suggest staying nearby at all times so that your I.D. can be used instead; it wasn't the original plan, but I'll contact Huwerd and let him know. It shouldn't be too inconvenient."

Eyareon gave Kal a thumbs-up. "Thanks for the help."

Argen gave Kal an affirmative nod before setting off into the field under the starlit sky. Where he would go, he did not know, but he would practise his steps before settling down. With such little light aside from that within nearby tents, Argen could scarcely see what lay before him, but Eyareon compassionately guided him whenever he faltered; his eyes had become slow to adjust to the darkness.

"Think we should stop by my tent?" Eyareon asked after a while of aimless treading. "Don't worry, I've had plenty of scrapes from time to time myself, so I know my way around."

"Actually, Eyareon, I've wanted to ask you something," Argen replied. While unsure if asking the question in mind was ideal with Yeula nearby, he would take the chance if only for his little time remaining.

"Yeah?" Eyareon asked, shortly afterwards snapping her fingers as her own memory served her. "It had something to do with my parents, didn't it?"

"Yes, it did. I wanted to ask if..." try as he could, he could not speak beyond that.

"Ha! Hey, don't sweat it; I haven't seen 'em in ages and probably couldn't answer much about 'em, but at least you don't need to worry about breaking my—"

"Are they alive?" Argen hastily interjected, encouraged enough by Eyareon's light-hearted tone.

Eyareon softly squeezed Argen's shoulder and came to a stop. Yeula followed her lead, her head lowered.

"What was that?" Eyareon quietly asked, her seriousness evident only in her expression.

"Your parents... Do you really think they're alive, or...?" Perhaps it was not such an appropriate question after all, Argen thought as he spoke, but there was no turning back.

Eyareon placed her hand around her chin as if to think. "Nothing gets by you, eh? Let's see... Well, like I told you, can't really remember much about them, so I can't say it's been on my mind that much. That said, it's not like I wouldn't mind seeing 'em again one day, y'know? Yeah, I get anxious when I think about how I'll be returnin' home without a family, so that's why I just keep it in the back of my head, mostly. Gotta focus on the now if it helps keep my hopes up; the day I give up on my parents is the day I grow a full head of hair." Eyareon sighed as she took her hand off her chin. "But really, that's a nice question. What else did Fortitude tell you, anyway?"

"The things they do... aren't safe for anyone there," Yeula murmured before Argen could speak. As she did so, she randomly paced around the two as though deep in thought.

The worry painted on Eyareon's face at least made it clear to Argen that she shared his feelings. "Yeula," she said softly, "that really wasn't my point."

Yeula shook her head. "I know; don't worry about me. To be honest, I'd always had a feeling that our families were sent to Fortitude for more than manual labour. Argen, I..." Yeula interrupted herself to look around. "Let's go to Eyareon's tent."

"Thank you, Yeula," Argen said. The cold air alongside the gloomy discussion had left him with a few chills; he was sensitive to the mounting tension and decided their conversation would be better continued within the comfort of shelter.

With Eyareon leading the way, the trio soon sat within her extravagant tent. An elongated dinner table lie in the centre, coated in a tattered beige sheet and lined with eight wooden chairs. The dim lanterns placed on each corner of the room atop respective stools gave the tent a cosy vibe. The tent was especially personalised between the lanterns with the presence of tall wooden cabinets and shelves lined and topped with various paraphernalia. Further down behind the tent's entrance —to the left of the dinner table where Argen was sitting— lay a smaller tent serving as a separate room of the conjoined tent, its bearings partially obscured with a transparent, ornately patterned blanket by the opening. Eyareon and Yeula were seated in front of him on the other side of the table, but only Yeula appeared to notice him; Eyareon, on the other hand, leaned into the table and gazed past the entrance with her head resting on the back of her hands.

"This is some home you've got here," Argen remarked, eager to dismiss the numbing silence with a little small talk.

Eyareon grinned. "Oh, yeah? Won it in a little bet with Huwerd, actually, but that's a story for another time."

"Huwerd? You really have seen him for yourself, then?"

Eyareon lifted herself against her chair. "Me and him go way back; known him since I was first taken here. He's like family to me, and you know how much that helps."

"All I had ever thought about was helping the others, even if that meant lying," Yeula said. "I never hated my father, but I..."

"Oh, that's right. Come to think of it, you never told anyone much about him."

"That's because I don't have much to tell. Just like you, I really don't know much about my dad, but not because I can't remember much about him. It was always as if I never even existed to him. And then mum left... I thought everything would change after that, but dad didn't care; he just obsessed over his job more than ever. And now he's probably dead." Yeula recalled her past as though it meant little to her in the present.

Eyareon gave Yeula a flustered look. "I—I'm sorry, I had no idea."

"It's okay. Besides, crying about it now won't change anything."

"But aren't you afraid of being alone?" Argen asked before Eyareon could respond herself.

Yeula shook her head. "Isn't that better than being with people you can't stand? You felt that way at first yourself, didn't you?"

Argen gave Yeula a smile, intent on putting her at ease. "My father died before I was born, so I only had my mother to look after me for most of my early childhood until I could finally look forward and seek friendship from others. In some ways, I was always powerless without anyone to stand by, even if I could not appreciate them at first. It was only after meeting you that I realised that, and I have yet to thank you for it, so... thank you, Yeula."

Yeula averted Argen's gaze, prompting another moment of silence.

"Hey, that's remindin' me of something," Eyareon said. "Argen, got any idea where you'll run off to after you're invited to Golem?"

Argen had hardly thought of his future within Golem, but he would make up an answer merely for the sake of discussion. "I'm going to be a writer," he said passionately. And indeed, he would be a writer with a magnificent story to tell. Although he had many other professions in mind, assuming Golem was at least a little like his homeland, he could gleefully look forward to inspiring others with his tale.

"A writer, huh? Well, like I said, I'm gonna be the best Fortitude officer there ever was! Hell, maybe I'll even end up runnin' this sector one day!" Eyareon seemed equally passionate as she professed her own dream.

Yeula chuckled lightly. "Where would I go, then? Didn't

you say I could stay with you?"

"Yeah, you could stay with me for a few years 'til you've got your own place, then I'll probably be leaving for Fortitude after that. Not like I'll be accepted right away, so we'll still have plenty of time together."

"Do you think you'll have any room at home for me?" Argen asked, smiling from ear to ear. "I'd certainly want nothing more to do with Fortitude but I'd be glad if we could all stay together for a few years."

"Was actually hoping you'd say that," Eyareon said, yawning and peering past the tent's entrance. "Looks like the sun's comin' up already, and I couldn't even find the time for a nap with all this excitement. How you feelin', Argen?"

"I think I'm too anxious to fall asleep even if I wanted to."

"Same here," Yeula quietly added.

Eyareon rose from her seat and waved at Argen as she left for the makeshift bedroom. "Just don't fall asleep on the transport, 'kay!?" she shouted from within the room.

"If everything goes well, that means you'll just be transferred early, right?" Yeula asked. "You're luckier than the rest of us."

Argen sighed. "I suppose so, although it would also mean I couldn't see you again for years or Eyareon. Without you, I'd have no idea where to start; I still feel as if I barely— Well, I had a mare with me, with that said. I suppose I'll be reunited with her earlier than I thought." He had spoken in an effort to excite himself at the thought of his impending transfer, to little avail. No matter how he daydreamed of his future within Golem, little more than emptiness swelled in his heart, and still, he could not fully understand why.

"What's wrong?" Yeula quietly asked as she leaned in closer.

"I'm still trying to figure that out myself. As far as I knew, all I really wanted since finding this place was to find a land where I could find my new home, like I said, with friends I could understand. I suppose I just never imagined I would find those friends in the very place I once hated so much, and now I have to leave them with no idea of when I'll have a chance to see them again, if ever at all. Maybe I'm just concerned with losing my friends again."

"Oh..." Yeula lowered her head for a moment. "So, you're afraid, then?"

"I've once experienced a fear that nearly killed the person I was. To think I would feel it again even if death is uninvolved..." Argen wrapped his hands around his head as he struggled for a solution. "I just... don't know what I'm supposed to do anymore —actually, I don't think I was ever able to change anything."

"I don't think that's true. You've already made a difference for all of us just by being here and showing us the world outside Golem, in a way. And when you become a citizen, you'll get to tell the whole colony about a world we couldn't possibly imagine before, and who knows where that would lead. If that isn't making a difference, what is?"

"In that sense, my coming here has made a difference, I suppose." Argen gazed directly into Yeula's eyes. "The problem is, I have no way of knowing if that's the right difference to make."

"There's only one way to find out, right?" With a smile, Yeula rose from her seat. "Just move on with your life and see what happens; forget about us for now."

As Yeula made her way out of the tent, Argen took his cane and followed her, greeted by the sun rising over the faraway walls of Golem, with nimbus clouds approaching from either side of it. It would be the first time he had witnessed the rain since the end of his journey; now, the mere thought of it left him shivering in trepidation. He took some solace in that what once heralded a chaotic beginning would now herald a favourable end. "It's beautiful," he solemnly commented to himself.

"It doesn't rain around here very often, I think," Yeula replied. "I wasn't allowed outside during a rainstorm when I was living with Mum and Dad, but now I can make my own rules."

"This would be... my third time actually in the rain," Argen said, recalling the times he had been introduced to rain in his homeland. Natural rain was so rare a sight in his homeland that few could ever witness it in a lifetime. The more fanatical inhabitants regarded it as an ill omen, and for a good reason— the rain would fall upon his homeland for many days and nights at a time, leaving floods in its wake. "So... how long is this rain going to last?"

"No rest for the weary, I guess," came Eyareon's weary voice as she walked forward beside the two. "You babies are too noisy."

Argen chuckled. "Sorry, Eyareon."

Eyareon yawned as she stretched her arms. "Oh well, just kidding. So, Argen, ya ready to depart?"

Argen nodded.

"Ya sure? The transporters just contacted me a minute ago; they said they were ready to pick you up."

"Okay," Argen replied after a pause. "Will you lead me to them, at least?"

"Someone's gotta guide ya, right? Yeah, I'll take you to 'em. Comin' with us, Yeula?"

Yeula nodded. "Let's go."

Argen began his final stroll alongside his new companions, his head held low. He exchanged quick glances with some of the children as the trio passed by numerous encampments, responding only with a smile to those who attempted to speak with him. While he had grown fond of each and every one of them, and them of him, he had little time to share thoughtful goodbyes. Eyareon would likely see to it that they knew of his departure regardless, and although he did not request it, he hoped that she would make it known to all of them how much he appreciated their acceptance and friendship.

The two transporters, men clad in black suits with sunglasses, awaited the trio in a barren expanse isolated from any encampment, with their method of transportation resting just behind them, one unlike any Argen had ever seen. Hovering above the air with a pair of large jets beneath it, the cerulean vehicle lifted open its sliding doors as if ready to welcome its newest passenger. Argen's first step towards the transport was acknowledged by the cloudy skies, with a single raindrop pouring onto the centre of his forehead the moment he looked up to marvel at the machinery. There was no formal greeting from either of the transporters—only a quick gesture to signal their readiness to depart with Argen in tow. Argen took a big step in their direction before turning to Yeula and Eyareon.

"We'll meet again in Golem, I guess," Eyareon sighed with a shrug, approaching Argen to hold him tightly in her arms. "Take care of yourself until then, okay?"

"Thank you for everything, Eyareon," Argen whispered in her ear before fixating on the seemingly troubled Yeula. Although he had found the time to engage her in a more personal discussion, he sensed that she yet kept something hidden from him. He opened his mouth as he tried to call out to her, but the right words would not come to mind—all he could manage to utter was his final goodbye. "Goodbye, Yeula."

Yeula remained unresponsive; perhaps she could not hear Argen from such a distance. With a smile, Eyareon released Argen and prodded at his nose once before turning him around, and he did not look back as he approached the transporters, who guided him to the passenger segment of the cerulean vehicle. Using a metallic flight of steps that had extended from underneath the passenger door, Argen made his way into the transport and rested on a long, cushioned seat to his left, placing his cane on his lap. The passenger door retracted its steps and shut behind him, abandoning the surreality of his situation—he was trapped in a transport leaving for Golem with no means to turn back; that was his reality. He was like a bird left to the mercy of a cage, but knowing that it was inevitability, and not his own powerlessness, that led to this turn of events somewhat comforted him as he reminisced of his peaceful days within the sector—Sector Two Seventy-Eight West, it was called. Two hundred and seventy-eight... it was a number he would never forget for as long as he remained separate from Eyareon and Yeula. And if, for whatever reason, they were to be kept away from Golem forever, perhaps he would actually find himself joining Fortitude one day, for they had somehow become as much a part of him as the family he had lost. He would never lose anyone again.

The small confines of the back of the transport came with little more than long windows on either side and although he leaned back on one just behind himself, he did not glance back at Eyareon or Yeula. The transport took to the skies above the walls of Golem and accelerated for the great colony at a speed Argen had never thought possible courtesy of its jet engines, the enormous power of which gently concussed the entire transport despite emitting little noise to add to that of the falling rain pelting its solid roof. Argen looked through the window after a moment of rest only to find that they had already flown above the walls at an altitude above most of the other vehicles prevailing the skies further ahead. There was no ground directly beside the walls on Golem's side, only a seemingly endless and bottomless man-made chasm segregating them from the rest of Golem. He could barely make out a massive bridge in the distance above the chasm against the gate of Sector Two Seventy-Eight West. On the other side of the bridge lay a militarised field fenced off from the streets of Golem. Directly below the transport lay what appeared to be a residential zone with little activity on the streets littered with bizarre, grounded vehicles of all shapes and sizes. Compared to the tall cities and skyscrapers that could be seen out yonder, wood and brick housing defined this relatively unimpressive district. His mind dazed with more questions than ever, he let out a quieted sigh at having no one to answer them, particularly not the two transporters hidden from the view of the front window behind the cockpit.

As the front window came to Argen's mind, he set his cane on the ground and crawled his way to it. Using the ridges of the window frame to balance himself, he rose to his feet and looked ahead to gain a view of the front window of the cockpit and thus, where the transport was to disembark. And there it was, standing beyond a rural area, the district of innumerable machines in the skies and towering ebony buildings. The most impressive building, one taller than nearly all the rest, lay directly ahead, and from that, Argen knew that he was to be taken to the capital of Golem—Prime District, it had been called. He softly planted his ear on the glass to eavesdrop on whatever words the transporters, yet hidden by the tall seats of the cockpit, exchanged to one another.

"This is Aerial Transport X Sixty-Four to the ASAS," the piloting transporter spoke into some sort of communicator after a discussion with the co-pilot. "Prepare for docking on port twenty-eight."

"Roger that, Sixty-Four," a male responded from the communicator. "Welcome back to Prime District."

All Argen could do was hope he was as welcomed there as they were and rest until the time came to prove himself to this new world. But as he turned around to crawl back into his seat, an abrupt disturbance from within the cockpit forced him aback. An alarm system had flushed the entire interior with a burning red hue, the intensity of which forced him wide awake. And this was no common occurrence, as the frantic pilot made disturbingly apparent. Reaching for the intercom again, the pilot yelled at the height of his voice, seemingly calling out to any channel his cries could reach.

"Aerial Transport X Sixty-Four to the ASAS! Aerial Transport X Sixty-Four to FOG Central! Aerial Transport X Sixty-Four to any nearby cruiser! Please respond!" With no response given, the pilot dropped the intercom and looked at his co-pilot. "Shit, the comms are offline."

"It's probably FOG Central's doing," the relatively calm co-pilot remarked before viewing a panel around the controls. "Look at this... This looks like—"

"This is a first-class global warning to every deployed aerial cruiser located within Prime District," a voice sounded throughout the entire transport. "Massive DEAS surge on radar within FOG HQ, Research Center. I repeat, massive DEAS surge on radar within FOG HQ, Research Center! All deployed aerial units perform Emergency Landing Sequence B and await further orders on land."

"What's going on over there!?" Argen exclaimed as he slammed his fist into the window, attempting to draw attention. DEAS—although he knew little of what it meant, he had already made the connection soon after he first heard of it, and in his new predicament, that was all he needed to know. Again, he was to witness the birth of a creature with power beyond what his own people understood, and again he would be powerless to stop it. How strange it was, he thought to himself, how he was more concerned with confronting this new threat rather than typifying a helpless coward, but he would stare down that beast with the hatred that only now flared within him, and he would do so even if it meant dying a bloody death and casting away his dreams for the future. Never before had he come so definitively to a decision—he knew what he had to do, for his own sake, for the sake of his friends, and for the sake of the colony in its entirety.

"Massive DEAS surge in Golem?" the pilot questioned, both he and his co-pilot ignoring Argen. "Is this seriously happening right now?"

"Emergency Landing Sequence B, now!" the co-pilot spat at his panicked partner.

The pilot hastily returned to his seat but hesitated with the controls. "FOG HQ, Research Center—it's happening over there, right? You thinking what I'm thinking?"

The co-pilot rubbed his chin. "If I recall, there was a suspicious—"

But he would not finish his sentence with the sudden uprising of a stream of black energy, outlined with a white radiance, from underneath the ground to the left of an isolated building yonder. The black stream sundered all clouds above it and cast aside the rain. It demolished all aerial presences in its influence, automatons and piloted vehicles alike. To his own surprise, Argen was also affected as his strength abandoned him, and he collapsed to the ground. The burning sensation throughout his body and his blurring vision indicated that his own power had once again turned on him, yet before he could lose consciousness, his body blazed with an insanity-inducing pain as the transport erupted into a ball of fire and ceased to exist. Smothered in undying flames even the rain would not douse, he tumbled downward with the aura of a meteor, destined to die before reaching the ground. He shut his faltering eyes to the sight of his scorched body with only his abandoned life at home in mind; this would surely be his final reminiscence.

Come to me. The soft voice echoed within Argen's dreams as though it were masked within them, only becoming clearer with each fleeting vision of a familiar locale. With what little time he had left, he subconsciously traversed from place to place within his own memory, searching for an answer—a source of the voice. Why it mattered to him, he could not say. As his memories grew blearier each time he revisited them, the voice continually faded off into a distance he could not reach. The final echo signalled the end of his dreams and a spiralling plummet into nothingness.

Come to me. And yet, there it was again, clearer than ever before, as if right beside him, and his visions returned in its wake, flashing before him faster than he could vet them. Why, he asked himself, could he not simply be left alone to die? And immediately afterwards, he questioned his own belief that he was to die. How could he be fated to perish with such a whisper binding him to life?

Then he came to a realisation—he had survived for this very moment. He had been left alone by that entity within the castle for a purpose only he could fulfil, and the purpose had been sealed, up until now, within the very crate his companions were tasked with delivering to Golem, and now it was calling out to him. It may very well have been the intention of his homeland to do away with Golem all along, and yet here he was, fighting to save it. With a vigorous cry, he returned his soul to his body, and the horrors before him became clear once more; now he would render the very flames meant to end him as helpless as he once was. Guided by instinct, he calmly righted himself towards the sky and outstretched his arms. As though he had grasped the might of the black mist pillar in the far distance, the clouds parted above him, and the sunlight shone upon his body, mending his flesh until his strength returned in full. The flames harmoniously enshrouded the surface of his flesh and tattered robe, taking the shape of a gleaming aura. Suspended in the air as though time itself were repelled, he directed himself towards the black pillar and conjured a phantasmal, three-point crest hovering inches from his back, to the sides of which spanned a pair of silvery wings, their auras biting at the winds.

No longer kept at bay by Argen's influence, the clouds stood anew between him and the sun, the rain falling upon his resurrected form doing little more than evaporating before his aura. Even with his power fully realised, he did not feel pain. Perhaps it was his fear of the unknown all along that pained him with each attempt to awaken this sleeping power of his. He closed his eyes yet again as visions of his final moments within the dark castle flashed before him. Back then, he did not have a say in whom was to make the final move, nor when it was to be made—he had been left at the mercy of that powerful being. And in the end, it had been that being which made the final move on him, throwing him off the castle and slaughtering his remaining companions as though he were unworthy of death alongside them. But now would be different, for he, too, had power—now he would be the arbiter to decide when and how to end his foe, and he had already decided it would end with a passionate glare into the eyes of the beast and sway of his own hand to sunder it to non-existence.

"This time, I will be the one to make the final call," Argen solemnly mumbled to himself before opening his eyes and soaring high into the air—into the darkness once more.

Chapter XXIV: Empyrean Wings

To the grounded spectators who could only await their fates following the uncertain finale, the glistening streak following the ball of light in the air was perhaps like an augur of a historical scene in the making. To the stream of darkness in the distance, that same light rushing to where it stood perhaps seemed more like an ill omen. But for the ball of light himself, he was Argen as he had always been. Although he had become a child stronger than he had ever been before, Argen would be his only name no matter how the citizens of Golem regarded him upon the end of the turmoil, for replacing that name, and every memory along its back would be to disregard the growth that had led up to this defining moment—the ascension to the peak of his own existence. He would accept his failings and move on no matter what.

He lifted his head to the sky as the black stream devastated its surroundings with growing intensity. Glowing wisps of darkness darted from the swirling stream and pierced away at surrounding buildings until they collapsed in blazes. And as if prepared to confront Argen directly, the stream tore a greater gap in the sky to call upon what appeared to be a black winged entity descending from above. Argen could not make out its shape from the distance between it and himself, but that distance would close shortly enough at the rate he and it rushed to intercept one another.

Time was short—if he were to protect the colony he had grown to cherish, Argen knew he had little time to reach whatever lay within the stream before an inevitable genocide took place, perhaps less time than he needed with his own efforts alone. With this in mind, he lowered his altitude just above most of the holographic billboards hanging from nearby commercial buildings and looked below at the chaotic streets as he approached the winged beast. Smoke lingered from the scrap of abandoned aerial vehicles and automatons in the way of a massive line of citizens fleeing the opposite direction, but the block was otherwise pristine, untouched by the fury of the black stream. Several automatons, mostly humanoid in shape, stationed themselves around building entrances, lacking the human instinct to flee from danger.

He could only imagine the confusion and panic as the people sought refuge from something so unknown to them. He squinted his eyes and suspended himself in the air to observe a party of specially clothed men and women approaching the crowd from an intersection. The suits these officers wore differed from that he had seen from Fortitude officers or the FOG operatives. Knowing he was to blame for the calamity, as the entirety of Golem's military was certainly aware by now, he knew better than to approach them directly, but at least he was not fighting alone.

As Argen observed the group of officers attempting to herd the civilians to safety, a wide shadow loomed ahead in the shape of an unfamiliar creature. Argen looked forward only to find himself staring metres from the wicked yellow eyes of the beast he had awaited. And before he could question how it had managed to reach him so quickly, the black beast opened its maw, a beak like that of a bird, in an attempt to consume him whole. He had only enough time to elevate high enough above the creature's maw to slide down its gleaming beak and land between its eyes, granting him an opportunity to jump forward from the top of its head behind its pointed ears as soon it swept upward in an attempt to throw him off. In the process, he had set the creature's head aflame with his aura.

Argen took one final glance at the streets below him with his back turned away from the beast as it let out a scream echoing that of a human infant behind him. Some of the soldiers had stopped to observe the chaos above, and while it was likely they considered Argen a threat as well, they had their own tasks to abide and rejoined their allies without a word. Turning around allowed Argen to finally observe the beast in full, excluding its inflamed face. It was a massive avian, its feathery wings spanning twice the length of its torso and a long neck a little over half that length. From its beak to the talons of its tall legs, the beast was swathed in black, the colour of its flesh differing little from its plumes.

It was the first time Argen had harmed any creature, and watching his feral enemy writhe in agony left him somewhat ambivalent, unable to deal a finishing blow. He rested his arms, standing and observing, believing his flames would consume the beast with no further action.

With a screeching roar, the beast expelled a pulse from its body, dispersing the flames and launching Argen backwards as windows shattered from nearby buildings. By the time Argen regained his balance, he was staring into the eyes of the beast again, its canine face unscathed and crumpled in fury. When the beast opened its beak in his direction and promptly regurgitated a thick rope of glossy black hairs, he stood too overwhelmed in awe to respond as the hairs swallowed and entangled his body, leaving him in silence and pitch-black darkness as though it had carried him to another world.

Eventually, even the repugnant, deathly odour was sealed away from his numbing body, but Argen knew that he had not yet died; indeed, he had felt this sensation before.

It was a dream, or so he thought, as a new world unfolded before his eyes—a world with a scene he was bitterly familiar with. Below his lofty, wingless body lay a dark corridor paved with beige stone, upon which stood seven individuals with their faces cloaked beneath hooded black robes, their circle highlighted by the radiant light of a white wisp hanging above. Only three of these individuals could be easily distinguished beyond their disguises—a woman with straight brown hair, an old man with a rough grey beard, and none other than a shade of

Argen himself. It was a scene drawn from his very own past as if meant to taunt him—yet this time, he was to play the role of a spectator, truly incapable of changing anyone's fate.

When the old man, Argen's late mentor, placed the wisp in his care and set him on his way as before, the Argen of the present remained alongside his mentor as he would have had he known of the outcome. He had been granted freedom he did not have before, and this would be his one chance to unravel the truth of what occurred that day.

When the light of the wisp following the Argen of the past vanished within the depths of the corridor, Argen's former mentor stood in the darkness, unaware of the light emanating from the present Argen standing directly in front of him. Only the sudden gasp escaping the old man's lips alerted Argen of a threat approaching from behind, one that had already run the old man through in the centre of his chest with a sleek black sword without Argen's notice, its influence burning away his mentor's robe until not a scrap of clothing adorned him. Argen lurched backward, landing on his backside, to find that the sword had pierced deeply enough through his mentor's body to end up with its tip phasing through his own forehead, flooding him with a familiar chilling sensation even as it left no wound. A veiny, pale, and disembodied arm reached out from seemingly out of nowhere to clench the back of the kneeling old man's neck before he could fall on top of his pupil.

Argen, frozen in shock rather than fear like before, gazed upon his mentor's sorrowful eyes until they rotted out from their sockets, falling through Argen's intangible body. The old man's already chiselled body deteriorated until his entire skeletal figure and some of his internal organs could be plainly viewed behind his thin and translucent layer of skin and muscle. With such feeble tissue supporting his shrivelled skeleton, the old man's body simply fell apart as his black-tinted abdominal organs slid onto the ground, and his liquefied cranial contents flowed out from his eye sockets, leaving a steaming heap of rotting human remains nestled beneath Argen which the maggots on the ground promptly infested. With a twitch of its fingers, the disembodied arm snapped apart what remained of the old man's spine and allowed his skull to shatter against the ground as a pile of ash. Absorbing the putrid stench of the otherwise illusory gore into his nostrils left Argen to roll over on his knees and gag violently.

By the time Argen regained enough of his composure to look up, the formerly disembodied arm had already joined the body of the same horrific entity that threw him off the castle before, but its face could be clearly seen this time. Staring up underneath the hood of its robe, Argen could finally see the entity's void eye sockets from which faint black smoke emanated, yet he could swear the entity was staring upon him. Having claimed his—or its—first victim, the entity turned around and began walking through the corridor at a seemingly frantic pace, with Argen shadowing it at a distance, only drawing closer once the entity began mumbling to itself.

"His valour is true," the entity spoke in a low tone. "That he may know the calling of the scourge which ails me, may mine ire be sown unto the bodies of his advocates. May he himself be preserved for the coming of the promised day, that he may live to grant her a soul anew. May this be the final act of King Daunger, that the meaning of Acantelieth may be at last understood. Art thou to speaketh not his dissent, having at last seen the truth with his own eyes?"

Argen stopped and looked away, believing he would find some sort of visitant to whom the entity—King Daunger, as he now understood—was speaking, only to find little more than the darkness of the corridor staring back at him. Argen's heart pounded in his chest as the truth became clear before he turned around to notice the king facing him with his arms folded. Argen overcame his fear and braced himself for a confrontation, but before he could even twitch a muscle instinctively, a pool of black liquid pouring from underneath Daunger's robes in every direction had already passed Argen's feet, overflowing around him and smothering his entire body in the shape of a spire.

Behind the translucent layer of otherworldly fluid, Argen could barely spot Daunger turning away and fading into the distance. Suffocated and enfeebled by Daunger's liquid, he could only prostrate his predicament before his body went numb, and he sat upon the edge of consciousness once more.

Before he could drift into unconsciousness, the liquid spire collapsed into the pool below him, leaving a floating sphere of residue smothering his head and denying him a breath. Freed from the spire that kept him in place, he fell forward without buckling his knees, colliding with the ground face-first. The weighty impact reduced the liquid veil to a fetid puddle against his cheek; the otherwise dry ground and feral winds whispering in his ear reawakened him with the knowledge that he was not where he had originally fallen. Laying before his eyes was the height of the castle where he was thrown back into the real world, that scene again taking its course. The Argen of the present lay helplessly at the feet of two of his companions to watch whilst King Daunger dangled Argen's past self over the edge of the castle with one hand clasped around his robe. With what little strength he had left, the Argen of the present planted his hands on the ground and attempted to rise, managing only to suspend his head from the ground. With his remaining companions standing close enough to touch, he reached for the ankle of the closest one—only to have his own intangibility thwart him. All he could do was await the inevitable and curse the powerlessness Daunger had so easily inspired in him. Even the power he had gained bathing in the chaotic flames felt far away, like a distant memory he could never relive.

Powerless, helpless, feeble... Argen vehemently cursed himself with those words until he no longer cared; in fact, berating his own weaknesses became almost comforting. It was the same as he had felt once he had been thrown back into the real world with the knowledge that only he remained, and from this, Argen realised that this dream world of his past had taken nothing from his own spirit. He was a child who had already lost everything and gained more than he ever had before, more than any threat could possibly reap from him—cherished friends, a land to protect, and above all else, a strength his old stagnant self would never have discovered. He was similar and yet different from the boy in Daunger's grasp and not bound to the quietus he had already experienced. And even if he was thrown back into a scene of his past against his own will, it was still his dream—his dream alone, and it would rightfully fall under his own mandate. To that end, he would become that helpless child dangling over the castle one final time, making amends for his mistakes and offering his companions a proper farewell; all he needed was to close his eyes and remember how he felt that moment in Daunger's clutches.

And so it was; in abiding by his own theory, however unlikely it was to be true, Argen opened his eyes to find himself right where he would be forced to continue on alone, having become one with his past self. Like before, he was terrified and enfeebled as Daunger paralysed his body and scrambled his thoughts, but now he knew of his dormant power, and to summon it, he would simply remember how he felt boiling in flames with a purpose unfulfilled. With that, Argen's body and robe ignited in flames of ivory, and his wings quietly erupted from his spectral crest, beckoned by a push from his indomitable will. With a glare in Daunger's direction, Argen called upon his flames to spread from the arm of the fallen king. When Daunger's lower arm fell apart as cinders, Argen remained in place, floating over the castle's edge to observe his enemy in his final moments. After nothing remained of his arm, Daunger's body was coated whole in Argen's flames, burning away his robes and unmasking his dilapidated head, the only part of his body which remained unaffected. It was as though Argen were staring at a statue; only the sight of the frail and tangled black hairs falling from Daunger's head from the heat of his searing flesh presented any sign of the pain he must have felt.

"Well met," was all the fallen king managed in his calm, deep voice before the ravenous flames submerged his head and reduced his being to flowing cinders dancing before the height of the castle.

With no master to claim the castle as their own, the thick black fog surrounding the premises faded away until the setting sun of the clear twilight sky could beam its light from directly behind Argen. Argen briefly looked below the bland beige castle to the sight of a boundless grassland dense with impressive oak trees. As his remaining two companions gaped with the knowledge that they had suddenly been spared an unsightly demise by none other than the child they had sworn to protect, Argen gaped at them as he struggled to put into words a final farewell. And although he yearned to turn back the clock and save his mother from a death he had not been offered a chance to prevent, he had found other people to look after—the time had come to move on.

"Forgive me," he murmured to his former companions, the meaning of those words he would leave for them to decide. With that, the entire world before him dissolved as flecks of light, leaving him suspended in an abyss of darkness until a curtain of light fell upon him, forcing his eyes shut from its effulgence. He awoke to the booming noises of heavy explosions and violent impacts upon surrounding buildings; he was in the midst of an all-out aerial war that had begun during his absence. Golem's defenders, piloting round, gigantic battle aircraft mounted with various weaponry, combated winged beasts similar to the one Argen opposed, but smaller in size. Shrapnel, ruined aircraft and mutilated human corpses littered the streets and damaged buildings. The downpour continued, and the void in the sky wrought by the black pillar long became a gateway for horrific creatures; countless black beasts now infested the skies, and many more could be seen continuously emerging from beyond the clouds. If he did not reach the black pillar soon, Argen thought, Golem's inhabitants would have no hope of survival.

Few aircraft persisted in Argen's presence other than a particularly large, seemingly unarmed aircraft hovering above the buildings and directly behind the beast Argen had successfully repelled, dwarfing it in size. How long the aircraft had been floating there observing the beast as it nearly swallowed him, he did not know, but the sight of the giant creature, screaming as raging white flames threatened to consume its head, and the long burnt strands of black hair falling from the sky made it clear that a subconscious outburst of his own power had saved him yet again. All that remained was to cull the beast before it could pray upon anything else and slay it he would no matter how much it screeched in pain, for never again would he hesitate against any foe.

With the aircraft above the two remaining stationary even as the beast yet drew breath, Argen knew the final blow would be his responsibility alone. He folded his arms in anticipation for the foe he knew was far from finished. And as he had predicted, the beast repelled his flames with the same mighty roar as before, glaring at him all the more menacingly. To his surprise, the beast furiously uttered his name, its screeching tone rattling his ears. With little a grace period, the beast was upon him yet again, savagely biting at him and screaming his name each time it missed and briefly set its own face aflame as a result of his aura. He remained calm and alert, weaving through the air out of harm's way each and every time the beast lunged at him. Eventually, the beast fell back, screaming his name one final time before lunging at him more forcefully than ever, throwing itself directly behind him once he had deviated from its path with little effort. Taking full advantage of his enemy's folly, he directed his hand to the beast and let loose a torrent of shimmering dust erupting from his own aura, engulfing the beast in the shape of a sphere and muffling its cries. Once the dust had faded, so too had the avian monstrosity—a quiet passing for Argen's second victim.

With little time to celebrate a victory, Argen ignored the curious aircraft and continued on his way to the pillar. He had only made a slight ascent before a massive ammunition shattered upon his back, the heavy impact dispersing the light comprising one of his wings and dimming the flames of the other before sending him spiralling out of control. The sudden assault left him gasping for air, a stinging pain spreading throughout his body from the centre of his back as he struggled to regain his balance with his remaining wing. Unable to stay aloft, he folded it around his body before tumbling as he collided with the damp pavement of the battered streets below, coming to a stop on his belly with his cheek against the ground. He lay still momentarily, staring solemnly at the aircraft responsible for downing him. Having anticipated Golem's taking arms against him did not make the revelation any less disheartening, but now was no time to ponder his bleak future. He carefully stood upright once his pain subsided, surprised to find that he had sustained not a single wound.

Before Argen could carry out his intent to disable the aircraft without harming its pilots and continue his journey to the black pillar, the presumed leader of the assault vessel spoke from within. "In honour of Golem's sanctity and the mandate of the Haizers, surrender yourself at once and brave the consequences of insubordination!"

Argen huffed at the leader's pretentiousness, but at least his message was concise enough to understand. "I refuse," came his rigid response to that message. "It was my own ignorance that caused all of this, and I intend to set things right before all else; that is my responsibility." No matter how reasonably he tried to justify his actions, Argen thought, the righteous leader would no doubt draw his own conclusion.

"Fair enough," the leader responded, his dry tone suggesting he had anticipated Argen's resistance and perhaps even desired it. "All right, men, hit him with everything we got!"

"Cease fire!" shouted a gruff, amplified voice from a farther distance away; the bulky aircraft obscured Argen's view of its source, but no matter where it had come from, the voice was vaguely familiar.

"That's funny," the leader of the giant aircraft responded after a moment of silence, "I don't remember Fortitude dictators having any command over RICOR-related operations."

"You RICOR donkeys'll look for any excuse to spill blood,

huh?" the voice behind the giant aircraft spat. "Must get real boring looking for trouble inside Golem's walls, I'll bet."

"Look, 'sir,' I'm just following orders. That 'boy' just absorbed some kind of power from an EL-H, and now he's headed for FOG Central!"

"Well, thank you very much for proving my point, dipshit. Our orders are to keep the outbreak contained in Prime District; wouldn't be much of a point defending the walls of a ruined colony, obviously. Me? As far as I'm concerned, that kid is my responsibility and probably our only weapon against that barrier over there. No way in hell I'm letting you dumbasses interfere even if FOG itself don't agree with me."

"This is no time to be fighting amongst ourselves!"

"Agreed, so how about you assholes agree to stay the fuck out of my way?"

"Sir, incoming transmission," another familiar voice said from behind the giant aircraft, prompting another moment of silence from both parties.

"Huwerd?" Argen instinctively murmured the name of the man whom the gruff voice reminded him of. Confident he had somehow earned the trust of the hardened veteran, he remained still in the midst of the confusion to assuage any doubts of his good intentions.

"Well, well," Huwerd said, "looks like FOG Central's had a change of heart. Must be gettin' rough over there."

"Who gives two damns anyway?" the leader of the giant aircraft growled. "I'll be back to settle things by myself after he dies." With that, the giant aircraft ascended higher into the air with the aid of equally massive jets beneath it, nearly throwing Argen off-balance from their sheer power.

As the giant aircraft moved in the opposite direction of the black pillar, Argen smiled at the sight of the smaller, similarly designed aircraft hidden behind it, and with that new allies to fight alongside.

"Huwerd!" he shouted at the height of his lungs.

Huwerd chuckled. "Long time no see, kid. Glad to see you

still got some life left in you, at least."

"But how did you find me? What are you doing here?" Argen's questions, though trivial in nature, would give all the answers he needed to prove to himself the reality of what was too good to be true for all he understood.

"Trying to help you out, obviously. Can't say for sure if you had nothing to do with orchestrating this mess, but hell, Golem can't get much more screwed than it already is without a miracle, and you seem to know what you're doing, so I'm going to fight with you even if it's my last job as a commander in Fortitude."

"Wesley here," the younger man who had spoken earlier greeted. "FOG Central has already briefed us on the situation. The contents of the package you delivered was responsible for the outbreak if you weren't already made aware. Because the DEAS outbreak coincided with your transfer to Prime District and incidentally destroyed all aerial transportation, with you being the only survivor, you have to understand if we're a little wary of your actions even if we've agreed to assist you. With that said, those eldritch hearts do seem hostile even to you. On another note, how much do you know about our government?"

"I was only told that FOG is responsible for Golem's protection, if that counts," Argen answered.

"Correct," Wesley replied. "From up here, we can see the DEAS barrier slowly moving towards FOG Central HQ. RICOR, FOG's subsidiary that normally handles internal DEAS outbreaks like this one, is collaborating with several other organisations over there to keep the barrier at bay. It's apparent that whoever sent or created this eldritch heart, or EL-H, is very familiar with our colony and is possibly targeting the Haizers specifically— the supreme rulers of our colony. With that said, eldritch hearts cannot be controlled nor reasoned with, so it's more likely that this EL-H was born from a hatred of our colony and is intelligent enough to act on its own. Its objective? Bring Golem to ruin."

"What?" Argen uttered. Not only had he forgotten much of his discussion with Huwerd, but now he was unsure if he ever knew what an eldritch heart was.

Wesley sighed audibly enough for the speaker to register it. "Well, none of that matters much anyway. All you need to know is that we need your help to breach that barrier and destroy whatever is hidden within it before time runs out. Can you do that, Argen?"

"I intend to try," Argen courageously responded as he took a step forward.

"Hope you've still got the strength to fly on your own," Huwerd said, "because we're going to need your power to keep us nice and safe if we're to journey together."

"Then say no more." Argen closed his eyes, focusing his might to restore the light and flame of his remaining wing as a new wing spouted forth to replace the one he had lost. Both wings radiated brighter than before. With his form restored, he sprang into the air alongside Huwerd's aircraft to a clear view of the black pillar approaching the isolated building he assumed was its target all along. "I'm ready."

"Stay behind us, Argen," Wesley said before the aircraft accelerated at a speed Argen easily matched from behind.

"So," another voice began, which Argen recognised as Creed's, "I get the sense of pride and duty and all—and not to disrespect it—but why have a couple of junior officers like me and Wesley tag along with you?"

"You two newbies were the only ones present when Argen first showed up," Huwerd retorted. "You were the only ones I could trust to join me after FOG Central gave the order to mobilise our forces."

"Hostiles incoming," Wesley stoically pointed out as a formation of five winged, black beasts that had freshly arrived from the sky altered their course to intercept the aircraft.

"Try to shake 'em off!" Huwerd roared. "We don't have time for this shit!"

"That will not be necessary," Argen replied as he elevated himself to clearly see the impending threat. And with a flick of his wrist, he called upon pillars of glowing dust from the sky to devour the foes before him. One by one, his power beamed upon each of them, disintegrating them to nothingness before they could cry out in pain. The dust persisted atop the steel of the aircraft as it bypassed the area unharmed by the spectacle.

"Way to go, kid!" Huwerd praised. "Looks like nothin' can stop us now!"

And for at least as long as Argen and his new companions had yet to reach the pillar, those words spoke truth. No matter how many hoards of aerial beasts dove in their direction, Argen banished every last one with unwavering ease. Some were incinerated by the dust; others were set aflame with little more than a glance; and a vast number of them diverted in other directions, having realised the folly of opposing Argen and the aircraft he passionately warded from any harm.

Once he flew beyond the urban area and near the vicinity of the source, Argen could finally see just how virulent a towering miasma it was. A massive trail of destruction and ruin—toppled structures and scattered bodies—exemplified the terror of the darkness gradually nearing a black mansion at a distance in front of the FOG Central building and in the centre of an expansive courtyard. There, Golem's final resistance struggled against the pillar's continuous emission of energy along with several-metre tall, eyeless four-legged black hounds leaping from out of its boundaries, devouring man and machine alike that stood in their way. Golem's forces were no less morbid, comprised not only of battle machines and RICOR officers wielding bulky silver firearms and pure white melee weapons such as knives and javelins but of seemingly feral humans clothed in tatters and metallic face masks, running along all fours, biting and clawing at their opposition while roaring savagely. A fewer number of Golem's allies were individuals in hooded coats unleashing power similar to that of the entities Golem knew as eldritch hearts; Argen vaguely recalled spotting such people in the crowd that awaited him the first time he stepped beyond Golem's outer walls, along with those who accompanied the woman known as Yona.

Argen gracefully landed a single foot on the damp grass of the courtyard with Huwerd's aircraft hovering above him, firing upon all abominations within reach. Two hounds were upon him before he could plant his other foot. An expulsion of will in the form of a repelling force sent them flying and crashing into the ground. The beasts tussled helplessly to stand upright before passing away as puffs of black essence.

"Just do something about the DEAS," Wesley said immediately once the beasts had fallen. "Don't waste time on anything else."

"I know." He could finally witness the full girth of the monstrosity his people had delivered to Golem, and he would savour every last detail as it centred upon his gaze—he would settle for no margin of error in his efforts to eradicate it. He would spend wisely the little time he had remaining before the shambling pillar demolished the mansion and whoever remained near or within it.

"Can you breach it?" Wesley asked.

Deep in thought, Argen could barely make out Wesley's voice and ignored him. The pillar—the towering cluster of DEAS, as Argen would now consider it—stretched so wide as to block his view of all else in its direction from the several dozen metres he stood away from it. Nothing surmounted its reach, not even the stars of the twilight sky above the clouds. He could see the winged beasts emerging from the darkness, soaring in different directions to waylay battle aircraft and squander any hope of aerial reinforcement. Even were he to breach the barrier of DEAS, he thought, he would be the only one who could challenge the entity within it; he had come to understand at least that much of the power that took away his friends and family. It was a surreal realisation that grasped at his heart and did not let go from then on. He could hear little else than the pounding at his chest along with the ravages of the pillar, real as it was philosophical to his entire existence.

"Keeper Lapine at four o'clock!" Shouted one of the RICOR soldiers, continually firing upon the DEAS cluster, snapping

Argen out of his trance. To his right, in front of the mansion, was an impressive fountain, a statue of a long-haired woman in a dress pouring into its stone basin from the chalice she held overhead. Strolling beside it was a regally dressed man a number of RICOR soldiers rallied around to fight off the beasts approaching his path, and holding his hand was a small boy with the hood of his gold-hemmed white robe lowered to reveal his silky silver hair. Upon glancing at such a strange child, Argen could not help but be reminded of himself.

"Who are those two?" Creed asked as Argen motioned to meet the strangers. "They look pretty important."

"That kid over there is Wrellord Haizer," Huwerd answered, "the next in line to become Prime Dictator of Golem, I hear. Keeper Lapine is most likely his keeper, obviously."

"Well, what the hell is he doing out there, then?" Creed asked.

"If you're talking about Wrellord, don't worry; that kid isn't as vulnerable as he looks," Huwerd replied in a low tone.

And so there Argen was, standing face-to-face with a couple of Golem's most important figures. All the questions he had reserved for such a moment would have to be set aside until peace was reclaimed. The expression on the keeper's unblemished face as his hazel eyes met Argen's told the tale of a man who had perhaps known of Argen for some time and had similar inquiries of his origins. With a mutual nod, the two agreed to set differences aside and focus on the task at hand. The stone-faced boy in Lapine's hand, Wrellord, shifted his gaze aloofly, undaunted by the sight of man against beast and even the DEAS cluster drawing ever closer. Only a single prolonged stare in Argen's direction testified that he was well aware of the importance of the fellow child before him.

"I trust you know what you are doing, Fortitude Sect. Dictator Bates?" Lapine asked, a question he enunciated slowly and deeply. He looked up at Huwerd's aircraft, prompting Argen to do the same.

"It's not my most thought-out idea," Huwerd replied, "but

hell, what do we have to lose now?"

"All right," Lapine hastily answered, furrowing his eyebrows and stroking his moustache at the sight of the dwindling resistance and the impending DEAS cluster, "we're going to follow Fortitude's lead for once."

"If I may ask, Keeper Lapine," Wesley began, "why have you not evacuated the Haizers from the mansion?"

Lapine chuckled. "Evacuation, you say? Golem's leaders needn't cower before an enemy sent to destroy us. It is a challenge we gladly welcome if to show friend and foe alike that it is we who are forged to be as rigid as the land we preside over, and we will not hide behind any shield of the people we oversee. That is what the Prime Dictator has decided." Lapine patted Argen's shoulder. "If you, Argen, would please aid our effort this once, we can surely restore Golem to the paradise she was made to be. Rest assured, she has survived many a strife like this one."

Argen nodded and set his sights on the DEAS cluster. "Keep everything else away while I do what needs to be done."

"Good luck out there, kid," Huwerd softly said. "We'll probably have a celebration waiting for you when you get back."

"Thank you for everything you've done for me, Huwerd," Argen solemnly expressed without turning away from the DEAS cluster.

"You heard the young man!" Lapine shouted to the remaining RICOR soldiers. "To arms and keep watch of the young Haizer!"

Side by side, Argen and Lapine rushed for the cluster like predators upon their prey. Lapine's otherworldly strength and disembodied force easily brushed aside any creature that drew near, and once Argen had made it as far as he needed, he dashed ahead of Lapine and leapt into the air with an arm glowing brighter than his own eyes could bear. Screaming at the height of his lungs, he threw himself into the cluster and thrust his arm forward at an invisible obstruction. With the sinister caress of the cluster's foundation blocking him from the world and threatening harm upon him he could only imagine, Argen struggled with his greatest might to force his palm through, his aura flaring outward like a dying flame with each push he made. By the time he had finally thrust his palm deeper into the void and out of his own view, it felt as if it had practically been severed from his body; the cluster had its limits just as he did, and to exploit that, he would simply need to realise his own limitations. With the help of another burning light, he threw his other arm into the unseen obstruction, drawing his face closer into the void until he had barely any room to breathe.

"I will not die by your command!" That rallying cry was all it took to bring out his last breath of power, embellishing his entire body with radiance growing brighter until his eyes could not tolerate it. A silence followed a comforting sense of weightlessness, nothing like the ominous clutches that held him in place just a moment prior—he had become a free spirit in both body and mind, aware of his limitations yet content he had discovered them, as he plummeted into a new world in which he opened his eyes only after he was sure his task was not yet fulfilled. Somewhere out there, below the calm, cloudy skies of dawn and upon the barren tundra, the entity that had called out to him watched and waited. Argen, bereft of his wings and much of his power, landed crudely into a small puddle among many dotted upon the land, the filthy water prickling against his exposed flesh. Left unharmed by the fall yet strangely numb under his forearm, he pulled his entire arm out of the puddle to find that the DEAS had wiped away his hand without so much as a drop of blood—where flesh had once been, only marred bone remained. He could not hope to replace his hand with what little strength he had left, but if that was his fate, so be it. Knowing he was strong could carry him on to the end even knowing he was a wounded mortal.

He stepped away from the puddle with a placid breath and looked yonder, out towards the cesspool of black fluid not several yards ahead. In the middle of it all was an unclothed woman, her skin snow white in contrast to the pool of black in which she bathed. Her long white hair draped over her exposed back, its length encompassing the entire pool in an indiscernible bundle of knots. And although she faced another direction, Argen could see she was parturient, a woman who had perhaps been corrupted just before her child could see the light of day. Noticing the presence of an onlooker, the womanly creature, possessing a face surprisingly ripe, looked at Argen with unblinking dark eyes and a stiff expression. Argen did the same—not out of hatred, but pity.

Change was of little significance to Argen in his homeland, a world which would never change its course and betray the child he once hoped he could remain forever. Not so would the ever-changing world of Golem accept a lost child if he remained so stagnant, yet his trials had taken him above and beyond the expectations of the colony. Having feared change for so long in his life, at no point until then did he ever know he would become one with the power to change the world by his own design. At a slow, deliberate pace, he limped in the direction of his lasting foe, the first steps taken towards a world he would create but perhaps never see.

Chapter XXV: A Vow Transcending Lifetimes

I must kill you all. Forgive me, whispered a voice in Argen's mind.

He took a step forward.

And by your hand will I accept my punishment, not only for the sins of my fellow Elegies but as well for the sins I will soon commit myself, the same voice continued.

He took another step forward, planting his foot gracefully as his pain subsided—the magic of his will.

We have awaited this moment for so very long—awaited the day you would return to us to fulfil your destiny as designed by your creator, a different voice spoke with an elderly crackle.

He took yet another step forward, his wings springing forth from the crest of light re-emerging from his back.

Are you one who chooses or one who is chosen? questioned the final voice, one too gruff to have belonged to a human.

Argen lifted his foot to take a step but paused. He had sampled the memories of a woman in flux—the profound thoughts of one driven by confusion and longing. What did she seek? Had she found that something in her final moments?

Or was he the answer she had long awaited—the sleeper and the awakened, entwined by a hand beyond his tiny comprehension? Never would he know until he outstretched his hand and grasped what she held dear even in death —that unborn monstrosity, bound in her womb since time immemorial.

If he was chosen to end her madness, then he would

choose himself to save her humanity.

Two locks that appeared to be comprised of silvery hair lashed towards either side of Argen; he had caught but a glimpse of the woman furrowing her eyebrows at him before the sentient hairs erupted from the puddle beside her, a mere finger's length away from doing as they pleased with his neck before he could react.

And just as he could react, a pulse in the wind sent him flying aback. He flipped himself upright and landed gracefully on his feet, safe from the locks of hair that were repelled and scattered about by the same impact before disintegrating as particles from their tips to their roots.

He reacted with a blank stare. If that was no doing of his own will, then whose?

"I was always looking forward to our reunion, my dear old friend," he heard a woman comment behind him. "And you're expecting! Who's that lucky man?"

He dared to look over his shoulder, but his view was obscured by the visor of a black cap worn over the lowered head of a woman with golden blonde hair and yellow skin not unlike his own. With a flowing garb swathed in black, she presented herself as a mourner dressed for a funeral.

"Did that sound overly jovial?" she asked with a smirk before lifting her cap, revealing her heterochromatic eyes—red in the right and orange in the left. "My mistake; I must be getting nervous."

"Who—" Argen cut his words short as a murmur flew past the ear directed to the pond. The woman had lifted her arms from the muck, holding within them what appeared to be a glaive extending over two metres in length, its mere aura pulling the warmth from Argen's flesh as though he had foretold being beheaded ceremoniously by its engraved blade. Yet as he dreamed of the blade's deathly embrace, a warm pair of arms embraced him in its stead, whisking him off his feet and away at a pace his eyes could not withstand. When his back felt the soil of the ground and the tickle of the grass, he opened his eyes to find himself surrounded in a field engulfed by gentle flames as black as night.

"Best we don't find out what those two are capable of doing with Halia's greatest treasure just yet," the woman cautioned, standing in front of Argen with a smirk on her face —before a subsequent frown revealed to him the gravity of their predicament. "Can you still fight?"

Argen lifted the skeleton of his hand, the flames dancing about its fingers before fading away without harm. "All I can do is fight back either way."

The woman crouched and closed her hands together to embrace Argen's own. From bone to muscle and muscle to flesh, he felt the sensations returning under the sphere of radiant dust enshrouding her touch. He pulled his arm away in awe the instant she was finished. "You're just like me!"

"A Halian, yes." The woman stood and turned to face the direction they had escaped from. "Who am I? Why are we both on fire yet perfectly healthy? I can't imagine how many questions must be flying around in your little head, but, unfortunately, we are short on time, and so I must be brief. One thousand years ago, I was a rogue Halian known as Cygna Aestatis. As a proud citizen of Golem, I am but a humble barmaid who goes by the name Floe Kaster. Yet, as the oracle of the Scion Finis, you could say..." She extended her arms to either side of her, alluding to the entirety of the paradoxical realm they trespassed. "... *this* is my obligation."

"Are you the one who sent me here? How could you have lived for so—"

"Halia betrayed my trust long ago. I don't know what business your homeland has to send my old friend over to the colony I founded, but I can sense the power of the Annulling Clasp within you. And if you possess the Annulling Clasp, the rarest of Halian treasures that has appeared only twice before your time, then I would assume they await the advent of Architect Acantelieth, just as we predicted." Floe extended her hand to Argen. "It's only a Halian's instinct to be terrified of the sight of the Regalia of Halia, but we must be steadfast."

Argen took Floe's hand and pulled himself to his feet.

"You and I, Argen, are dealing with an eldritch heart the likes of which we scarcely encounter in Golem. Even two powerful Halians together would be unfathomably lucky to survive such a threat, let alone stop it. Fortunately, we have our own eldritch heart."

"Do you—" Argen paused to closely inspect the flames nibbling at their legs—the verve of sentience present but not traceable.

"If you, a mere Halian, would stand brave before even the Architect, then I will serve as your blade 'till lost is your body to the soil, Cygna."

And there it was, a voice accompanying a profound presence a short distance behind him as the flames were swept from beneath his feet, coalescing in that direction. By the time Argen turned around, the flames had solidified into the shape of a large hound not unlike those ravaging Prime District, with the exception of its eyes—one gold and the other blue as though night and day stood alongside one another.

Floe gripped Argen's shoulder as he stepped back in trepidation. "Rest assured, 'Regbith' here is our ally—at least for as long as he exists in flux between one persona and another. Actually, I think both Aerbith and Regnal would have desired this outcome regardless." She frowned, exhaled deeply, and looked into Argen's eyes. "You and I can't run away from this. If we do, even when Golem wins this war, Watcher's suffering will never come to an end. Either we liberate her soul, or she liberates our bodies from our souls."

Argen nodded. "Do you mind if I ask one question?"

Floe opened her mouth to speak, but her gaze deviated forward, where a recess had formed in the soil. From the soup of black liquid and bundled white hair, Watcher lifted her face; the Regalia of Halia followed, exhumed by her hands and pointed towards the clouds.

"What is she to you?" Argen asked while readying himself,

glancing at Regbith as it moved to guard his side.

Sentimentality painted Floe's face amicably as though she were an old woman reminiscing of better days. "Those were lonely days, my childhood. I was taken from Halia when I was an infant; I was among people who could not understand my eccentricities. When I met Watcher, not only did I learn that I was not alone in this world but that I could use my power to make this world a better place. In her human life, she was a companion; as a cursed nobody with no memory of that life, she was my best friend; and now, as an undying monster who can't so much as beg for a release, she is the only friend I will ever need." She tilted her head at Regbith with a smile. "Well, she along with the 'doggo' next to you, that is. I'm no less powerless to change her fate than I was all those years ago. Am I selfish for using you to accomplish what I was never meant to?"

With both arms raised above her head, Watcher pointed the Regalia of Halia towards the trio. A stream of hair darted towards Argen's face—this time from the knob at the base of the regalia's blade.

Regbith took a rising swipe with one of its three long tails, scattering the hairs and pinning them in the grass with the all-consuming flames of the One Ideal.

Argen extended his palm in Watcher's direction, and a ray of Halian dust crashed into her den from above the clouds, detaching the hairs from her regalia and gradually burning her flesh as she writhed in hurt.

As Regbith charged to deliver the killing blow, Watcher vanished from the recess as abruptly as a flash. The Regalia of Halia plunged into Regbith's torso, cast from a far distance to the side, and the tainted amalgam fell to the ground, trapped in place by the regalia's influence.

Argen traced the trajectory of the regalia and vaguely spotted Watcher far away in yet another recess. "I need to get closer," he whispered before summoning his wings and approaching Watcher quickly but cautiously.

One hundred metres before he reached the recess.

Watcher obstructed Argen's view with several ropes of hair fast approaching him. But Argen, reacting well from such a great distance, blasted them into disarray with a pulse of Halian dust before dodging to the side and continuing onward with a clear view of his destination.

Seventy metres before he reached the recess. Watcher's response was similar to before—two ropes of hair travelling tightly together before dividing in an attempt to engulf Argen from both sides. He extended both palms and cancelled her attack with two concurrent pulses of Halian dust before leaping over the writhing hairs and suspending himself in the air.

But before he could rain down upon Watcher from above, his neck and wrists felt the tight embrace of three finer ropes of hair that had concealed themselves behind the first two. A single pulse scattered them all by their root, but such was not Argen's doing.

Sixty-five metres before he reached the recess. He mentally thanked Floe before flying ever forward, his palm extended to reach for Watcher's face. Watcher's hair extended from the black water yet again to reach for Argen's body in the shape of a single rope—only for her efforts to go wasted as Argen gathered his dwindling strength and repelled her yet again before rolling further to the side and continuing on his way.

Fifteen metres before he reached the recess. He stopped and let out a yelp; two strands of hair had embraced and burrowed into both of his ankles from behind before coming to a sudden stop; they had been severed from Watcher's control by an unseen assailant.

He flew several metres beyond the recess, a mere arm's length away from coming to contact with Watcher's forehead. Alas, his palm met with the tepid liquid beneath her and his entire body followed shortly thereafter; Watcher was gone like a flash. "This is impossible," he muttered to himself.

"Good job, you two!" Floe shouted while approaching the recess alongside Regbith, the Regalia of Halia in her grasp.

Argen, frantic and frustrated, ignored Floe and whipped

his head back and forth in search of Watcher. "Where is she?"

Floe pointed in Watcher's direction with the regalia while offering her free hand to Argen. He took her hand and struggled his way out of the recess, wiping his face with his sleeve as he did so. "Don't despair. We've already gathered all we need to win."

Argen directed his gaze yonder where Watcher and another recess awaited him. Doubt began to loom over his conscience until he squinted his eyes and took a closer look. Watcher's silver hair, once glistening and bountiful, had become worn and sat scarcely atop her head.

Floe dangled the regalia over her shoulder. "Yes, it seems poor Watcher has already expended much of her strength to keep our friends in the real world busy. You and I both only have so much resistance to give, but time is more against her than it is us." She tipped her cap over her eyes. "Best our next strike settles this. She deserves to die with her beauty intact."

"You can still be so carefree at a time like this?" Argen huffed, grimacing. "I can barely stand on my feet right now!"

"Oh, my heart is racing with worry and woe, I assure you." Floe pounded the regalia's pommel into the ground and beheld its blade as it pointed to the sky. "Now, how do you suspect an eldritch heart would come to wield the Regalia of Halia, a treasure which is only born in a woman selected by fate to govern Halia as the shepherd of all Haliankind? Halia has never known another shepherd since the passing of Caevin, the last shepherd, has it not?"

Argen shook his head. "Halia was never the same since she disappeared—at least that was what my old mentor told me."

"I was there to witness Caevin's death by the hand of an eldritch heart known as Enlenea, but the fact that her regalia was since never inherited by a living Halian suggests that she never truly died. Enlenea was the catalyst to give birth to Acantelieth, and Caevin chose to give her life to impart the regalia to her. The fact that I am able to wield the regalia against its owner proves that Caevin's will lives on; she, too, has long awaited the advent of Acantelieth."

The lost shepherd the Halians would petition to salvage their homeland—such was the only description Argen could recall of the entity said to possess enough power to make any dream a reality. Having witnessed his every realm of comprehension shattered time and again since the moment he set off on his journey, the reality of Acantelieth itself was no surprise to him. But such a reality did leave him to wonder: What conflict could such a profound existence herald upon the future of all living beings? Was he right to heed the words of Floe, a woman who had come long before his era, yet he himself knew so little about?

"But Acantelieth is of little concern to you, is it not?" Argen asked, recalling Floe's obsession with Watcher's humanity.

Floe extended her arm, bringing the regalia within Argen's reach. "That's correct. The Halians may worship Acantelieth as a fine means to an end, but for me, Acantelieth is just another monster. If that monster ends up on the deep end of the lake, then I'll look forward to drowning it in its place—with Watcher by my side." She tilted the regalia towards Argen. "Take it, Argen. Feel the power of Halia's rightful ruler swell within you. Let's concern ourselves with the now and see to our own selfish desires together."

As Argen wrapped his own hand around the regalia's shaft above Floe's, he felt the weapon's authoritarian influence surging throughout his body as if he had been crowned ruler of all creation. Once Floe gently pulled her hand away, he struggled against the weight in his grasp—until it suddenly began to feel like an extension of his arm. He held it lengthwise in front of him, wasting no opportunity to inspect it closely. It was a glaive the likes of which he had never seen before, weighted with a golden crescent-shaped guard and two large silver knobs comprising the pommel and the outermost guard serving as the base of the engraved blade. Dark wood comprised the centre of the handle—beyond the crescent guard above and a golden pincer below, the handle was gilded as it extended towards the blade and pommel. Ordinarily, any mortal would be challenged to hold such a weapon, let alone swing it with grace.

Argen glanced under the regalia's handle as a glossy hoof landed beside him. His gaze climbed the figure's fluttering flesh until he discovered Regbith's eyes worn upon the head of a large stallion moulded in flames. "Ride my back, bearer of the regalia. I will glide in place of your wounded legs."

"To Watcher, then," Argen replied with a nod of confidence, stroking the oddly silky texture of Regbith's flesh before climbing atop his saddle. Regbith's flame lingered around his left forearm, and once he extended it to his side, he felt two handles press against him as the flames coalesced into a weightless ebony heater shield.

Floe had observed it all like a doting parent. "The Regalia of Halia, said to possess a sharpness capable of rending the boundary between dream and reality, and the gluttonous flames of the One Ideal, said to devour anything its wielder desires. An unwavering blade and an immovable shield to match—wield that power you hold in your arms with pride and cast aside your doubt forever."

Argen nodded, tears swelling under his eyes. "I guess I do still have something I need to prove to myself."

A shield held out towards his destination, a blade extending beyond the length of his steed, and wings spread out and booming with gleaming radiance—Argen had obtained power far transcending the Halian rulers of old, and Regnal was eager to guide it to the throat of their mutual foe; Aerbith would guide it to the heart of his anguished master. And gallop they did towards the final resting place of Watcher's corruption. Whilst Argen glared with decisive intent, he could see the lack of resolve in Watcher's movements as the distance between them grew ever narrower. Did they desire the same outcome all along?

He continued onward, uncontested by her.

Closer...

And closer...

And there it was, another tendril of silvery tresses, comprised of what remained embedded in Watcher's scalp. They drew so far as to impact the front of Argen's shield—before their entire length was instantly engulfed in a gluttonous flame that then retreated back into the shield without a trace of their meal remaining, sparing only Watcher's bare scalp.

A cackle and a giggle—Argen's mind was inundated with a woman's joyous titters.

A tear trailed down his cheek. Had he reached the precipice of anger or happiness? Were his emotions even his own?

He found himself staring down upon Watcher—Regbith leaped over the recess.

He readied the regalia as he came directly below Watcher, her tearful expression opposing his own.

He lowered the regalia under Regbith's feet and swung upwards, the blade glimmering like a star.

And before Regbith landed on the opposite end of the recess, he looked behind him.

There, Watcher's body collapsed, void of life, her head cleft in twain.

A victory or merely a beginning?

The scenery became an incomprehensible swill; he climbed down Regbith's back before the abyss overtook his sight thereafter.

And so, too, did it begin to claim his awareness.

A linger of bliss—before the plunge.

Chapter XXVI: To Another Life

Argen lifted his head from the hardwood surface, opening his eyes to find himself staring down at a busy work desk. He noticed a pen clasped in his hand and laid it beside a paper scrawled with a jumble of thoughts and descriptions, highlighted under the morning rays piercing the tall window to his right.

He wiped the cold sweat from his brow, cleansing his memories of a dream's unrelenting musk. He had woken up early in the morning to eat breakfast before commuting to his day job in a local nursing home, where he spent a better part of his shift lamenting his woes with the elderly while tending to their physical needs. When evening came, he returned home, cooked dinner, and spent the night in his room accompanied by his pen and paper as he envisioned a fantastical world in writing, just as he had done countless other times in his young adult life. As midnight passed, he drifted off to sleep, and his dream whisked him off to a different fantasy, one in which he, a child not unlike his real self over a decade ago, was taken from his homeland and sent off to an isolated nation booming with technology. The journey had cost him the lives of his dearest people, and he wallowed in depression before persevering under a new purpose—to live on in the names of those who had sacrificed themselves on his behalf and to watch over those who had taken their place in his heart. He had gone as far as to suffer a gruelling battle on behalf of the latter, even if doing so meant acting against the wishes of the former; he would be forever stranded in a foreign land if such was the price to pay for amending his mistakes as a helpless pawn with no direction other than that presented to him by those who had sought to use his power for their own ends.

He had done well to take power into his own hands and see to his own selfish desires, proving his strength and wielding it to salvage a woman who once had power but refused to wield it—powerful and influential, yet no less helpless than he was.

Alas, the dream came to an end before he could witness her future as a consequence of his actions. For everything he had done to save her humanity, he could not even recall her name.

A cackle and a giggle—the faint sound of a woman's joyous titters roused Argen's ears, yet he could not trace its source. Carried by instinct, he rose from his seat before leaving his room and walking quietly but hurriedly down the stairs to his living room. Instruments and antiques littered the ground and cabinets; a grand piano stood to the far corner of the left, partially obscured by a woman seated in front of it. All he could see was the back of her white dress and greenish-blonde hair, long enough to reach a pin's length short of touching the carpet beneath her feet.

"Good morning, Watcher." Immediately after he questioned her presence, he uttered her name casually as if he had known her for years.

No response.

Before opening his front door in search of the voice's source, Argen leaned forward, attempting to catch a glimpse of the woman's face, hidden behind her dangling tresses as it was. Only after he turned the doorknob in surrender did the woman startle him by abruptly shifting her head in his direction. Try as he did, he could not look into her eyes—indeed, he could not find her eyes at all. Her skin was like a sheet of white, pressed and unstained, yet vacant without a face to peer from within its snuggle.

Even so, she looked oddly familiar.

"I'm off work today, so I'll be back inside shortly," Argen said with a smile, his confusion gone with the wind of altruism. As he opened his door, the fair morning breeze greeted him, sweeping across the autumn grass of his front yard. The sound of planting his foot upon the hardwood of his porch came along with the familiar sound of a woman's cackling. To his right, a rocking chair swayed back and forth; the black dress and long crimson hair of the young woman riding upon it flowed with the wind, and an infant lay quietly on her lap, its faded green hair coiling around her entire waist.

As fitting as she was amid the scenery, Argen had never seen anyone like her before. Who was she? What was her name?

The woman, unmoved by Argen's presence, doted on her child with a loving smile, laughing as though she had claimed a great victory. "How long have I been dreaming?" she breathed. "How long have I looked forward to this moment? It's all here; it's all in my arms, all I've ever wanted for so damned long." She looked at Argen while maintaining her smile, tilting her head with a hint of curiosity in her emerald eyes. "You don't look all that gloomy yourself."

"Who are you?" Argen asked, having waited long enough for his fragmented memory to answer the question for him.

"Who am I? Funny; just a short while ago, I would have strained to answer that question myself." She coaxed a giggle from her infant with a light finger stroking its nose. "But damned if I start speaking in riddles like a tainted. I called myself Watcher back in my rebellious days; if you pestered a human to dig up something about me worth saying, they'd probably sing praises about a 'Blade of Humanity.' My goal? I just wanted to resist the inevitable. I wanted to make my enemies bleed as much as I could until I died. And in my final moments, I *did* wish I could have just died."

Argen froze in shock before mustering the courage to respond to the dream that was coming to life before his eyes. "Your name is Watcher? If you're Watcher, then—"

Watcher briefly lifted her palm in front of Argen's face. "The whole world once revolved around me; I want to retch just thinking about discussing that life again." She exhaled a sigh. "So, why don't we have a chat about you?"

Argen timidly pointed to himself. "Me? What about me?"

Watcher looked yonder. "It's so peaceful here, isn't it? Nice breeze, too. It seems to me like you have everything you've ever wanted—a cosy place where you can write and study at your leisure, free from society and its incessant chaos. I caught a good glimpse of your own misfortunes moments before you cut my head open. You remind me of an old friend of mine."

"You can't be real," Argen breathed, squinting his eyes as he took a step closer. "That was in a dream; I woke up in my room and—"

Watcher lifted her palm again, her smile drooping into a frown. "Argen, what we are experiencing right now is nothing more than a fleeting fantasy conjured by Caevin's Regalia of Halia—our thoughts and fantasies, linked as one. I couldn't tell you how we ended up here since everything went dark for me in an instant. Dying tends to do that to you." She snuggled her infant under her face. "Well, that's not to say that death is ever permanent for a tainted like me. That's probably why you were brought to me—this world in front of us is some kind of deliberation towards the future of me and this child I hold in my arms."

Suddenly, Argen could no longer question why he had reacted to the woman by the piano with little intrigue; he could no longer question why he shared a home with two women and an infant he shared no relation to.

And no longer could he question why his dream had ended so abruptly when he had slept restfully and without disturbance. As far as his thoughts were concerned, he went from an aspiring author with few worries to a child with heavy burdens and questions unending, no different than he was before he was imprisoned in this fantasy. And now, he had all the time he required to gain the many answers he sought. "That child is still human, is it not?"

"Not completely, no. In fact, at present, this child barely has a mind to call its own. Were it allowed to mature as things are, this world would change forever, and I don't think for the better. This child represents a pact between myself and a certain someone a long, long time ago. I wasn't completely sure about trusting her; she took her sweet time accomplishing what she had died for, but this is it. It's all here, right in my arms—this child is my humanity, soon to be freed from the whims of the Scourge."

"And the other Halians sent me along with you, knowing that you would awaken in Golem and that I would save you," Argen added, recalling Floe's words. "Floe told me that I have something called the 'Annulling Clasp.' What is it? How do I use it?"

Watcher smirked. "I normally wouldn't have known anything about that. Thankfully for you, that damned Caevin is a part of me now; I know all she knew." She stood up from her rocking chair, cradling her infant in her arms. "The Annulling Clasp is in your dominant hand. With it, you can halt—possibly even reserve—the effects of the Scourge on living people. And should you be its wielder, the Scourge will never reach you no matter how much you expose yourself to it. This infant contains a power that is, and always will be, unstable. It may not ever have the fortune of living like any regular human, but with the Annulling Clasp alongside it, we can at least prevent it—her—from becoming a monster."

Argen glanced twice into his right palm, struggling to grasp the weight of responsibility dormant within. "To save that infant's life, I would need to stand by it for the rest of my own."

"Use the Annulling Clasp and save the world; don't use it and watch the world go to ruin. The choice is obvious, isn't it? So obvious, in fact, that using the Annulling Clasp is not what I'm going to ask of you."

"What?"

"The previous wielder of the Annulling Clasp died around the same time as Caevin. I killed him just as he had used it to trap me in stasis, but he was unable to reverse my transformation. With that, it probably became clear to the Halians that even the Annulling Clasp could only contain my power temporarily."

"So that's why you awoke in Golem."

"That's it. The Halians, knowing that I would eventually break free, had only one option: To wait and pray that the next wielder of the Annulling Clasp would come just before my resurrection. Merely twelve years before I was reborn, you were here for me. The Halians would probably call that a miracle; I call it dumb luck."

"But why send you to Golem? Why endanger the lives of so many innocent people?"

Watcher chuckled, bitterness evident in her expression. "I don't have a clue. The Halians had always been a surreptitious, narrow-minded, and self-serving lot towards me. They never cared about the innocents in Proto-Golem, a nation that may or may not still exist today; they don't seem to care about the innocents in New Golem either. They stalked me to use my power for their own purposes, knowing well they could have possibly saved me instead; they sought to kill Cygna because her mother went rogue and escaped to Proto-Golem. I hated, hated, hated, Halians; I thought all of them were the same before I met Cygna. She turned out to be one of the most kind-hearted people I've ever known."

"You mean Floe?"

"Yup. Little Cyggy's grown so much that I can hardly recognise her, but I can't wait for a proper reunion." Her expression grew sombre as she looked at the slumbering infant. "Unfortunately, Cygna, I've decided that you're going to have to wait for me a little longer."

"Wait, what are you talking about?"

"Caevin's memories weren't the only ones I inherited that day. A long time ago, there was a particular tainted. What distinguished her from her kin was that she was born from a painting depicting a woman without a face. She wandered and wandered without a mind to call her own until she stumbled upon the Garden of Mercy and touched a lyaphend —a black flower said to be the physical manifestation of the hopes of previous wielders of Halia's four treasures. It's probably nonsense, but touching it was when she became sentient. She wasn't after human blood like most other tainted; in fact, she sympathised with us. You know a thing or two about her yourself, don't you? It seemed like you mistook her for me back there."

"What?"

Watcher bobbed her head towards the front door as it opened to reveal the faceless woman who sat by the piano. She looked ever forward as she stepped between Watcher and Argen with her bare feet, transfixed by the sky but seemingly unaware of the presence of either of them.

"Her name was Enlenea, the Painted Woman," Watcher continued. "She was my enemy, but she sacrificed her sentience to preserve my humanity. If I leave her as she is, she will be reborn as a tainted with no memory of what made her special. With my humanity returned to me, she will wander aimlessly again and eternally with no way out—this was the outcome she promised to me." She looked at the slumbering infant. "She was too pure to deserve that kind of fate. What I hold in my arms is the only means I can give to preserve *her* humanity. And I want her to live as a human from now on because I will grant her wish to suffer this world as I have."

Watcher held the infant with one arm and gently uncoiled its hair from her waist before approaching Enlenea and holding it out towards her. Enlenea held her forearms out without a hint of awareness and wrapped them lightly around the infant's small body as though a distant plea had possessed her.

Argen flinched; Enlenea shifted her weight erratically like a sleeper pulled abruptly from a nightmare until she noticed the infant sleeping in her grasp, then Argen gazing with shock, and finally Watcher smiling upon her with joy.

"Wakey, wakey, sleepy-head," Watcher greeted, placing her hands on her hips. "Can't thank you if your head's empty as a drum, can I?"

"You!" Enlenea uttered, her voice echoing without a clear source.

"No, you," Watcher chuckled. "That's right—I've decided that I'm just too good to accept your help. I may live on as a tainted, but damned if I won't regain my humanity my own way."

Enlenea lowered her head towards the infant in a moment of silence. "Watcher... why condemn yourself to the oblivion of insanity without an end foreseeable after what strides I took to give back the humanity we stole from you? Do you yet loathe me so?"

"Oh, yes, I hate you; I hate you so much that I'm giving you what you envied so that I can hearken your wailing when I come back whole. But, honestly? I see this more as an act of requited kindness. Enjoy."

Argen watched the road ahead as a yellow vehicle, with a livery bearing the word 'taxi' adorning its hood, came to a stop beside the paved path to his porch.

"Ladies and gentlemen, it's time—time for me to head back to the forefront, that is." She placed her hands on Enlenea's shoulders. "You and I are likely to forget this moment, and if I'm really messed up, I'll end up chasing after you to take back what I had willingly given to you. You'd better be ready for me if that time comes."

Enlenea shook her head. "This power, Watcher—how will I stay this madness if I am to become human?"

Argen took Watcher's stare as an invitation to speak in her stead. "The both of you were asleep for a thousand years. You were stopped thanks to someone who wielded the Annulling Clasp, a power we Halians have—something I now have. With it, you can possibly restrain your power as much as necessary to prevent yourself from running rampant again."

She would restrain her power—not he, but she. Argen displayed his confidence before Enlenea with a faint smile before shifting his eyes to Watcher, hoping she had grasped the meaning of his words—what he had designed for his own future.

Relieved he was when she shot a resolute glare his way,

a gesture of gratitude and her only farewell for him. Hopefully, she would do him a service and prolong her stay enough for him to decide for whom he had endured up to this point.

Watcher lowered her hands. "You hear that, Enlenea? I imagine living as a human will be damn scary for you, but at least you'll get to stay sane enough to realise that you're damn scared."

The following bout of silence between the two was all Argen needed to make up his mind. Cravenness had dwelt in his every action long before he set off from his homeland. His colleagues, who joined him in an uprising resistance against the rebels terrorising Halia, laughed and jeered as he struggled with the most basic of tasks as a fledgling warrior. When he was selected for a special task to deliver a package to a foreign land, surely it was more of a mistake than a privilege, but he would prove himself to everyone nonetheless.

It was neither a mistake nor a privilege, but Argen had no time to ponder why he was there while his friends and family were slaughtered before his eyes, and he was left to stand powerless and watch. From the moment his wings carried him from the cusp of death, he sought to save himself, protect his new homeland, and, most importantly, prove his mettle and unwavering resolve. He resembled Floe in that while his actions would benefit others, they were born from his own selfish desires nonetheless.

And he had proven himself quite well. His decision—this final decision—was not one of self-interest but pure empathy. He had his trials to thank for that empathy.

"Thank you, Watcher," Enlenea finally said.

Watcher patted Enlenea's shoulder. "If someday the new you ends up remembering this conversation, be sure to say hi to Cygna for me." She turned away, lifted the skirt of her dress above her ankles, and proceeded to daintily leave for the taxi. "Also, give Aerbith a good pat for me. He's still a good doggo. And Regnal? I'll be ready to kick him extra hard in the nethers next time as a token of gratitude."

"Wait, Watcher!" Enlenea shouted, stopping herself from chasing after her. "What truly is your name?"

Watcher paused, looking over her shoulder with a smirk. "Our memories are linked, remember? It'll probably come to mind if you ruminate on it long enough. If not, there's always next time, right?" She continued on her way, waving her hand over her head. "Keep that monster at bay, Argen! You know which one I'm talking about, don't you?"

Argen stood beside Enlenea as the taxi, with Watcher in tow, drove off behind the scenery. "You'll remember her name when you see her in person."

Enlenea rested her hand on her temple. "But perhaps not for the fiend she will doubtless become as consequence of her arrogance."

Argen grunted as the sky gradually adopted an unnatural reddish hue. He extended his right hand to Enlenea. "Let's go."

As Enlenea bound his hand with hers, soft yet cold to the touch as it was, his eyes attentively followed the collapse of his fantasy—and the advent of his final nightmare. His neighbourhood fell beneath the horizon, leaving his house stranded on a grassy island sailing an infinite, starlit blood-red sky. As though a fog had settled in the distance, the twin moons presiding over the real world, one silver and the other gold, appeared on opposite sides of the desolate landscape.

An orb of Halian dust gathered into Argen's left palm, scattering and coalescing into an elaborate shape until the Regalia of Halia, in all of its solidity, sat in his grip, the flames of Regnal worn over its blade. He narrowed his eyes in anticipation. The time had come to stand before the greatest monster of all.

A gigantic right hand, pale as the Halian snow, shot forth from just beyond the landscape, its palm positioned beneath the golden moon as if holding it in place; the unseen creature's left hand shortly followed, clinging to the silver moon standing opposite. Finally, a dark mound arose—or so it appeared to be a mound before a foreign symbol, an arcane tattoo of sorts, presented itself in the middle of a dome of flesh as the mound continued to rise. The symbol was elevated well above Argen by the time the mound had completed its ascent, staring down at him from the forehead of a woman with eyes as lifeless as an abyss, the black roots of her hair extending and warping around her bare chest as a translucent white garb. A vertical, eight-pronged halo materialised behind her back, and within its glow spawned a glistening pair of black wings smothered gently in white flames. As her bloodshot eyes fell softly upon Argen, her mere aura tugged at his sanity, threatening to rend from within the transgressor who bore no edict to stand against the grand order embodied.

But who would Argen be to ever kneel to a dictator?

"Fie, is it my fate to be slain anew where I stand?" Enlenea whispered, clenching Argen's hand as she stepped back.

"Enlenea?" Argen said calmly, transfixed by the entity's gaze.

"Yes?" she responded with some hesitation.

"When you've grown up as a human, please watch over 'her' for me. You know whom I'm referring to, don't you?"

"Yeula? But I—!"

Argen watched Enlenea from the corner of his eye. While he could not read her emotions from her facelessness, he was keen to the fear and hesitation in her voice, for such was a weakness he once possessed. Now was her turn to awaken the fighter within her, and he would serve as the guiding hand he did not possess—an expression of empathy and a desire to impart all he had learned to his successor. No foe from before could compare in the least to the inconceivable, perhaps omnipotent, entity that stood before him, but at the challenge of facing her, he managed a confident grin.

"And you will live to give me your word—you will live to do as I humbly ask. This abomination has no fucking clue what you and I are capable of!"

Chapter XXVII: The Gift of Empathy

I had stumbled upon this land and its people by chance as I wandered the desolate beyond in search of an interesting spectacle. I clung to the shadows, concealing myself as a mere mortal cloaked by the hood of a robe long enough to drape my horns until I found myself lost amid a calamity. A tainted, whose influence I deemed vaguely familiar, appeared as a pillar of scathing blackness. I had yet to remember this sensation as the downpour of black beasts commenced upon the city, and I, so I thought, was its only saviour imaginable.

I, a saviour of mere mortals... My stomach churned at the irony, but if I was to preserve my own interests, I would gag my way through each lick of tainted blood until I reached the delicacy of enlightenment at the centre of the unknown. I pondered my actions, and the inevitable consequences to follow, for what felt like several generations before I noticed a stunt in the flow of the Scourge, the pillar halting as though time itself had confronted it. I threw myself towards the anomaly to discover a gateway to another world—the den of my quarry, reachable, so I thought, only to those who had long foregone their humanity.

Evidently, the flow of time was convoluted, for the battle had already concluded before the moment of my arrival. I had readied myself to take a stand against another tainted, only to end up with both knees buried in the tall grass as I elevated the body of a Halian boy into my forearm. Floe and Regbith stood closely together, looking upon me with anticipation as I awaited their explanation.

Read his memories, they told me with their eyes.

And read them I did. I permitted his left hand, all bone as it was without Floe's transient restoration, to rest upon my own before I plunged my spirit into the faint recess, carelessly stowing every wisp of knowledge within reach into my breast. I had only surmounted the hip of the hill that was my arduous task when I found darkness laughing at my folly. I allowed my consciousness to float back to the surface of reality. The boy had passed on before I could amass all his knowledge as my own.

"The Annulling Clasp..." I uttered from instinct, attempting to fill the lapses in my memory with my own reasoning. I waded through the mundanities of his upbringing and escaped into the deathly wasteland traversed by him and his companions. My curses to the forgotten king of the North, for if not for his interference, I may well have ascertained the territory of New Halia. I carried dismay over my shoulder as I soared to the land of Golem with Argen underfoot. I staved off the boredom of overseeing his captivity and was as excited as he to be let free into the sky above Golem's capital city.

I made it as far as to observe the slightest of Argen's battle against Watcher, but after he lifted the curtain that was the regalia's blade into her chin, I stumbled, perplexed, with the greatest lapse of all having fallen onto my lap. Something had occurred to entrap both Argen and Watcher in what I could only assume was the domain of the slumbering Architect Acantelieth. The inevitable battle to follow would be one to decide the fate of Watcher's tainted womb—whether an innocent newborn or the herald of my journey's end would emerge from within. Alas, the profound nightmare would reach a depth even my own perception could not penetrate; I could not witness the end of that battle.

Given that the newborn now slept soundly in Floe's arms, its hair surrounding her within the grass, I could only assume Acantelieth had been bested, and I was gazing upon Enlenea's human incarnation. How was such a feat even possible for a mere Halian and one tainted to accomplish?

I exhaled a sigh and concerned myself with the consequences alone. How Argen and Enlenea vanquished Acantelieth mattered little, for regardless, the Era of Enlightenment had been adjourned for another generation, and perhaps such was for the best.

I gently pulled my forearm from Argen's back and laid his body to rest, raising my bloodied hand on display for Floe and Regbith to gawk at. "What is the meaning of this?" I muttered, my attention fixed on the stab wound in Argen's chest, distinct enough to identify as having been inflicted by the regalia.

Floe's eyes dilated, the woman herself realising my question should have been an unnecessary one. She disguised her bewilderment under a faint smile. "Oh dear, you couldn't reap all of his memories before he died? Maybe I shouldn't blame you for your bloodthirsty tone, then."

I stood up. "What became of the Regalia of Halia?"

"It disappeared as soon as Argen stabbed himself with it. That's right, he stabbed himself. I don't know how cognizant he was of his own actions, but rest assured that none of it was my doing. Why would I prepare to keep New Halia's secrets from you when I hadn't even foreseen your arrival?"

Floe's eyes deviated to Argen as I bore into her mind to exhume something she had neglected to mention. The boy's youthful body was ill-suited for his own power; alas, he was fated to die soon after they awakened, with or without a sound victory. "Regardless, you may be disappointed to hear that the one you hold in your arms, which now bears the Regalia of Halia, the Annulling Clasp, and the power of Regnal and Architect Acantelieth all at once, is not Watcher."

"Enlenea, then?" Floe chuckled. "I know how well you can read minds, but I think I still knew Watcher better than you did. She wouldn't turn down the chance to become human again unless she was certain there was another way to do so. I'm sure she wanted this for Enlenea as a way of thanking her, or maybe it was simply out of the pride I've always known her to possess. I've waited a thousand years to see her again; what does it matter if I need to wait a couple of decades more?"

"Your stubbornness is acknowledged, Cygna." I turned my attention to the hound with one blue eye and one golden eye beside her. "At last, we meet again in the flesh, Regnal. Ne'er could I have expected that next we would meet it would be with kindred goals."

Regbith's golden eye shifted to resemble his blue. He spoke with the all-too-familiar voice of a wind's whistle. "Ne'er could I have expected we would draw within a stone's throw to joining arms against a common foe, but 'twas not that I shared in your desires, Vaharja."

I bobbed my head in agreement. "And what of you, Aerbith? Will you withdraw once more until guardianship is again required of you? Or is your fixation more of he who wishes to wrestle his will from Regnal's influence?"

Regbith's blue eye shifted to resemble his gold. He spoke with a booming voice, "Be damned with your meddling, overseer. My affairs I shall keep to myself."

I quickly withdrew the smirk that crept upon my face. "As ill-mouthed as ever you were, I see."

"On another note, Vaharja, I should congratulate you for having found New Golem," Floe said. "Does this mean the other Elegies are here, too?"

"Astot and Inguis are near, but Constius is as away as he was a thousand years ago. Where he has gone, I cannot say." I shifted my attention to the recess behind the duo—the resting place of Watcher's tainted form. Her half-sunken body idled harmlessly in the dew of blood and water, a severed umbilical cord resting on her swollen belly. "And we, I had neglected to mention, had best away from this world afore it collapses upon us."

"Fair point," Floe chirped before focusing towards Argen's body. "Would you kindly take him along with you? The people of Golem deserve to know what became of their hero."

"As you wish." I lifted Argen's body into my arms, careful

to not disturb his blood-soaked wound. I gently laid my influence onto his lifeless gaze, sealing it forever with his own eyelids.

Floe turned to the side. "Regbith."

Regbith condensed his form to that of a tiny hamster and climbed Floe's garb until he was atop her shoulder. He took refuge at the back of her neck, kept hidden under the drape of her long hair.

"You seem undecided as to what you will do with that child," I remarked, having delved into Floe's thoughts.

Floe smiled at the infant. "Unfortunately, attempting to raise Enlenea in Golem myself would just cause trouble for me in the long run. I'll 'lend' her to FOG until she's old enough to decide her own future."

"You will not return her to the Elegies?"

"I hope you don't take that the wrong way, but Enlenea sympathised with humanity, didn't she? I'm just granting her what she would have wanted—freedom of will alongside those who share in it. We can worry about what that will mean for Architect Acantelieth another day. For now, all I ask is that you join me in overseeing a journey all her own."

"Astot may not agree to that."

"So what if he doesn't? You've been more than capable of acting on your own whims up to this point, haven't you?"

I walked past Floe, eager to move beyond our conversation before the subject became I. "Should Astot agree with you, I will not interfere; should Astot oppose you, I will not interfere. You alone will brave the consequences of your actions, and I shall not exist as part of those consequences. Now let us make haste."

Floe lowered her head, concealing her eyes beneath the visor of her cap but not the fullness of her smile. "Thank you, Vaharja."

I briefly looked over my shoulder as a gesture of acknowledgement towards her gratitude. "To the precipice of this world we go, you two."

With that, Floe followed me along an elated stroll upon

the landscape with Regbith in tow, humming a song with the infant cosy in her arms and eager for the journey as well as the destination. With a moment of silence, she said to the infant, "The people of Golem deserve their newly arisen augur, little one. Our moment together will be fleeting yet memorable. And wherever you may go or whomever you choose to follow— however new experiences and olden memories will shape you— we will one day meet again when you become our 'Acantelieth'; that, I promise you."

Chapter XXVIII: The Dove in the Rain

Ingrive 48th Reign, Year 999 I.G.R.

"This is Caevin's Regalia of Halia," Lyaphend breathed with the sword in her grasp, staring vacantly into the sky, overwhelmed by the excess of old knowledge exhumed to the surface.

Wave gave Lyaphend a blank expression. "Pardon?" she whispered.

"Caevin. This is her sword, her regalia. I really was born here eleven years ago." She cackled at the lunacy of her origins, beads of sweat pouring from her temples. "I'm a child with the body of a woman and the mind of a relic!"

Wave wrapped her hand around Lyaphend's wrist. "Lyaphend, I understand the gravitas of what you must have experienced, but I require your focus—focus on the present. Look into my eyes and start from the beginning."

Lyaphend exhaled deeply before reawakening to the familiar sights of the present—the rooftop of the King's Tower, the drizzle of the cloudy night sky, and the illuminated city of Prime District overlooked by the building's precipice. Then, she looked into Wave's eyes as ordered, sympathetic to her obliviousness, and recounted the life of Enlenea with intimate detail. As she remembered the pact between her and Watcher, her eyes began to burn with sorrowful tears.

Wave lifted her palm to silence Lyaphend, gently pulling Caevin's sword away from her grasp. "You have said more than enough," she softly declared. "Collect yourself, and we shall continue."

With a handkerchief tucked away in her pocket, Lyaphend gently patted around her eyes. "For so long, everything has been out of my control."

"And here I stand, offering you a chance to finally gain a semblance of control."

"What do you want from me?"

Wave leaned over the railing, looking over the city. "It regards your old friends, the Elegies—or, shall I say, one in particular. We Haizers are the last of King Daunger's lineage; through his trickery with Constius, we possess a portion of the Elegy's power. Daunger had hoped to expand upon his kingdom by gambling with the arcane, but Constius himself was deceitful and very vengeful."

Lyaphend nodded, tucking away her handkerchief and leaning alongside Wave, her gaze sharp with her usual composure. "I know. Constius had his power stolen by Daunger, but he got even with him twenty years later. Everything fell apart when Constius used the existence of Daunger's own power to turn his own kingdom against him. In the end, he became an eldritch heart. Constius told me—told *Enlenea*—that story."

Wave put her fingers over her lips, stifling a chuckle. "My ancestor rotted upon his just reward for his arrogance, but I suppose it is because of him that I stand before you now."

With a moment of thought, Lyaphend ventured to guess Wave's predicament. "Constius' revenge didn't stop at that, did it? He must have gone after all of Daunger's relatives. He's coming for all of you now, isn't he?"

"Constius was quick to eliminate all of Daunger's immediate relatives following the destruction of his kingdom, but what he failed to realise was that Daunger had an affair with a commoner at some point after inheriting his power, and his illegitimate daughter was exiled to a faraway settlement. His daughter would go on to bear two illegitimate children herself; those children, a boy and a girl, would pass the gift of their bloodline, diluted twice as it was, to the next generation by committing incest. And thus began the cycle that birthed my family."

Lyaphend gave Wave a quick look-over, her eyes wide in astonishment. "You look normal enough for an inbred girl."

As Wave began to shiver from the cold, the guard beside her offered her a hooded coat. "Excuse me for one moment," she blurted, throwing on the coat with haste. She cleared her throat and straightened her hair before answering, "Yes, well, my brother and I are rare exceptions. There is a reason my father never shows his actual face in public, so I am thankful I have only my grey hair to lament." She leaned slightly closer to Lyaphend. "Anyway, I suspect that Constius has close ties to the Scion Finis, a cult whose members have similar power to our own. In other words, he is hiding within Golem, biding his time until he may turn its people against my family, destroying Golem with deceit as he has done with so many nations before it."

"And you want me to eliminate him before he does," Lyaphend added.

"Correct. If what I heard from your fight with this 'Watcher' on the Great Divider is accurate, then Constius should be no match for you."

"Provided I can find him first."

"You are resourceful—a woman with ties to FOG, the Dalka Clan, and even the Scion Finis. Someone of your standing has the means of reaching places that the proper authorities cannot. If anyone can lure Constius out in the open, it is you."

"I see," Lyaphend said with half-interest, lost in her thoughts as she pondered Wave's motives. "Would you mind if I ask a personal question?"

Wave shook her head. "It would only be fair at this point."

"Your words and actions tell me that you aren't particularly close to your father. Are you requesting my help more for your family or for yourself?"

"Without my father's influence—and soon, that of my brother—I am nothing. I wish to employ you because I wish to preserve my own life and standing, nothing more, nothing less."

"You want power?"

"No, I want to claim a life I can control however I see fit. I, too, know what it is like to be led on a leash if you will excuse my crude analogy. I am sympathetic to your plight because it is one we both share."

"And arranging this privately is your way of feeling like you're in control," Lyaphend mused, her tone softening as she began to feel as though she were conversing with a close friend.

"Now you understand that power and control are not one and the same. I am the most powerful girl in the world where influence is concerned, but what I may do with that power is, at large, decided by the men of my family. You are undoubtedly the most powerful woman in the world where sheer might is concerned, but you lack the influence to use that power as you see fit. Without one and the other, we are bound to undesirables and their selfish whims, but together, we have the power and control to do as we please." She turned away from the city, resting her back against the railing while gazing at Lyaphend excitedly. "We could rule over Golem ourselves, in other words. Why not change the nation for the better rather than attempt to leave it?"

Lyaphend glanced at Wave before looking skyward solemnly, less trusting of herself than Wave. Misfortune was bound to follow the likes of her wherever she went. Her fear of losing friends far supplanted the joys of making them. "Because every time I attempt to make a difference for the better, it turns out things would have been better off without me."

"Failure justifies hesitation, but not stagnation. You can either walk forward or stand where you are and break your back under your own dead weight."

"Well, a buckled back sounds like a fine excuse to laze about in safety," Lyaphend smirked, chuckling bitterly.

Wave shook her head. "Everything we do entails risk. If you wish to linger in safety until you die, then, truly, why live your life at all?"

I'd say not to stress over your teammates too much and just worry about yourself. Those words, gifted to Lyaphend by a friend who had perished in saving her, would perhaps confront her for the remainder of her life as she continually pondered the worth of camaraderie. Watcher wished for her to suffer as a human—to succeed and gain so that she could fail and lose everything. Argen wanted her to live—to forget her tragic past and begin anew so that she could look after his friend. Progression was suffering; protection was stagnation. She would have gladly isolated herself with friends and family if stagnation did not mean abandoning Watcher to her fate.

She was a human above all else. Her transient existence would carry a world of suffering, but she would suffer it gleefully among creatures she could suffer alongside. Watcher was much too noble to deserve the fate of suffering alone and forever.

Alone… That word clung to Lyaphend's mind like a lucid dream. Where was the red-eyed blonde? Where was the feisty magic cur? Where were those two individuals who shared Lyaphend's desire to see Watcher well? Her answer partially came in the form of memories she was certain neither Argen nor Enlenea could have possessed. Aerbith merged with Watcher's old rival, Regnal; he and Cygna journeyed to Golem, where they, alongside Argen, conquered Watcher and Enlenea's warped fusion before going their separate ways—Aerbith to the East and Cygna to the South.

Lyaphend herself had already defeated the resurrected Watcher mere months ago, but FOG had dealt the final blow; without the touch of Architect Acantelieth, she would continue to reappear in Prime District every eleven years. Eleven years would be all Lyaphend needed to free Aerbith from Regnal's influence and adopt him for herself before the fated reunion, as much as the thought of seeing Regnal again caused her heart to race.

If Cygna was no less reliable than she was in the past, then Lyaphend would not need to concern herself with finding her—

she would reveal herself when the time was right.

And with a sliver of luck, Constius would reveal himself only after Lyaphend had rescued Watcher's prized pet. Regnal was a more immediate threat to both Aerbith and her, but if protecting Wave meant clashing with Regnal and Constius at the same time, then so be it.

"You have yourself a partial agreement," Lyaphend finally answered. "First, I need to pay my dues to the Dalka Clan and look for someone out in the East District. Once I've done that, we can find Constius and the Scion Finis. Sound good?"

Wave nodded. "*Very* good. My time is still in abundance, so settle whatever business you have with the terrorists, and I will return to you within five months to see if you are ready. I look forward to having you under my employ." She extended Caevin's Regalia of Halia to Lyaphend. "And as promised, this sword is yours to do with as you please."

Lyaphend looked at the sword with disinterest, seeing nothing more than a rustic relic of broken times. "Actually, I already have a similar weapon of my own. I'd rather move on from those days." She turned towards the city. "Besides, the Regalia of Halia is a ruler's symbol. If we are to rule over Golem together, wouldn't it be more fitting if we both had one?"

"I believe this is more your way of discarding your past, but I appreciate your gesture!" Wave laughed, handing the sword to her adjacent guard.

"So, what happens—" Lyaphend cut herself off as her phone began to vibrate and looked at her texts.

ARE YOU STILL ALIVE? I'M CALLING IF YOU
DON'T ANSWER ME WITHIN THIRTY MINUTES.

Lyaphend shifted her eyes to Wave. "Do you mind?"

Wave shook her head, looking on with a childishly inquisitive expression.

Lyaphend let out a groan before calling Yona. "Yes, I'm still alive. I'm standing here next to Wave; she had what I was looking for."

Yona uttered a strained breath. "And no worries if she

hears our conversation?"

"No."

"Well, at least keep my name out of your mouth while you're there. Now that you have your objective, what next?"

"She and I will be working together once I've fulfilled my contract with the Dalkas. I have business with the Scion Finis, but first, I'm going to the East District as planned. I'll explain everything later."

"Friends in high places, eh? Well, I think I've more or less finished babysitting you throughout this little excursion, as we agreed. I hope you're ready to pay it back with interest, little partner. Goodbye."

"Bye, Yona." Lyaphend paused for a moment to silently lament her stupidity before putting away her phone.

Wave pinched her chin between her fingers. "Was that... Yona Igens, by any chance?"

"Yes—I mean, no!" Lyaphend paused before deciding to answer honestly. "Um... yes?"

"Is that so?" Wave mused, lowering her gaze slightly. "I would love to have a moment to ask her what became of my mother, but perhaps I should wait until we can better trust one another."

Lyaphend took out her phone again as its ringtone began to play. "Hello?"

"Lya!" a high-pitched voice shouted loudly enough for Lyaphend to pull her ear away in pain. "Where in the fuck did you run off to? I already told you to call me before you disappear for long periods of time. Your twerps wouldn't stop texting me about you."

Lyaphend chuckled. "Did they tell you to meet them there? Sorry, Yeula."

"Just haul your ass back home ASAP, all right? And don't forget your damn contract!"

"Yes, of course," Lyaphend sighed, nodding slowly.

"Hey, is that Lyaphend?" another individual questioned in the background with the voice of a young boy. "Tell her about—"

"Oh, right, sure. Tredy wants you to teach him how to draw or... whatever."

Lyaphend envisioned Yeula rolling her eyes. "Yes, yes; I haven't forgotten," she sighed.

"Are you talking to Lyaphend?" an older individual questioned beside Yeula.

Yeula groaned. "Irosis, I'm trying to wrap this shit up! Fine, get it over with."

"Lyaphend, I'm glad to see that you're okay. I can't seem to find Argen, that stray cat you brought in earlier."

"Hello, father. Did you check around the vase in my art gallery? He seems to like the scent of lavender."

"Ah, the art gallery. It hadn't even occurred to me."

Yeula exhaled another groan. "All done? Okay, so—"

"Yo, is that Lyaphend?" the voice of another young boy interrupted.

Yeula promptly ended the call, leaving Lyaphend to simmer on her giddy thoughts of seeing her family's faces again.

"And I presume that was your family?" Wave asked.

Lyaphend pocketed her phone. "You could say that. I see them as nothing less."

"I see." Wave approached the railing, looking skyward. "Perhaps I should envy you. I would have enjoyed the experience of a loving family; alas, my brother and I were raised apart from one another, and I would become his mere stepping stone in the eyes of my father. Now here I stand atop his tallest building, alone and plotting to topple his empire. If nothing else, I inherited his apathy for family." She faced Lyaphend, expressing herself sternly. "Lyaphend Farwalth, another matter: You said you have a weapon similar to this 'ruler's sword.' Is there, by chance, a way I could have a look at it? Can you summon it here?"

Lyaphend surveyed her surroundings, unsure of the consequences of summoning her regalia atop a populated building. She had only done so twice before; on both occasions, she had little control over its volatile radiation. "You mean right now? That might be dangerous."

"No one is up here but the two of us and my four men; we have twenty-five floors of vacancy between us and the guests. Do not forget that I, too, have some control over the DEAS. I understand your hesitation, but I must witness your power with my own eyes."

"As you wish." Lyaphend backed away from the railing until she stood several metres away from Wave and her men. "Stay back."

She stuck her right arm in the air. The Regalia of Halia was a mutable weapon, shaping itself according to the spirit of its wielder. To draw it into their hand, the wielder needed to delve into their past and meditate upon their greatest desires. Caevin sought to imbue a broken world with order; Lyaphend, above all else, sought to defy her dormant madness. Casting aside her fear of the unknown, she envisioned herself diving headfirst into the blackness within the furthest reaches of her heart, extending her arm upon reaching the crux and grasping the light of defiance.

"But please *mind* the building!" Wave shouted, shielding her eyes from the torrential winds.

And with a tremor extending alongside a burning flash of light, the war against order manifested itself within Lyaphend's grasp, solid enough to sunder anything in the material realm. The length of the regalia extended well beyond even Lyaphend, its appearance unchanged from eleven years ago, but with an aura dancing about its blade like a whirlwind of snow.

"Without further ado... this is *my* ruler's blade." At odds with Lyaphend's playful tone, the regalia flickered in transparency as she winced, struggling to maintain its presence amid her fluctuating emotions. To manifest the Regalia of Halia was to submerge herself in her deepest desires; to maintain it was to remain there without drowning in them. Without a medium—an entity upon which she could unlade the flow of madness—she would eventually be unable to reemerge as herself, and everyone around her would bear the consequences.

But before she could surface to the fresh air of calm, a

quiver ran down her body from her right arm. She had grown familiar with this sensation months ago, an augur telling of an existence resonating with her own—an eldritch heart who leered from a place unseen. She traced the faint verve of malicious intent, guiding her eyes beyond the railing and above the building where a vaguely humanoid silhouette hovered in the darkness.

"Wave!" she shouted, having already determined the entity's intended target. With unnatural impetus, she sprung forward with one leg, instantly closing the distance between herself and Wave with her regalia poised as a shield against the Haizer's would-be murderer. She had swung the regalia's blade mere inches towards its intended target before the entire glaive reverberated with the impact of a swift object she had barely reacted to.

She glanced downward. A severed leg lay by her foot, its flesh writhing about its muscle and bone as though it were malleable and possessed a life of its own.

"Hostile! Open fire!" one of Wave's men shouted, beginning a round of fusillade from all four men present on the rooftop.

Lyaphend turned to face the direction the assailant had crashed into the rooftop. There, on his remaining leg, stood an unclothed, dark-haired man, his mottled flesh writhing like that of the leg she had claimed from him. She could faintly see his beady eyes looking at her from their deep sockets, his body unfazed by the unrelenting gunfire as though he were but an apparition. She had made herself known to him; she was his target now. With that, the sea of hatred within her released its grip from her lungs, satiated with the knowledge she would soon draw blood as tribute.

She drew the men's attention by raising her left hand, her words and actions subsuming her training as a weapon of FOG. "Cease fire!"

Before she could lower her arm, the assailant rushed forward again, the severed leg by her feet having somehow reattached to his body; but Lyaphend herself was no less nimble. By her will, the regalia vanished from her grasp in a flash of light. She jerked to the left, avoiding a blade salivating with black blood that had emerged from the centre of the assailant's palm. The short distance between her and the edge of the building came to mind. With the momentum from her dodge, she pivoted backwards and leaped onto the railing, balancing herself on one leg.

Then, the assailant lunged, aiming for her throat. She planted both legs, jumped out of the way, then flung herself away from the railing, rolling into a crouched position as she landed back on the rooftop with the assailant plummeting over the edge. She shifted her eyes to take in her surroundings. All four of Wave's men were alive and well, their weapons lowered in helplessness; Wave herself had crouched on all fours until the assailant disappeared under the railing, and she picked Caevin's regalia off the ground before frantically rejoining Lyaphend.

"By the forefathers, what is an eldritch heart doing here?" Wave gasped.

"Keep your guard up, Wave," Lyaphend quietly responded, her focused gaze unwavering. She took a deep breath before submerging herself into madness once more, conjuring her regalia into both hands, its blade pointed forward as a mop of glistening white hair dangled from the knob of the blade. She struggled briefly to maintain it while questions swam alongside her. From where could such an eldritch heart have spawned unseen? Was it acting on its own whims? Had someone sent it to eliminate the ruling family?

Regardless, this much was clear—she would need to settle this before FOG did it first, and without alerting the citizens below.

The assailant—or the Mottled Man, as Lyaphend would name him in her mind—emerged abruptly from below, only to be suspended in the air with his entire body bound in several ropes woven of the regalia's extending hair. Lyaphend stood up, positioned the regalia's blade perpendicular to herself, and willed its hair to contract back into the knob, pulling the Mottled Man towards her while she put her leg forward and swung.

She felt a slight resistance mid-swing, the blade having connected with some part of the Mottled Man's body, before coming to a stop with the blade above her head on the opposite side. She kept her sights on where the Mottled Man originally was as the ill omen wrought by his existence gradually retreated from her body and back into her right arm.

But the ill omen remained regardless. She looked over her shoulder to find the Mottled Man in two places—one occupied by his lower body, and the other by his torso. Dark fluid pooling beneath both pieces mingled with the rain; the Mottled Man lay on his back, watching the downpour with a dead expression befitting his bottomless eyes.

Lyaphend squinted her eyes for a closer look. With more time to think, she had enough time to vaguely recognise the man's face, dignified in spite of its gaping blemishes.

Wave rejoined Lyaphend, having retreated the instant the Mottled Man reappeared. She cautiously circumvented his body. "Did you kill it? Thank the forefathers! Are you hurt?"

"I've met him before," Lyaphend mumbled, keeping her stance.

"I beg your pardon?"

"This man..." She lowered her regalia and faced Wave. "I know him from somewhere, this man. At least, I think I do."

A dark miasma began to form close to the ground surrounding the two, lingering gently before surging into the fallen tainted's remains. The ill omen spilling into Lyaphend's body was stronger than the last.

She widened her eyes, this much having become obvious through instinct—she needed to help the others escape the rooftop.

"Everyone, jump the building!" she shouted, throwing her regalia high into the air like a javelin with its extending hair coiling around her waist. She caught Wave into her arms before the latter could protest and ran for the edge of the building.

Wave dropped Caevin's regalia and held tightly onto Lyaphend's shoulder. "What? Unhand me at—"

But Lyaphend jumped over the railing before Wave could finish. Treating her regalia's hair as a rope, she grabbed on with one hand and suspended herself against the wall of the building after descending two floors down, a balcony visible a moderate distance parallel to her. Her regalia hovered high above her, rigid like an obelisk.

Wave screamed. "Lyaphend! Drop me and you're a dead woman!"

"That would make two of us," Lyaphend smiled, wincing at Wave's tight grip while looking up. A torrent of the dark miasma surged from the rooftop, expelled by a silent eruption. Three of Wave's men dangled safely away, having taken leaps of faith after she caught them in her regalia's hair as well.

But in maintaining her regalia while loosing it from her palms, she had created a mental paradox. To manifest the Regalia of Halia was to submerge herself in her deepest desires, to maintain it was to remain there without drowning in them, and to linger in the sea of madness without a hold on the warmth of its heart was to fully expose herself to its frigid touch threatening to keep her there forever.

She could already feel herself succumbing to it; she yearned for the warmth of freshly drawn blood. She could not say if it was Caevin's discipline or Enlenea's determination that allowed her to maintain her sanity in spite of the odds, but she was grateful she could smile and jape even in the presence of an adversary. She was stronger and wiser than her demure and immature self who was left at Watcher's mercy mere months ago.

A warm draft of air pressed against her front. She lowered her head to find an elongated, weapon-mounted transport in front of her, the driver looking concernedly at Wave.

"My chauffeur!" Wave shouted, desperately reaching for the transport while her chauffeur opened the front passenger door.

"She's yours," Lyaphend said to the chauffeur before carefully handing Wave over to him. At the same time, she controlled her regalia's ropes to swing Wave's remaining men onto the nearby balcony before retracting all of them but the one around her waist, granting her some relief—some warmth —from her looming madness.

Wave swiftly closed the front passenger door and breathed a sigh of relief. "Lyaphend, if you wish to end this matter privately, we should do so in the remoteness of the North District, only a few kilometres away," she calmly said. "FOG's border control will ignore you and that fiend so long as I give them my signal."

Lyaphend nodded, looking up as she sensed a familiar presence shooting into the air from the rooftop, its shape silhouetted under the darkness of night, yet no longer resembling that of a man. She kicked the building to swing herself into the transport and climb onto its roof before unsummoning her regalia and breathing her own sigh of relief. She grabbed onto one of the transport's crossbars as an anchor. "He's mine. I can keep him occupied from up here."

"Do it properly or you and I are dead *women!*"

Lyaphend felt the transport press against her side as it ascended above the King's tower before steadily flying towards the North District. She sat up, observing an object closing the distance from behind.

She rolled up her sleeves and extended sideways her right arm, now crackling with what appeared to be purple electricity as a dark miasma emanated from its exposed marking. She needed more time; she needed to gather her strength within her sea of madness; she needed to remember how she felt against Watcher.

The shadow in the night grew larger, the distance between her and it narrowing further.

She journeyed into her subconsciousness, marvelling at the black sea's ripples of anticipation before taking the plunge once more, tugging at its heart to revive the Regalia of Halia in her right hand.

She widened her eyes as the shadow approached a distance where she could clearly make out its features. It wriggled through the air like a salamander in water, a bloody cloak that appeared to be made of human flesh, bone, and organs flowing atop its elongated back, concealing the crown of its mangled, oversized head.

Perhaps Mottled *Monster* would be a more fitting name, Lyaphend thought. A monster to be sure, yet nothing unlike that which she had already suffered and conquered.

The Mottled Monster opened a maw full of pointed teeth; Lyaphend shot several tendrils of hair from her regalia's knob. With or without Acantelieth's influence, defeating such a foe would have been a trivial affair if not for her concern over human life. She would take no chances of the creature plummeting into a crowded city upon death, and so she would exert herself only enough to keep it at bay until she reached the North District—the place of her upbringing, present only in her memory since joining FOG at a young age.

She directed one tendril into the creature's chin like an uppercut, forcing its mouth shut and knocking it off-course.

The creature recovered quickly, gaining enough speed to approach the transport from the side, intending to batter it out of the air; Lyaphend redirected another tendril into the top of its head, knocking it underneath the transport.

The creature resurfaced farther away on the other side, opening its maw with its head angled slightly away from the transport. Lyaphend, like all eldritch hearts, could perceive the emotions of others, and, to a lesser extent, their intentions. She preemptively knocked its head upwards with another tendril into its chin, diverting its aim as a dark spike the length of a man's arm darted from its throat—sending it into the clutches of another tendril positioned above the transport, which she promptly brought down into the creature's back, stabbing it with its own weapon.

The creature lurched downwards before reclaiming its

position alongside the transport. It bored into Lyaphend with its hollow eyes, a glint of nobility yet alive within them—the sole vestige of the man the creature formerly was.

"We're almost there, Farwalth!" the chauffeur announced.

Lyaphend briefly took her eyes off the Mottled Monster to glance at the scenery far below. She returned her attention to her foe only to find him beginning a slow descent into the North District, its greenery now visible beyond the tall wall separating it from the industrialised capital of Golem.

"Fuck, where's he gonna go?" the chauffeur asked, panicked.

But Lyaphend, having already read its intentions as it did hers, smiled at the circumstances. "We're all right. As far as he's concerned, this has got personal." She stood up, tracing its movements with her eldritch senses and predicting its destination before relinquishing her hold over the heart of her madness and ascending to the surface, having offered enough bloodshed to behold her palace of tranquillity. And so faded her regalia once more.

But with a victor yet to be decided, her madness hungered for resolution, and she could only linger for so much longer before it erupted of its own accord.

"I'm descending into the North!" the chauffeur announced.

Lyaphend balanced herself on the edge of the transport's roof. "Stay right where you are, sir."

"Holy fuck!"

"Lyaphend!"

But neither the chauffeur nor Wave could stop Lyaphend before she adjusted her glasses and sent herself freefalling into the North District, the brisk air pressing uncomfortably against her. The Annulling Clasp was among Halia's esteemed treasures, but Argen had only touched upon its potential inadvertently. Beyond halting the flow of the Scourge, the Annulling Clasp could negate force in its entirety upon its bearer and either rebound or scatter it. By touching either the ground itself or the leg that would land upon it at the instant of impact, she could divert all the resulting force into her surroundings, leaving her unharmed.

Or so, that was how Lyaphend suspected it would work, having tested it once before on a short fall. She chuckled. Evidently, the memories of Argen's boyish brashness had yet to wear down on her.

She extended her left hand, where the Annulling Clasp resonated, towards the approaching ground, clenching her teeth with some anxiety.

The moment of impact drew close enough that she could see the Mottled Monster staring at the crash-zone-to-be from the ground—a dirt road sparsely surrounded with trees and shrubbery. Her left arm grew almost unbearably hot as she imprinted her will onto it.

She closed her eyes and counted the final seconds before impact.

One...

Two...

Three...

Impact! Lyaphend's planted palm indented the ground surrounding her; she had scarred the land, yet her body remained intact. She flicked the tingling sensation out of her left arm before standing up with both arms folded in front of her, staring down the Mottled Monster awaiting her several yards away, pounding the ground with its tail. She stepped forward before turning away, pausing to bask in the atmosphere—the gentle cadence of rain, the nature dancing amid the breeze, and the humidity against her every breath. She was comfortably distant from the noise and fetor of the drab city and immersed in her childhood memories, as fleeting as that childhood was with how her own body rushed for maturity.

She smiled faintly, shifting her eyes to the Mottled Monster, pitying both of their circumstances. She would have given up her powers without hesitation to reclaim that childish ignorance. She yearned to be that little girl who believed the monsters would never reach her.

And she yearned to believe there was more than one monster.

"Interesting," she said, facing the Mottled Monster. "Rattled your ego up there, did I? Or is this your way of telling me you still have some humanity left in you? If you were after Wave, then coming down here shouldn't be in your best interests."

The Mottled Monster brought one front leg forward, licking its lips slowly, its expression void of emotion other than that of a predatory beast salivating at the sight of its prey.

"I know he's in there somewhere—that noble man you used to be," Lyaphend continued, lowering her arms. "Is this how he wants to die, then? So be it. It's getting late and my family is waiting for me, so I don't intend to keep you waiting. You already know that, don't you?" She extended her right arm, still crackling with wicked energy—an invitation to the closing step.

The Mottled Monster exhaled, its dark breath mingling with the air, before lunging. It engulfed Lyaphend's arm in its maw but paused, unable to clamp down on the invisible force locking it in place. The scene shifted red in Lyaphend's bloodshot eyes. To manifest her power was to submerge herself in her deepest desires, to maintain it was to remain there without drowning in them, and to linger in the sea of madness without a hold on the warmth of its heart was to fully expose herself to its frigid touch threatening to keep her there forever. But even in the case she remained above its surface and did nothing at all after having tempted it, the madness would spill and consume her of its own accord.

And there it would remain until she gave the proper tribute—the nihility of the enemy in front of her. Then she would remember her proper name: Architect Acantelieth.

"Sorry," she said softly, bringing her thumb and middle finger together, "I'm the real monster."

With the snap of its fingers, her right arm erupted with the same gluttonous black flames that once claimed Enlenea's arm, freeing it from the Mottled Monster's maw and obliterating its lower jaw in the same instant. Her Halian power flickered inches behind her back, manifesting as a pair of disembodied auburn wings, an aura in the shape of an eight-pronged halo radiating between them. The Mottled Monster reeled backwards only for its forehead to be ran through by her regalia, summoned into her left hand.

But before she could tear out her regalia's blade, her mind flung her back to the past in the body of another. She stood beside a boy with white hair, observing a strife between FOG and black four-legged beasts raiding the courtyard of a mansion. In front of her was another boy with short blond hair and a tattered black robe, his hazel eyes alight with resolve, yet flickering with curiosity. She stood stoutly amid the danger, her bewilderment overshadowed by her sense of duty.

She would give her life if necessary to protect her homeland's ruling family; she would abide her master's every order without question. She would cast aside her individuality and desires, for how else could she atone for the crime of her existence?

"You don't exist."

The scenery sailed away like the wind, leaving her alone in a dark room, meditating to the voice of her master.

"*You* do not exist; you're an extension of my will."

Indeed, she may as well have not existed as an individual. She was a slave; her life was her master's to do with whatever he pleased or dispose of when he deemed it appropriate. Her body was his weapon, a mere extension of his will.

"And my will is as such—my sister will die rightly, slain quietly by its living extension."

Lyaphend blinked, the sights and sounds of the real world returning to her in that instant. Her regalia's blade ignited with its frigid aura, and she gripped the shaft with both hands before tearing the weapon free from the Mottled Man's forehead, leaving him to disintegrate in a spectacle of flowing ash and mock snow. Her regalia, too, steadily crumbled into the wind, coinciding with the blood fading from her eyes as Acantelieth returned to slumber, her madness satiated. The elation—the moment of absolute clarity—that followed was like surfacing from a dark sea of muck and taking her first breath in a fragrant grassland, basked in the sunlight.

Beyond engraving into her soul her identity as Lyaphend Farwalth, she relished another victory against the Scourge. She was her own woman, nurtured by the fire of Watcher—her living miracle, forged at the crux of despair.

"Don't move!"

A squad of men approached Lyaphend from her flank, rifles rattling into position as one of them shouted a command. Standing motionless as ordered, Lyaphend shifted her eyes in their direction, recognising the suits of RICOR, FOG's Internal Special Affairs Division.

"Put your hands in the air and face me!" another RICOR officer demanded.

Lyaphend attempted to reposition herself only to be interrupted by the officer who shouted first. "I said, don't you fucking move!"

"Enough!" someone else shouted from behind Lyaphend. She recognised Wave's voice but dared not turn around to be sure.

"It's Wrellord's sister!" an officer shouted.

Wave stepped between Lyaphend and RICOR, her chauffeur raising an umbrella behind her. "Did 'Wrellord's sister' not warn you to ignore this? Put your arms down this instant or I will kill you all myself."

"Ms. Haizer, that's the runaway subject from Operation Nightfall."

"And I am Wave-fucking-Haizer. Leave this woman be and fall back. I will not repeat myself a second time."

"But, we—" the officer cut himself off; Lyaphend looked away and heard the squad marching away seconds thereafter, followed by the humming of several transports speeding away from above.

Wave stepped in front of Lyaphend alone, looking concernedly into her eyes. "Did you win? Are you hurt?"

Lyaphend paused with her mouth open, struggling to find the right words. "Wave... your half-brother is dead."

Wave tilted her head. "I beg your pardon?"

"I said, your half-brother is—" Lyaphend paused to breathe out whatever influence her vision still had upon her. "Fifty years ago, your father had an affair with one of his 'keepers,' and she gave birth to Theo Lapine. Gede abandoned his own son to the streets of Prime District, and he was eventually discovered and raised by the Scion Finis. Gede had a change of heart when Theo was a young adult, and he was welcomed back into the family under the condition he kept his heritage secret and served under his father as one of his keepers.

"When Wrellord was born, Theo became his keeper. He served his family with loyalty and thought of nothing more than following his duty. He was an extension of their will, and he gave up his own identity along with the only thing he ever wanted in life—to be loved and accepted by his father. He hated himself—his flesh and blood along with his history with the Scion Finis. In his eyes, he was an abomination, denied the purity of royal blood; he might as well have been a decrepit monster. And that's what he became in the end."

Wave averted her gaze as though she felt a pang of guilt. She gestured to her chauffeur, taking his umbrella and holding it over Lyaphend. "I knew about Keeper Lapine only what I learned from Wrellord; he spoke to no one else whenever I saw him, not even my father. And I absolutely did not know we were related! By the forefathers, how do *you* know this?"

Lyaphend furrowed her eyebrows, presented with a dilemma she was unprepared to face: Lie to Wave or tell the truth and risk arousing suspicion. Freedom was a privilege most took for granted, but she would not have it if it came to her at the cost of putting an innocent girl's life at risk. "Wave... I swear to you on my soul that I did not plan for any of this to happen when I met you. I'll have nothing to gain if you don't want to trust me, but at least give my words some thought."

"Of course, Farwalth." She softly clenched Lyaphend's forearm. "You most certainly saved my life, so the least I can do is hear you out."

"That monster was Lapine. Your brother did it—Wrellord changed Lapine and sent him here. He was trying to kill you, indirectly."

In contrast to the reaction Lyaphend expected, Wave grinned, a small chuckle slipping between her teeth. Was this her way of coping? "Oh, dear brother, you always were too impatient for your standing." She let go of Lyaphend's forearm, clenching her fist more tightly. "So, Wrellord considers me his rival, does he? As he should. But then, who is to be his wife? Did you glean anything regarding Mr. Gede's intentions?"

Lyaphend shook her head. "Nothing."

"As far as I know, Wrellord, Gede, my mother, and I are the only ones left with pure Haizer blood; my mother saw to that. You may possess some connection to the Haizer lineage yourself, but you are too old and powerful to submit to him. Are there perhaps more illegitimate children such as Lapine?" She handed Lyaphend the umbrella before flipping her own hair and stamping in the direction of her transport, her chauffeur in tow.

Lyaphend reached out for Wave. "Wait. Where are you going?"

"I will... make myself absent after I have prepared properly, then we will proceed with our partnership as discussed. Even the Prime Dictator must answer to FOG should he err from the laws cast in stone by our nation's very founder. If you seek justice for Lapine's death, then know that what my brother did to him is technically within those laws to permit. He signed a contract wavering his rights as a living person; a Haizer can do with their keepers whatever they please. Weaponising DEAS is also legal as long as it is used by officials against other officials.

"Lapine's mother, or Gede's young mistress, was but one of many mislead into signing that contract only to be abused under the sheets and disposed of as soon as they grew too old for his liking. If you are as sickened by my family as I now am, then join me and help me restore it for the better. Oh!" Wave hastily returned to Lyaphend and clasped her hand. "Actually, it occurred to me that RICOR has likely I.D.'d you now. My transport has a dampener in place so that all attempts by cameras to scavenge data from the chips of those inside produce nothing. You will need to come with me if you wish to return home unfollowed."

Lyaphend smiled. "Thank you, and I'm sorry. This night got a bit more hectic than both of us were expecting, didn't it?"

Wave extended the courtesy with a smile of her own. "For you, perhaps. I summoned you with only a faint idea of your intentions, and I considered the possibility that this night would be my last, whether I was to be killed by your hand or my brother's. Thank my intuition for trusting you and predicting my brother's betrayal."

As Wave offered her hand, Lyaphend hesitated for a moment before shaking it to their kinship as fellow outcasts. She lagged behind Wave while the weight of her responsibilities began to sink into her chest, and, for but a sliver of a second, she questioned her resolve.

I see you.

And that was all it took for her heart to freeze, enslaved under the grip of an all-encompassing hatred, its deep voice piercing her flesh like reams of long needles. By the time Lyaphend whipped her head around in search of a dead-eyed figure breathing into her neck, nothing was there to greet her but the rain, the bleakness having settled back into her heart as suddenly as it spiked.

For the first time, Acantelieth had spoken to her, invigorated by the power she reaped from Lapine.

"I know," Lyaphend whispered in acknowledgement, shrugging off her embodied madness with a faint smirk. "Now go back to bed."

Final Chapter: The Crow in the Sun

Ingrive 50th Reign, Year 999 I.G.R.

Ding, ding.

Lyaphend sluggishly reached for her phone and set off its early-morning alarm before gently peeling away her blanket and exposing her face to the morning rays peering by her bedside window. She brushed aside her ruffled hair and sat up to look over her recent texts.

Two days had gone by since her encounter with Wave. Yesterday was spent in harmony alongside her family—no serious errands, no suspicious contacts. In two more days, she would set off for Golem's East District, where Watcher's lost companion awaited her, not only to claim him as her own but to meet with the mysterious client responsible for revealing her existence to the Dalka Clan whilst she was hidden away in FOG, fulfilling her obligation to the clan before switching allegiances yet again.

She reached for a pen and notebook lying atop her bedside dresser. She was a busy outcast in a world that could never afford the likes of her a moment of rest; she could only abide by its flow until she saw the opportunity to err into the vast waters of liberation, her hand clasped within Wave's own. She wrote down her pending tasks in a bullet-point list:

- **Go to the East District**
- **Speak to the Dalka Clan's client as agreed**
- **Rescue and adopt Aerbith**
- **Eliminate Regnal?**

She paused after writing Regnal's name, ailed with many questions yet to be answered regarding the shapeless one's intentions. She remembered Enlenea's insight into its origins—she remembered the little girl clinging to its distorted arm. If only she knew who that was, perhaps she could save Regnal from itself with the mercy it refused Enlenea?

Regardless, Regnal was not her enemy; it was but an obstacle in the way of her sanctuary. As it was, however, she lacked both the power to vanquish Regnal and the fortitude to stand against it at all. She furrowed her eyebrows, continuing her list with some hesitation.

- **Accept Wave's proposal and leave the Dalka Clan**
- **Convince Yeula to leave the Dalka Clan**
- **Investigate the Scion Finis with Yona's help and eliminate Constius**
- **Rule Golem with Wave**
- **Bring Watcher back**
- **Do *something* about Acantelieth as soon as possible**

"Good morning, Master Lyaphend. You have a visitor on the way."

Lyaphend gave her partial attention to the intercom above her as one of the maids spoke through it. "A visitor?" she whispered, considering the possibilities. "I wasn't expecting anyone today."

"Lyaphend, it's me, Yona!" a woman shouted from behind the front door before banging her knuckles against it thrice. "You and I need to chat in person—urgently."

Lyaphend put her notebook aside and stumbled out of bed to open the door. Yona Igens stood in front of her in a buttoned-up green trench coat, glaring at her with the uncompromising sternness she had come to expect from her always. Time itself cowered before her image, leaving her face barely less sleek than that of a young adult despite her over fifty years in life. She had tied her long hair into a crude bun, suggesting the haste with which she arrived.

"Yona?" Lyaphend questioned, her jaw hanging open in disbelief. "What are you doing here?"

Yona pointed to Lyaphend's bed. "Sit down right now."

Lyaphend sheepishly followed Yona's pointed finger with her eyes before obeying her command as if her own body were moving of its own accord. She sat on the edge of her bed with a straight posture, awaiting Yona's word as she leaned against the wall with her arms folded.

Neither Yona's stern tone nor stoic expression changed as she remarked, "You look like ass. Did you just wake up?"

Lyaphend ran through her hair with her fingers, keeping it away from her face. "Do you mind explaining why you're here?"

"It's about Wave Haizer."

Lyaphend paused, searching Yona's eyes for some hint of her intentions. All she could see was that Yona was attempting to do the same to her. "We talked about it yesterday. What of it?"

Yona's gaze dulled after a moment of silence, the woman herself apparently satisfied with Lyaphend's reaction. "Well... I have good news and bad news. Which one did you want to hear first?"

Lyaphend subtly cocked her eyebrow, suspecting another test. "Whichever one you'd rather tell first."

Yona's response proceeded from a peeved utterance. "Have it your way. The good news is that Wave is alive. Word's got out she was assassinated yesterday morning in her private estate, but that's just Wrellord's cover story, and he's parading Wave's keeper's head to make it look legitimate. That means he was either intending to kill Wave or he's aware of her scheme and is trying to prevent her from consolidating power over the masses, or both. Only Wave's men are aware of what happened to her, and Wrellord is going to keep them quiet one way or another." She looked out the window. "The bad news is that she's waiting for you outside. She wants to speak to both of us."

Lyaphend jolted up. "Here? Right now?"

"That's what I just said. I'll be waiting for you outside. At least make yourself look presentable before joining me."

Biting her tongue before she could utter a witty remark regarding Yona's own rugged appearance, Lyaphend waited for Yona to leave, dressed herself in a simple gown, tied her hair in a crude ponytail, and sauntered outside into her mansion's expansive courtyard. Yona awaited her on the veranda, leaning against a spiraling pillar beside the stairs descending into a paved walkway leading to a bench and a three-tier stone water fountain, surrounded by a maze of equally towering hedges.

Lyaphend leaned to the side to closely inspect the bench past Yona, narrowing her eyes to inspect the young girl sitting upon it, her long brunette hair flowing down her raised white hoodie like a waterfall. Upon noticing Lyaphend, she put both hands against the bench and strained to lift herself before shambling towards the porch.

"Wait!" By instinct, Lyaphend rushed downstairs and caught the girl into her arms before she could collapse onto the floor. She gently lowered the girl's hood, revealing a familiar pair of alluring blue eyes behind her ruffled hair, albeit with reddish sclera from exhaustion. "Goodness. Why did you even come here?"

Yona walked up to Wave, lighting a cigarette between her fingers. "You're in safe hands now, so take it easy, Lord Haizer," she sarcastically said.

Wave glared at Yona while she spoke before shutting her eyes and clenching her teeth as Lyaphend helped her back onto the bench. "My dearest keeper lost her life, and I could do nothing to save her," she muttered. "I have lost everything and have not slept in days. On behalf of your welfare, I beg you, Yona, do not anger me."

Yona glared at Wave, unimpressed with her as far as Lyaphend could tell from her expression. "Is that a threat? I would very much like to see you act on it, little girl."

Lyaphend looked at Yona and raised a finger to her lips. "Yona, please," she murmured.

"You've always been too caring for your own good, Enlenea. It's as she said—her brother took her power away from her. Wave Haizer is dead as far as the world is concerned, and she has nothing on her to prove otherwise. Her influence is net zero. She's of no use to any of us now, so why even bother?"

"If you have something against her, then I would love to hear it." Lyaphend retained the calm in her tone, standing to face Yona as an equal.

While not daring to lift her head, Wave chuckled softly. "What, did she never tell you? She is a genetic freak harvested from my mother."

"Stay cheeky while you're able," Yona scoffed. "We all know that's all you can do now."

Lyaphend erratically shifted her eyes between Yona and Wave. "Can one of you please enlighten me right now?"

"Yes, Yona, do enlighten us," Wave added. "Tell her—tell her what you are. Tell me what FOG did to my mother."

"You want me to start from day one? Fine." Yona stopped herself short of taking a puff from her cigarette. "I was one of FOG's lab rats like you, Lyaphend. I was cultivated in vitro with genes from several legendary figures, including Wave's mother, then I was raised as the daughter of one of their volunteers before being forced into FOG Central at the age of sixteen. I was there for twenty years before I defected to the Scion Finis at thirty-six. Your mother went flying off the handle five years after that, Wave; it was immediately after you were born. She massacred almost your entire family and never took kindly to my existence either.

"Unfortunately, she made one big mistake: She came after me directly. I turned her in to FOG after teaching her some manners; I don't know what they did with her after that, and neither does Gede."

Wave lifted her head, eyes wide with excitement. "Then she still lives?"

Yona shrugged. "I never gave enough fucks to look into that. She's dead business as far as I'm concerned. What I never saw coming is that I'd end up looking at her equally demented spawn, close enough to spit on."

"She had no part in her mother's actions," Lyaphend quietly interjected.

"In case it wasn't already obvious, that woman came closer

to killing me than anyone before or after her. You're in over your head if you think her daughter isn't cut from the same cloth as her and Wrellord. All of them are selfishly thirsty for power; the only thing setting her apart from the others is that she's offering to help you. You're better off staying out of the Haizers' business."

Wave smirked. "I will correct you on one thing: Power by itself says nothing of the one who possesses it. What matters is that I intend to wield my power for the betterment of our people. And..." She struggled to stand until Lyaphend assisted her. "And do not speak as if you were a victim. You were arguably FOG's most prized operative, the most feared initiate in the Scion Finis at one point, and now you are a legendary mercenary, not to mention you are good-looking even at fifty-five years old. Your life is a privilege most could only dream of."

"Spoken like a true one-dimensional comic book villain. Well done." Yona folded her arms. "Gede said something like that about power in his inaugural address before any of us were born, when the government was more authoritarian than it is today. He reclined in his chair and transferred many of his duties to FOG; now their power has gone out of the Haizers' control, and we can only guess what that means for Golem's future."

An epiphany had struck Lyaphend at the mention of the state of the government. "Before I go after Constius, I would like to speak with Wrellord directly," she declared, addressing Wave. "If Constius is targeting him, then I can bargain with him to help both of us."

"He won't let you anywhere near him under normal circumstances, so you'll need to earn his trust somehow," Yona responded. "Just get your own problems sorted out first before you end up killing all of us; go to the East, meet the client, get your dog, and come back here. We need to get rid of Acantelieth somehow before you go insane. I'll keep an eye on Wave in the meantime."

"Before I go insane? So far, I feel okay." She glanced at the birthmark on the back of her right hand. "Besides, she's my leverage against FOG. I'm too valuable to kill as long as I have what they need."

"They'll ensure you stay locked up until they have your secrets, then quietly dispose of you. You're as good as dead with or without Acantelieth if they catch you, so don't get cocky." Yona snuffed out her cigarette against the back of the bench, having not used it once, before glaring at Wave. "Just looking at you takes me back so hard that I almost fall back on bad habits, kiddo."

Lyaphend interrupted Wave before she could respond, attempting to keep the two on agreeable terms. "Do you think FOG will lock down Prime District again after what happened with Lapine?"

"Not likely. Lapine was nothing compared to Watcher, so they wouldn't be expecting a dangerous spike in DEAS levels. That works well for all of us." Yona walked past Lyaphend and turned around. "Why don't you take another day off? Enjoy your free time and try to forget about your problems as long as you can. Spend some more time with your family; you don't know how much longer you'll have that opportunity." She continued on her way before pausing again.

"One last thing, Lyaphend: Choose your friends and associates more carefully from now on. I'm not saying this just for the sake of people who might end up dead because of others who want something from you, but also for the sake of you who might end up directly dealing with the latter. A woman like you is bound to run into all kinds of scum who will say anything they think you want to hear just so you give them something they want—intel, power, money, or sex. I don't give a rat's ass about you or what you think of me, but I'm 'using' you to keep Acantelieth under control. At least I'm honourably bitchy enough to admit it."

Lyaphend sneered, offended but relieved. As intimidating and unfriendly as Yona was, she was equally reliable and genuine—so much so that Lyaphend could shamelessly voice her own disdain. "That's a relief because I couldn't give a rodent's rear end about you either."

"You heard her," Wave added, throwing her middle finger up towards Yona. "Nobody cares about you, so get gone already!"

Yona nonchalantly extended the courtesy with her own middle finger. "We'll be seeing each other a lot from now on..." She flicked back her finger like a switchblade, exchanging it for a thumb pointed at her face. "... so get used to this good-looking face. I'm going out to get some coffee, then I'll come back for you tonight and take you and your chauffeur to one of my hideaways. You're all hers until then, Lyaphend; just don't sign the keeper's contract."

"She is my employee," Wave pedantically corrected before Lyaphend could assert herself. "Worry less or you are prone to grow as many grey hairs as I."

Yona rolled her eyes. "I'll let her simmer on this advice, then: Do what your job requires of you, but don't roll out the red carpet for your little 'employer.' It won't be long before that carpet begins to blend with the red-tile floor; then it'll be your blood drawn to enrich the colour all over again."

As Yona turned away and jogged towards the front gate, Wave gently loosed herself from Lyaphend's arms and crouched under the bench. Lyaphend observed her, pausing short of lifting her back up. "Are you okay?"

"I had nearly forgotten this," Wave elatedly said, standing up with Caevin's regalia in her arms. "I am still one step ahead of my brother. This sword was given to me by our father; I can use it to lure FOG's attention and prove to them that I am Wave Haizer. I can make my brother pay dearly for lying to them about my whereabouts if necessary."

Lyaphend chuckled. "You could have made my job easier by showing that to Yona."

"Lyaphend!" Before Wave could respond, the two were approached by one of Lyaphend's adoptive brothers, a small, spectacled ten-year-old boy who stumbled down the stairs shouting his sister's name.

Lyaphend looked below her brother's auburn bowl cut and

acknowledged him with a wide smile. "Good morning, Alco!"

"Did something happen?" Alco asked concernedly, looking at Wave. "Who's she?"

Wave meekly waved at him. "I am—"

"Oh, she's just a friend of mine!" Lyaphend interrupted. "Wave, why don't you go inside and rest? Our maids can help you with anything you might—"

"Maids!" Wave exclaimed, rushing for the entrance before Lyaphend could finish.

"But please don't disturb my father!" She stepped forward but paused, held in place by two tiny paws brushing against her leg.

Alco pointed downward. "He was meowing by the front door. I think he wants to follow you to the garden."

"Was he now?" Lyaphend chuckled, bending over to lift a slender white cat into her arms. One look into Argen's hazel eyes assuaged her of the fear her uncertain future brought upon her, and her heart was ready for the task at present: To stroll through the fragrant garden of the courtyard alongside her exuberant brother and simple-minded feline. She would suffer these precious moments together with everyone—her gift to the sufferer who sought to suffer anew and the guardian whose will lived on in her soul.

What kind of woman was she? She was kind but strong, selfish but genuine, indecisive but determined. What did she want in life, and how was she planning on getting it? She sought freedom but did not yet know how to acquire it. What did she have then that was most valuable to her? She had her father and brothers, her mother and her mother's guardian, she would soon have, and the courier from Halia she would never have, but they had parted ways amicably and she would remember him always.

I could only speculate the profundity of Acantelieth's slumber within the body of this painting granted human life, but perhaps that painting deserved to relish her humanity, a gift she may well deem a curse with time in these fleeting moments of harmony and stillness.

Enjoy life as you are permitted, Enlenea, for happiness was never yours to claim.

Epilogue: A Good Night in Water

For most living creatures, sleep is harmony—a respite from life's woes and a moment to reclaim one's vigour. Sometimes, their fantasies run rampant in their minds, weaving tales far removed from the reaches of reality. Their waking moment would be but a boon to their senses or a boon and a welcomed escape from a gaol warped of their dormant fears.

But for Lyaphend, that experience had drifted farther than day and night—as far as her childhood and the moment she awoke as Architect Acantelieth. A sort of purgatory awaited her each night in bed, a gateway behind the brim of madness and depths of slumber. She was alone beside her sea of madness, isolated on an island of grass burning auburn against the blood-red sky. Thunder roared along the virulent storm as lighting cut through the clouds. Nightmarish phantoms broke the surface of the water—clammy hands and forearms belonging to unseen giants, brimming with scarlet auras yet suspended in various positions as their sickly-sweet stench sailed downwind. She never failed to imagine, to her horror, of being bound against her will under their cold fingers and sinking into the sunless deep, never to return.

The sight of deep water had always caused her imagination to flourish in disturbing ways, but she had only begun to understand why. The horrors of the deep recited tales of her insanity, beginning from the moment she—Enlenea—massacred the Halians. She furrowed her eyebrows as she stood barefoot upon the shore overlooking that representation of hatred too vast to understand, her determination at odds with her milky pyjamas.

Even the depths of infinitely paled against her will to stay true to all she was, but she had nothing to stay its growing urge to betray her.

She lifted her hand, conjuring her regalia into her palm with effortlessness possible only in this divide between wake and slumber. Every night was a trial to restrain the Elegy of the End; Lyaphend's every phantom of fear and hatred clawed against the water's surface amid the hands that surmounted it. Occasionally, they would spill onto the shore, leaving her to fend against the inevitable until the ripples faded, permitting her one more moment of rest.

But no terror arrived from the shore this time. Innumerable lashes of dark smoke approached downwind, coiling and conjoining a distance beneath her feet, and stacking atop each other until they solidified into the shape of a clawed black bull towering over her. She steeled herself for a confrontation, holding her regalia's shaft above her head with its blade directed to her anonymous enemy.

As this anonymous enemy opened its beady red eyes, however, it suddenly became recognisable, but not upon her memories as a human. She remembered a tower isolated in the wilds—she remembered the adherent of wisdom abandoned to its prison, like a flickering candle alone in the dark.

And she remembered the name of the creature who inspired her to act for herself. "Madcow?" she whispered as she lowered her regalia. "Is that you, Madcow?"

Madcow wobbled his head as if gathering his bearings; then, he studied his front legs, perhaps as taken aback by his own presence as Lyaphend.

"Do you remember me?" Lyaphend continued while drawing closer, unsummoning her regalia. "You and I met in your master's tower. I..." She hesitated, straining to refer to herself with her abandoned name. "I'm Enlenea. Well, that's not to say I'm exactly who she was. That was so long ago, but... you're still my friend, are you not?"

"So long ago, you say?" Madcow feebly grumbled, focusing

his eyes on Lyaphend. "And yet I am weak in both body and spirit, as though I had fallen mere moments ago. You carry the scent of a human; so too, an influence I have felt before. Enlenea... what has become of us both?"

Madcow turned around and sat beside the shore; Lyaphend took her old friend's invitation to sit beside him and tell her story as she had done when they first met. She began from Enlenea's encounter with the Halians and ended at the moment she vanquished Lapine and apparently reclaimed enough of Acantelieth's power to summon the spirits of Regnal's victims—at least in her purgatory. She fell silent for a moment to bask in Madcow's comforting presence before continuing with what awaited her next. "I know where Regnal is; I know he's waiting for me in the East District, so that's where I'm off to next. I'll knock him silly and get you and Aerbith back. It should only be a few more days now."

Madow briefly shifted his eyes to study her resolute expression. "Do you not fear him?"

Lyaphend shook her head with a smile. "I'm no less afraid of him than I was back then, but if I don't come to him, he'll come to me. It would be so much easier if I could just ask nicely for his cooperation, but here we go again."

"How fares the other Elegies?"

"I don't know. I have memories of Astot talking about me to someone after the Halians put me to sleep—I don't understand why—but whatever they've done up until now, I don't know for certain." She planted her hands on the ground and leaned back. "Astot is still looking for his 'Begetter,' I'm sure. I don't know how I feel about that."

"The Halians declared him a man; if his Begetter was mortal, ne'er will he know him."

"And he'll never evolve because he has all the time in the world. When I stop Acantelieth from controlling me, so will I."

"You do not wish to die?"

"No; not anymore. Watcher wanted me to suffer as a human; I have suffered a few times, but all in all, I'm having fun.

I have a family that loves me, and I have people who count on me; I *have* the power to stand against my foes. I won't take my life for granted no matter what happens."

Madcow's eyes flittered about the grim sea. "Alas, is this what the world has become without me?"

"This is just a manifestation of Acantelieth's power, or my madness, you could say. I'm not terribly familiar with Golem myself, but it's a nice place to live. And, speaking of living..." She stood up, diverting Madcow's attention from the sea. "... we should plan things out a bit before I set you free. I say we start by giving you a name more fitting and less... laughable."

Madcow stared into Lyaphend's eyes, baring his contemplative thoughts before he put them into words. "Aye, to go by 'Madcow' as I stand today would be a laughable folly. Though began I did as a mad slave to the hunt, I am now content to pursue wisdom and joy along my fellows." He stood up, obscuring his face with the bulk of his front leg as he watched the sea. "Upon the day I am again set free, I will make myself known as 'Happycow,' a tribute befitting to all I have learned."

Lyaphend barely managed to stifle her laughter, preferring not to ruin the moment. "Very good, but what about something a bit more different? What about... Freesia?"

Madcow bucked his knees slightly to tilt his head at Lyaphend.

"Oh, it's just a flower that came to mind when I thought about what you'd gone through. Freesias symbolise purity and thoughtfulness."

"Is that so?"

"It's up to you in the end, of course, and you'll have all the time in the world to make up your mind. Until then, my dear friend..." She extended her hand to Madcow. "... wait for me a little longer. I promise you that your life has only begun."

Madcow tilted his head the other way, evidently perplexed by Lyaphend's gesture, before gently lifting his leg, bringing his dark claw into her grasp.

And she laid her other hand above his claw, stroking its

sleek surface. "Goodnight, Madcow."

"Goodnight... Lyaphend Farwalth," Madcow replied as softly as his booming voice would allow. Lyaphend took a deep breath and proceeded to walk towards the sea with courage as her guide, but Madcow called out to her as she dipped her feet, "Who is wiser—she with no anger, or she with anger aplenty who knows to tame it? I know what it is to beware the monster inside one. For cycles uncountable, I was naught but my hatred; I nurtured it, and it coddled me. And though it decides for me no longer, it has not left me; I accept it as part of my being. 'Tis no shame in embracing one's anger; let it be part of you, but do not let it *become* you. Only then might you conquer it."

"Accept Acantelieth as part of myself, in other words?" Lyaphend faced Madcow's fading form with a smile, putting her palm against her chest. "I might consider it one day, but not while I'm the only monster I know."

And hello, she thought, to her sea of madness, that which empowered her, that which thirsted for her body, and that which she would give herself to for but a short while. She walked forward, closed her eyes, and allowed herself to sink into the abyss. She felt the cold embrace of an elongated arm against her waist and hands gripping her arms and legs, tugging at her with impatience. Her visage and consciousness began to bubble away from her until she was the faceless woman whence she was birthed. Her madness would settle for this fleeting taste of victory, the silence in which it could exist sans a mind contorting it.

Until the canvas was painted once more.

The End

Acknowledgements

After many years planning this particular story of mine and several more years making significant revisions from my original draft, I can finally say one of my many literary projects throughout the years has reached its completion. *Epitaph Proven: Foedus et Monstrum* has proven to be a difficult and mentally draining endeavour; oftentimes, I wished I had never begun the journey at all. I was inspired to push forward with the glowing reception I received towards an earlier draft along with my desire to challenge myself and overcome my dreary mood with this project constantly in my head.

While I was on my own for a better part of this journey, I do have others to thank for setting me on the right path. I would like to thank my editor, Destyn Hehr, for providing me with insightful feedback that led me to drastically alter my trajectory for the plot. I thank my dear friend, Christina Saget, for advising me during the publication process and being the much-needed confidante with whom I could share my triumphs and woes.

And lastly, I thank you, my dear reader, for giving my writing a chance, as new to authorhood as I may be! I do hope you enjoyed this book and continue to follow the lives of Lyaphend and company throughout other related works to come.

Glossary

Annulling Clasp

A power that randomly manifests in the dominant hand of a newborn Halian male. It can alter the flow of DEAS within living organisms, negate any kind of force upon the user's body, and immobilise anyone the user touches with their dominant hand.

ASAS

Alpha Security Air Station. FOG Central's primary base of aircraft telecommunications and docking in Prime District.

Before Golem

Alternatively B.G. A label for every year in the Golemian calendar occurring before the founding of Golem.

Begetter

A man believed to have been the first "wielder" of DEAS. Considered a god by Astot.

Dalka Clan

The largest cyberterrorist organisation in Golem, owned by the Dalka Family. Their ranks consist of orphans, renowned hackers, fugitives, aristocrats, and ex-government employees. While widely considered to be highly dangerous, the clan does not endorse violent crime and specialises more in government espionage and charity. None of its members are aware of the existence of DEAS with the exception of Lyaphend.

DEAS

Destructive Ashen Scourge. The modern term for the Scourge. A mysterious energy responsible for changing a living or recently deceased organism into an eldritch heart. It mutates the power and physical form of those infected in accordance with their desires. While believed to be omnipresent, its concentration varies according to location and quantity of eldritch hearts present within the location. Infection can be prevented by remaining calm in areas high in DEAS concentration. An individual with sufficient discipline can infuse inorganic materials with it, creating weapons that can be used to temporarily kill eldritch hearts.

Eldritch heart

Also known as an EL-H. A phantasmal entity resulting from either a human or animal succumbing to DEAS. The power of an eldritch heart varies according to the desires the individual possessed in life. They are normally driven by instinct and cannot recall their former lives. Although immortal, they can be temporarily killed with either DEAS or Halian sorcery.

Eldritch brain

Also known as an EL-B. An evolution of an eldritch heart that occurs when a self-aware eldritch heart acts against the desires responsible for their creation for a prolonged period of time and succumbs to complete madness. Unlike eldritch hearts, who often retain at least enough self-awareness to identify threats and focus on individual targets, eldritch brains always attack everyone indiscriminately. Although significantly more powerful than eldritch hearts on average, eldritch brains are considered a lesser threat to Golem compared to Elegies due to their inability to focus their power.

Elegies

A group of self-aware eldritch hearts, led by Astot and given names according to a fable by the Begetter.

Elegy

Either an eldritch heart belonging to the Elegies or any self-aware eldritch heart.

FOG

Forerunners of Golem. A branch of Golem's government, divided into several subsidiaries.

FOG Central

FOG's general division, tasked with handling public relations, making deliveries to FOG's subsidiaries, experimenting with DEAS, and eliminating special targets.

Fortitude

One of FOG's subsidiaries, responsible for protecting Golem's border, delivering supplies to allied colonies, mining materials beyond Golem, and organising expeditions to uncharted lands.

Halians

An ethnic group of humans with mysterious powers unrelated to DEAS. Believed by the Elegies to be responsible for the creation of DEAS. They commonly possess yellowish skin and light hair; some Halians possess red eyes.

In Golem's Reign

Alternatively I.G.R. A label for every year in the Golemian calendar occurring after the founding of Golem.

King's Tower

The tallest building in Golem, functioning primarily as the government's lookout and secondary storage facility.

New Halia

The new nation of the Halians. Its location is unknown.

Old Halia

The original nation of the Halians. The cause of its destruction is unknown.

Regalia of Halia

A supernatural weapon wielded by the shepherd, or ruler, of Halia. It is randomly born in the soul of a newborn Halian female. Its exact form is dependent on its wielder's personality. Upon the wielder's death, her Regalia of Halia will either become inactive or vanish, depending on whether it was summoned or not before her death respectively. Only one active Regalia of Halia can exist at a time.

Reverentia

An organisation tasked with combatting DEAS in Proto-Golem.

RICOR

Responsive Insurgent Covert Operations Regiment. One of FOG's subsidiaries, responsible for combatting DEAS-related threats within Golem.

Scion Finis

A religious criminal organisation comprised of humans capable of manipulating DEAS.

Scourge

The archaic term for DEAS.

White Monument

An obelisk engraved with the names of Golem's former rulers.

www.ingramcontent.com/pod-product-compliance
Lightning Source LLC
Chambersburg PA
CBHW051940220626
47052CB00004B/736